S0-BBO-452

Hanging On

Hanging On

a novel by

Robert G. Beason

HARCOURT BRACE JOVANOVICH, PUBLISHERS
San Diego   New York   London

Copyright © 1984 by Robert G. Beason

*All rights reserved. No part of this publication may be reproduced or
transmitted in any form or by any means, electronic or mechanical,
including photocopy, recording, or any information storage and retrieval
system, without permission in writing from the publisher.*

*Requests for permission to make copies of any part of the work should be mailed to
Permissions, Harcourt Brace Jovanovich, Publishers, Orlando, Florida 32887*

Library of Congress Cataloging in Publication Data
Beason, Robert G.
Hanging on.
I. Title.
PS3552.E176H3   1984   813'.54   83–12861
ISBN 0-15-138440-1

Designed by Karen Savary

Printed in the United States of America

B C D E

Hanging On

Here I sit, mad as hell.

An old geezer put in this woeful place by my one and only daughter, the lovely Norma, little brat.

They call it Eagle Arms, a Retirement Residence, twelve amorphous gray-brown stories revealing an acute shortage of backbone in the architects. When it came time to make a statement, as the saying goes, a mole's squeak was the best they could do. From down the hill Eagle Arms could be taken for a low-profile mental institution or some minimum-security place where the bars don't show. I myself favor the second reading; you come here only when your candle is guttering, and the usual sentence is life.

I'm not yet resigned to a need for inmating. It depends on where you're coming from, as my grandson Rodney says. Another brat, sixteen going on sixty and beset sometimes with the smarts. My driver's license claims I am seventy-three, which means I am fortunate to still have it. I'd be even luckier if I had a car.

Even as a septuagenarian I can't say I feel old. About the same as at forty, or perhaps it's that my memory has a garbled picture of what my life was like those many years ago.

Sometimes Norma treats me as if I'm pushing ninety, and from the far side at that. I'm still trying to get a fix on her, this daughter of mine who has been off here in the East so long. I seem to detect changes in her, and not all for the good either.

Just yesterday she sat in that red chair over there and analyzed me for the benefit of her friend with the big boobs who was sitting on the love seat. That is a piece of furniture hardly in keeping with the diminishing figure I cut these days. But aged or not, I like to think I'll make use of that love seat; banked fires have burned down houses, you know.

"Oh, Papa's not senile or anything, Gladys," Norma said. "Still as bright as a penny. Just couldn't live alone any longer, that's all, and we couldn't take him in. So I brought him here."

A sack of bones heaved into the back room.

"Such a lovely place," tinkled Gladys, looking with admiration at my off-white walls that have all the warmth of a charity ward.

Have you noticed how, when people are up in years, their juniors sit right under their noses and talk about them as if they weren't there? You could as well be the family hound. "Rover? Oh, he's a nice old chump, 'cept when he pees on the rug."

Then there's the matter of names. When you are grayed and wrinkled people reduce you to Al or Joe or Ben. But you must call them Mister; they insist on it by not supplying their given name. "Hello, Ben, I'm Mr. Harmon." Thus our Executive Director introduced himself to me, and he keeps practicing his art. "Ben, this is Mrs. Willikers. Mrs. Willikers, say hello to Ben." As if my surname, like a vestigial tail, had dropped off somewhere in the vague past. At fifty I was Mr. Carpenter. Now I'm back to plain Ben, same as at ten. Mr. Harmon of course is a pretty sorry representative of our species.

I could have booted Norma's butt when she kept on about the shape I'm in, and I thought of starting a counter-

2

offensive. Such as how her buns are getting overstuffed, or when did you give up bras, my dear? Naturally, I kept quiet. We old folks have learned how to lie low, especially when our benefactors are around.

"He still has his own teeth," Norma announced. *"Don't you, Papa?"* A shout so I'd be included in the conversation. I could hear every damned word. It's not my ears going bad, only my vintage. It used to be considered a good year too.

At my age Norma figures I'm deaf as a stone toad, and she won't let herself be persuaded otherwise. People hand out characteristics by age. Remarkably, I still have my own teeth. Think of that.

"You want me to go over and bite off the doorknob to impress your friend?" I asked Norma.

They laughed at the old geek sitting in the corner. "At least he's kept his sense of humor," commented Gladys.

To tell the truth, I hardly followed their conversation, being busy staring at Gladys's magnificent bosom. She's a slim girl too, though more woman than girl, about my daughter's age. I still think of Norma as that little girl with strawberry hair and frank blue eyes. Her hair is still the same, doubtlessly helped by some druggist, but my child is getting on. Staring truculently now at half a century, and waiting for it to blink first.

They're all coming to look young to me. I'd probably be marked for senile if they caught me casting whistling eyes at ladies of fifty, but there you have one of the few advantages of age. At eighteen a man's range is as narrow as a tax collector's smile. He might wink at a girl as young as sixteen but would never pinch (they still do that?) a lass of fifteen for fear of being thought her age.

My selection at seventy-three is veritably wool-worthian. I find blondes of eighteen delectable, but hardly more so than comely specimens three times that age. We have one stunner at the Arms, who turned sixty-two last time and is still more beautiful than most women half her years. Emily her name is, Emily Walrod, and she has clear tight skin, big brown smiling eyes and hardly ever wears glasses. It's true she can't see a hell of a lot without them and keeps bumping into things. She's vain, I suppose, but with a face like that, who cares?

You have to be sixty-two to get into Eagle Arms, and Mrs. Walrod just made it. She actually likes it here, a view by no means universal amongst Residents. Mr. Harmon says the average age for the Arms is seventy-four. You have to admire Mrs. Walrod for adjusting to a bunch of fuddy-duddies many years her senior.

The specific reason for that visit by Norma and Gladys may never be known. They came. They sat. They talked. Mainly about me. Norma took grape pop, Gladys a beer, from my shoe box of a fridge. I managed two brews myself, feeling a powerful thirst. It was like a session of the Geriatrics Committee, Norma Kemp presiding, on the condition of Benjamin Osro Carpenter, old fogy. Meeting over, they got up and departed. Maybe Norma wanted to show her friend what a heller she has for a father.

In which case Gladys was quite disappointed—unless she reads minds.

Any visitor is welcome to my digs here on four. If Fidel Castro came along pursued by a posse, I'd hand out a beer and cigar. In a place like this the voices you miss most are those of youth, and you long to talk on an equal level with the really young, like a teen-ager.

This country of the aged is new to me. We Residents find ourselves shrouded from the real world by a misty veil, and we dream of going back, if only for a day, to kick up our heels once again. But kicking is not a big sport for a man who has to sit down to pull his pants on.

Last evening before supper—known as dinner here in the East—Fletch and I were sitting on the cushioned bench outside the dining room waiting impatiently for the gates to open. We were hungry as a pair of desert rats, and it not yet five. He is a retired dentist from some town in Massachusetts, Dr. Fletcher Pepper, DDS, a trim little bird with a fringe of snow for hair and a bow tie, always a bow. They kid about his name. "Take Dr. Pepper at ten, two and four," the ladies say, no doubt wishing they could.

Fletch and I have become best friends, like boys at boarding school. He's a right guy, to my mind, and has a laugh that's close to a cackle. You know, spontaneous and full of joy. Once I said, "Fletch, I'll bet you'd like to get your hands on the man that named the pop."

"Not him," he said. "It's my mother I should have throttled."

"Your mother?" I said, as if on cue.

"Yeah. She was the one who wanted me to be a dentist. I always hated being up to my wrists in somebody's mouth, but Mama got what she wanted and I turned into a tonic. What I always fancied being was a plumber, plain Fletcher Pepper, specialist in sweating copper, putting in elbows and unstopping sinks for grateful ladies."

All this took place more than half a century ago but he makes it sound as fresh as last week, and I admire that. Not like those people who keep dating everything. Was that in sixteen? Or was it early seventeen? Then they forget what they were going to tell you, and you get the feeling that everything interesting happened way back when. Tell the tale, I say, and forget when.

Fletch seldom delves into the past, because his memory is frayed, like an old flag. He wears little rimless specs and suffers from some strange ailment. I once heard him name his disease but it stayed in my mind about as long as the begats in the Bible; the effect is a diminished supply of blood to the brain that slows his thought processes and recall. You don't notice except when he gets excited.

Almost nobody here is without some plague or other. High blood pressure, arthritis and bursitis, those badges of old age, are as thick as chiggers in July back home. You hear complaints of back pains, deafness and failing eyesight, ailments with no more class than constipation and flatulence. At least my friend Fletch has a distinguished disease.

Our dining-room gates open at five and Residents form up as if we're going to dash into a rock concert. After an exhausting afternoon of doing nothing, we're starved. Some keep snacks in their flats but you can't cook anything for yourself. Our kitchens are in the wall, no bigger than hints, and there's nary a range in sight. Eagle Arms contracts restrict Residents to electric saucepans and fryers, that sort of thing. Hot plates are more feared by the Owners than tax audits, and the line in the agreement that forbids them is the only one in the whole long mess that is underlined. The Owners tremble and quake, I suppose, at the idea that one of us might incinerate their Investment or, almost as frightening, sauté a fellow Resident, which could lead to Nasty Lawsuits. Considering my own culinary history in Illinois, with flaming skillets and scorched walls, they might be right. Besides, we get three squares a day at the Arms. Just like the penitentiary at Stateville or the Army.

Fletch and I were getting edgy last evening, feeling starvation drawing nigh, when along came Mrs. Walrod, she of the neat face, and took a seat beside me. "Evening, boys," she said with a big smile. "Notice anything different?"

And I did. "Sure," I said. "You got your hair done by that Mrs. Bernice. Looks lovely."

She fairly beamed. "How sweet of you to notice, Mr. Carpenter." We old folks still have family names amongst ourselves.

"He didn't until you brought it up," said Fletch with one of his patented laughs.

Mrs. Walrod ignored him. "It's not Mrs. Bernice though, Mr. Carpenter. Her name is Bernard."

"Same family obviously," chirped Fletch.

"Could be Bernard, all right," I said. "I don't go to her often myself."

"Coulda fooled me," Fletch said.

With his own head near cue-ball status, Fletch often teases me about my hair. I still have every one I was born with, maybe more. It is white as a ghost's underwear but thick and wavy still. I keep it neatly combed, on my mother's theory that you make the best of what you've got. The belles at the Arms are unlikely to be bowled over by the virility of my figure but they just might notice the nice part in my hair.

Mrs. Walrod, beset by the talkies, next got onto how skinny she is, a big subject for the ladies—how skinny, especially those overflowing their girdles; how gray, just after a dye job; how poorly clothed, while wearing a frock that cost three hundred. It is a form of self-preening, like a peacock working over his own tail.

"I'm just getting too awfully skinny," she said. "Don't you think so?"

Being forever accommodating to beautiful women, I said, "You're just right, Mrs. Walrod; shouldn't lose another ounce."

"Why, thank you. What a nice thing to say."

Fletch was looking around for somebody, anybody, to start a new conversation with. His malarkey threshold is lower than an ant's knee, and he once told Mrs. Bombard, on seven, that her coat was all right but must have looked better when it was stuffed with mink guts.

Mrs. Walrod crossed her legs and patted her calf. "I think maybe I need about a pound right there."

"Whyn't you try lard?" Fletch said over my shoulder.

The biggest laugh came from Mrs. Walrod herself, which was pleasing to me. A conscious effort is required, once you are over the hump, to keep yourself from becoming too self-centered. You have to be able to laugh at yourself or you'll be a pain to everyone else at your Retirement Home.

The idea that an Eagle Arms or worse is waiting down the line can scare middle-aged folks silly. But there it lurks for all of us.

I never intended to grow old. A fiery wreck at Indianapolis or a plane crash in some distant land seemed plausible alternatives to having my life run down and stop in some sick-bed like a tired clock. Well, I saw Indy exactly once, and flew scarcely more. What happened was starkly simple: I went on living one day and then another and another until, powerless to hold back the tide of time, I found myself an old man.

Life's last great challenge is facing up to the big numbers with some degree of grace and dignity. A few do it easily, others struggle, some fail. That great American he-man Ernest Hemingway got the better of wounds and critics and overbearing women but, unable to accept what time was doing to him, he took a shotgun and blew his head off.

I was hoping last evening for Mrs. Walrod's continued presence but Jackie, our hostess, steered her away and later brought over a woman named Jenny Biggs I barely know. That was our party then, the three of us. Jackie figured

Mrs. Biggs alone was enough for Fletch and me to handle, and she was.

She's a regular clothespin of a woman, going about ninety-five in pounds, seventy-five in age, always appearing in a flowing white dress with youthful blond hair piled up like the back of a shearing shed. Her immunization against the years.

"We have such lovely food here," she said with a little smile to please her male companions. Mrs. Biggs is quite nice, I'm sure, but sometimes her eyes show an unnerving gleam.

"Beats Spam any day," Fletch said, returning the smile. We were having fried chicken with rice and gravy, pitchers of red and white wine on the tables.

"You must have been in the service," said Mrs. Biggs, thinking of I don't know what war. "My sons always hated Spam, all three of them. I had one in each branch. All my boys served their country."

I feared long tales of the heroics of the three little Biggses but when she didn't go on I said, "What I think Dr. Pepper means is that life could be worse."

"Dern sight," Fletch muttered.

"Then you like it here, do you?" she asked him.

"No, I hate it, but it's the best I can do right now." Fletch can be a care when he wants to.

"Well," she said, understandably confused, the gleam in her eyes becoming more noticeable, "if you don't like it here, where would you rather be?" A reasonable question for the doctor.

"Outside, anywhere outside," Fletch answered, using the term as they do at San Quentin, "outside and away from the Arms, about forty years old and driving around in my plumbing truck."

"Oh, my," said Mrs. Biggs.

3

Norma, my child, where the devil were you?

Thursday, not quite eight o'clock, a month to the day since I moved in. Norma promised she'd come see me yesterday but never showed. I might have called but didn't, not wanting to intrude, or get her on my case either, in the words of my grandson.

I've come up from a breakfast of prune juice ("Advised for regularity," says the buffet menu), eggs and sausage and toast. I'll write a while to pass the time, that being my lifetime's work. Not your great American novel, no. More like *Two pedestrians were killed yesterday . . . Fire destroyed a tenement . . . Magellan's former Chief of Police announced from his prison cell . . .*

I find it difficult to break old habits.

Later I'll pay some bills and go for a walk before lunch. Then a nap. A frenzied existence.

At Eagle Arms we have no problems of inadequate diet or a leaky roof. Trouble is, until we became Residents none of us knew the others existed, and cared less. Oh, we're decent enough, typical of those on the far side of the hill, and as compassionate to each other as defeated stragglers who fall in together on the roads of retreat.

We have 94 Residents now, 11 of them men. That seems a perverse ratio but I've read that on average single women over fifty outnumber men fifty to one. The same piece said these ladies think of sex every twenty minutes. Sometimes in the sitting room I look at one of our ladies and say to myself, What's a nice person like you doing with thoughts like that?

Mr. Harmon says we're one big happy family, though I judge he claims no kin. To him we are livestock: feed them regularly and keep a roof over their heads and you turn a profit.

My own family dwindles. Norma and her husband, Clyde, their son, Rodney. My youngest child, Christopher, is in the picture business on the Coast and has lost his first name. Those people ripped the capitals off Christopher and Carpenter and turned him into C.C. I get as many letters from him as from Ulysses S. Grant.

My wife, Dorothy, died eight years ago February. My brother's gone too, and so on. You get into a dreary recital if you start listing all your relatives who are dead. Turns out damned near all of them are.

On her early visits Norma told me she was delighted to have me near; lately she's been adding thoughts of how I can help her with her problems. I'm not certain I want to know what she has in mind. Clyde is away a lot, as she's complained for years, and now she says she can't do a thing with Rodney. With a teen-ager, who can?

I am coming to know my grandson as something more than a little water-head who jabbered all the time at Old Farm. He seems a decent kid, despite Norma's dark hints, his tongue now more controlled, a good-looking child with the raven hair of his grandmother.

Clyde Kemp is hard to know; comes from a family of Germans, an electrical engineer turned wheeler-dealer. His schedule leaves no time for me. He came once with Norma, has not returned, a bright man hustling to keep his family in steaks and cars. Clyde works for Universal Business Machines, one of their key executives. Said so himself.

Norma was twenty-five when they married and moved to Marlow, on the distant Connecticut shore. It might not seem far if you are in Jersey but from the Illinois plains Marlow is halfway to forever. In a month they'd bought the house where they still live, up on a ridge in North

Marlow, which appears to be something of a social distinction. Back home we had South Magellan, where the climbers went to hauteur it up after the second war. Dorothy and I stuck it out on the East Side, neither having a taste for pretension.

I knew little about Clyde when they married, learned hardly more later because they left so quickly, driving to New York in their old Ford coupe. He had been hired by UBM, and hasn't left yet. Clyde, like his father-in-law, has staying power. My whole working life was devoted to *The Magellan Times*. I wish I were sure that dogged tenacity is a virtue—to other than pit bulls.

We got things all wrong when they went east, thinking they'd hang around New York a while, sowing their wild oats, then come home with grandkids in tow to set up a serious home. Not necessarily right in Magellan. Perhaps a country place outside of town. Even a house in St. Louis, an hour away by motorcar. We could imagine nothing farther. We were what you call "provincial."

They had no wild oats and after a few years we realized our kids were not coming back, were actually happy in the East. We were mistaken about grandchildren too. None arrived.

"Maybe he has no oats at all," I said.

"We must give them time," Dorothy answered. "They're in a strange new place, you know." As if geography affects fertility.

After nine years Rodney appeared and we said it was a good beginning, not knowing it was the end as well. I'll take him for a grandson any day though. On visits out home he called me Grandpa every other word. Norma said it was because he got to use the word so seldom.

They came on flying visits, Norma alone, then Norma and the baby. Clyde is in Europe, she'd say, or South America, or couldn't get away. I used to picture him in a green eyeshade slaving away at his desk, the moon peering over his shoulder.

You know how flying visits go. They come on the afternoon plane, look up friends next morning and leave the day after. There are set conversations too.

"But do you really *like* the East, Norma?"

"Oh, sure, Mama, and it's where Clyde's job is."

"Looks like he could get something closer home."

"That *is* our home now, Mama. Marlow is home to me."

"If Clyde is gone so much, why don't you come spend some real time with us while he's away?" This from me.

"I have things to do, Papa, redecorating, entertaining, being social. Clyde's business associates, you know; it's what you do if you want to get ahead."

People from the *Times* used to come to our house. We'd feed them fried chicken and roasting ears fresh from the garden, beer to wash it down. Hardly food for getting ahead, nor the guests either. Three special friends from the back shop came often, and there were fellow reporters too. The talk without fail ran to that tight-fisted Clint Bradly ("It's l-y, you idiot, not l-e-y," he shouted at me in my first week on staff. "Look it up in the phone book if you don't believe me!"). Mr. Bradly was Owner.

Whatever the reason, we saw little of Norma and in my mind she remained the same girl who drove out of Magellan one morning on the long trip east. They'd returned from a four-day honeymoon in Memphis, stayed the night and left as the sun rose. No slugabeds they, honeymooners or not.

Well, my little girl is not the same. Still pretty enough, but these days she has more grit than Bon Ami. I see a cosmopolitan flair, wife of a big shot, an Easterner through and through. She smiles sweetly when she gets what she wants, and I have this unsettling feeling that you'd see the identical expression while she, if you crossed her, whacked off your head. Scary.

In Clyde there is less change. Pounds have been added to his already stocky Teutonic frame and there is frost in his sideburns. He's basically a kind man, gentle with his family, but edgy and hard-driven in his job. He goes in and lays out computer systems for clients, and draws a big salary.

Enough of this. I've typed away a suitable segment of time, during which clouds blew up and now rain is falling. So scratch the walk; I'll read a while instead. I'd prefer walking and fresh air, but not if the price is pneumonia.

🍂 4

The wine pitchers went dry last night, and from that alone I would have known it was Friday. Though none of us goes out to business—a local colloquialism meaning going to work—we all feel an end-of-week letdown, as if we'd been eight-to-fiveing it since Monday. You cannot simply forget the routine of a lifetime when they tell you to stay home and collect Social Security. Probably three-quarters of our Residents went to bed tipsy, happily contemplating the weekend, it never occurring to them that Saturday at the Arms holds no more magic than Monday or Thursday.

Mrs. Walrod joined Fletch and me for supper, the doings of Jackie, our hostess, an olive-skinned little thing of Italian heritage and a tendency toward icky sweetness. I have been wanting to talk more to Mrs. Walrod and was delighted, Fletch less so, as it turned out. Jackie was doing no favor to me of course, merely following what seems to be a staff trait of pushing people together like mothers presiding over a sandbox. Not a few would dine alone if given a choice, but no, that is what Mr. Harmon calls "withdrawal," a no-no amongst his flock of ancient chickens. So we dine together.

Later Jackie, with a smile like the white keys of a piano, brought over Mrs. Cardoza, widow of a Cuban sugar planter, and said, "Look, Mrs. Cardoza, what handsome men you are joining!"

That kind of sweetness might be divinely inspired, but not when it's insincere. You know if God is watching he has noticed how the sweetness holds only so long as you stay docile as a winded milk cow. The staff's efforts to turn you into a vegetable go so far as telling you how wonderful you look when you know damned well your appearance suggests you have just finished shopping for a mortician. Everybody does that to old folks though, telling us we don't look a day over forty while thinking we probably died three days ago but forgot to fall down.

Mrs. Cardoza smiled as if she believed what she heard. She is rich, very rich, has a neat little mustache and doesn't care whether school keeps or not. She and Mrs. Walrod talked of Mrs. Cardoza's many grandchildren and then Mrs. Cardoza and I got into Havana in the old days. I was there twice in Batista's time; she goes back when Cuba was still Spanish. She's eighty-nine.

While listening to tales, in nicely accented English, of beautiful riding horses and fast speedboats, I could hear Fletch spinning one to Mrs. Walrod about, in his words, pulling an old widder woman's tooth. The roots were so strong and, in those days, his arm so powerful that when the tooth came out it brought along a chunk of jawbone with a couple of snaggly molars clinging to it. A flush spread over Mrs. Walrod's face, and later she turned down dessert.

"She give yez d'exhibition table, I see," said a low voice in my ear. It was Margie with our baked bananas. She is our waitress—waitress as opposed to Jackie, our hostess-waitress—and her allusion was to our having the table right in front of the gates. Jackie seats people there if she thinks they will make a suitable picture of old coots at supper, should outsiders happen by. The Kremlin could learn from that girl.

Margie is into as many games as Jackie, except hers usually skewer other members of our staff, and Residents become spectators. She's a pretty young girl, a freckled pink Irish face with pug nose, and one of my favorites even if she does have a New York accent that can curdle milk. "Y'know what I *mean*?" she says nasally, and is disliked by some Residents who are epicures in voice intonations. I simply treat her with decency. She thinks I'm kind, so I get her little confidences, and sometimes especially good dishes too.

After supper Fletch and I went off to the card room on mezz to get up a bridge game. "Fletch," I said, "why did you tell that terrible tooth story? It was sickening."

"Oh, you were listening, eh?" he said, his eyes flashing mischievously. "Well, I figure it served her right, Ben."

"Why, Fletch? She's a nice woman."

"Nice nothing," he growled. "Why, Ben, you're as naïve as a fourteen-year-old virgin. That woman is laying a trap for you and you don't even know it."

"You sound loony," I told him. "Besides, I could always say no."

"Oh, Ben, that would be such a mistake. You don't want to take up with these old widder women, get married and the rest, not at your age."

I found no answer to that. Fletch, I gather, sees a threat to our friendship. At our age you make friends easily, all being of a piece in our ancient condition, but the jealousies of friendships are akin to what you might see at a junior prom. That gory story was to tell Mrs. Walrod to buzz off and leave us old buddies alone.

We got into a game with a Greek-looking Resident named Lloyd Axelrod and the snappy dresser Andy Kelly, late of Wall Street. We took them by better than twelve hundred points, which delighted Fletch, mainly because we set them three times. Winning is all right with him but setting the competition is twice as much fun.

It is getting on for supper again and now comes a rapping at my door. That will be Fletch, who has it worked out so we'll drink a beer here and arrive as the gates swing open, thus avoiding the dangers of entrapment by wily females.

Hold on, Fletch, I'm coming.

5

Never ask for too much; you might get it.

So said my grandmother, and I know what she had in mind. I have been wishing for a visit by Norma, and yesterday I got it, with Rodney to boot. Oh, I was happy to have them with me, even if only for a few minutes, but my daughter has a way of leaving disturbing thoughts on my door sill when she departs.

They'd been doing Saturday shopping and dropped by for a few words and a bottle of pop. When I opened a beer my grandson demanded one for himself.

"Rod, quit acting bigger than you are," said Norma, primly.

"Ah, Mom, all I want's a little." The age-old whine.

I poured two fingers in a glass and handed it over. "Might grow some hair on his chest," I said. Norma scowled.

What can you do with a boy whose features remind you of your dead wife, who spouts forth in French, shows impudent brashness and settles for a sip or two of beer? You know grandpas, always seeking in their grandsons the streak of grit they wish they'd had.

"*A son santé, Grandpère,*" Rodney said, drinking the brew like a Viking refreshing himself. "*Magnifique, mon ancien!*"

"Oh, Rod, you and your French," Norma complained. "What you need to do is learn decent English."

I laughed myself into a coughing fit, pleased immensely at having a youngster acting goofy around here. I understood none of his French but he wrote it down for me. Since age eight Rodney has been enchanted by French. He loves the language, reads the classics in the original. Unfortunately, says his mom, his interest in such mundane subjects as history and math is around two on a ten scale.

What the heck, I say, nobody can be perfect. I'm torn between spoiling Rodney and telling him to straighten up and fly right. Spoiling seems to be ahead on points.

They'd barely got comfortable when Norma took up a new tack. "They sell *The Marlow Mail* downstairs, don't they, Papa?"

"Usually have a stack at the front desk. Why?"

"I want one, and we don't get home delivery, you know. Rod, trot down and pick up a copy. Here." She handed him a quarter.

"We can get it when we leave, Mom."

"Never mind, Rod, just do it now and we won't forget."

"Ah gee whiz, Mom." He slunk out.

"What's with you?" I asked. "Seems to me he was right."

"Listen, I want to talk to you about something, Papa, about Rod."

Wily Norma, the former child so sweet. I could see there weren't going to be many laughs in this one, whatever it was. "It was only a little beer, hardly two sips," I said. "Have a heart, child."

That didn't throw her off the trail a bit, or raise a smile either. "Papa, Rod is very fond of you."

"Some grandsons are like that, Norma. No accounting for taste."

"Papa, please stop being funny. This is serious. Rod is turning out to be just worthless, no good at all."

"It seems a little early to write him off, Norma. What's he done at age sixteen that's so awful?"

"It's what he doesn't do, Papa. He sits around and reads and talks on the phone, does nothing constructive at all."

"You want him out in the yard building a condo or something? For heaven's sake, he's on vacation."

"Listen, I tell him to mow the lawn, and he won't. Oh, he finally gets it done, after all these excuses and being reminded fifty times. Yesterday I told him to help me clean house and all he got done was empty the waste-baskets."

"About normal for a teen-ager, my dear. I don't recollect you working your fingers to the bone helping your mother."

"Stop making excuses for him, Papa." Sternly.

"So what do you want of me?" Leery Papa.

"I want you to talk to him, that's all. Set him down and talk some sense into his head, tell him he should start being helpful to his parents."

"Me? Do that? You've got to be kidding."

"No I'm not." I could almost hear her foot stamping the floor. "I'll send him next week on the Connbus and tell him you want to see him."

"Norma, this is a bird-brain idea. You're the one who's supposed to discipline and motivate your son, you and Clyde. Especially him. You know, man-to-man talks."

"He's away so much, Papa."

"So you've said for years, but what about right now? I'll bet he's out there at the house this minute."

"But he's working, Papa."

"On a weekend?" My irritation was feeding on itself.

"He's writing memos and things, and I don't want to disturb him. Come on, Papa, you can do it and you know you can. Don't disappoint me now, after all those years when I wished you lived close so you could be of some help. Now you're here and you don't seem to want to do anything for me."

"It wasn't our fault we weren't closer, Norma. You are the one who moved away, you and that husband of yours. Your mama and I stayed put, and don't you forget it."

I am not fond of my daughter's attitude these days. Here she came flying out to rescue me from self-immolation, threw me into this awful place and now wants me to straighten out her son. I thought I was the patient; Norma is bent on turning me into the doctor in the case.

"How about Tuesday or Wednesday, Papa? That all right?"

"All right nothing. I'm telling you, I'm not your hatchet man. You send him down and I'll hand him a six-pack and tell him to enjoy it."

Our discussion ended quickly when Rodney reappeared in my hall as if materialized by Houdini and, right on his heels, came a crashing whomp-whomp that sounded as if my door had been hit by a wrecking ball. The knob turned and Rufus, known hereabouts as Rufe, entered with his passkey.

Rufe is our giant super, standing about six and a half feet, the shoulders of a pulling ox. He must weigh three hundred, the color of high-grade anthracite, from somewhere down in the islands. Rufe wears a uniform of green shirt and pants with a New York Yankees cap perched on his head like a Dixie cup on a bowling ball.

"Mist Horrmonn say y'air out," he announced with a big grin, his wonderful accent making the words nearly unintelligible to me.

"What?" I asked.

"Your air conditioning, Papa," Norma translated.

"She out, Mist Horrmonn say."

"Good god, Rufe. I hate the stuff myself." And I do. This Eastern weather stays so beastly cold that I find my needs for cool air met nicely by one open window. We're into July, for godsakes, and my sweater is still out.

"I check'r," said Rufe, who, when I made introductions, tipped his cap to Norma and reached out a paw the size of a catcher's mitt to Rodney.

"Hi ya, Rufe, how're ya doin?" I thought myself that my grandson could do better.

"Fine sahr, jess fine." He went into the bedroom, ducking at the door, and I had visions of my furniture in splinters after he'd passed.

I was in the red chair, Norma on the love seat, Rodney what they call "hanging out," standing, leaning, sticking his head in to watch Rufe. Norma, seeming to forget our altercation for the moment, took a self-satisfied look around. "It looks so nice," she said. "Didn't we do a great job of packing you up?" She likes to relish that adventure.

"More like chucking me out," I grumped. "You threw away some of my best stuff."

"What a lot of things you had jammed into that little house, Papa. I wanted to keep more too, but we couldn't, even if I am more of a pack rat than you."

We both have trouble ridding ourselves of possessions merely because they are broken or useless. Out home though she set her teeth and heaved like a longshoreman. A fine time to reform, when her hands were in my stuff.

I heard Rufe crank a window shut and the whoosh of air conditioning. He came through into the living room and got this one going too.

"She work now, Mist Cahponter," he announced.

"Great news," I said, "but don't forget to turn them off before you leave."

"Turn er off?" Hurt puzzlement on his face.

"Rufe, I can't stand air, as they call it here. Isn't that right, Norma?"

"Saying 'air' for 'air conditioning'? Yes, but Papa . . . ."

"Mist Horrmonn say she heffal."

"Healthful," Norma translated.

"How does he know whether mine are on or off?"

"Clean lady, dey reparts."

"But Rufe, I *like* heat."

A smile spread across his face. "Yessah, Mist Cahponter, she be cold f'us come fum warhm place, but she ninney yistdee. Mist Horrmonn say hard on olderly."

"Elderly."

"You want drive sohmplice jess call Rufe, Mist Cahponter." He sometimes chauffeurs what we call the Eagle Crate, a station wagon with Olde English on the doors. It takes you anywhere in town for a dollar and a half and Rufe is eager to drive us, expecting big tips.

"Christ amighty," I said when he had gone, "that nitwit Harmon even wants to decide when I run my air conditioners."

"Now, Papa," Norma said soothingly, "he may be right about it being healthy. We've had it hot, you know."

"Hot, fiddlesticks. What's happened to you, child? Where's your St. Louis blood? Out there your juices don't begin to flow until it hits ninety."

"Exactly what it was, Papa. Didn't you hear Rufe? He said it was ninney yistdee."

They hadn't made the parking lot before I had the air off and a window open to warm up my digs.

I am not sure what happens next, but I suspect Norma will have her way and Rodney will turn up at my door. Once in a while my cheek is brushed, as if by a breeze, and there are rustlings telling of trouble just over the horizon. If I get my way I'll pass on by and pretend I didn't know. I've already experienced a lifetime of problems; surely the Almighty is not going to drop a bunch of new ones at my door. And that Norma, did she bring me a thousand miles so I could meddle in a boy's life?

⚡6

I was reading the paper in the library on mezz this morning when in walked Mrs. Walrod, chipper as a schoolgirl, and with her Mabel Moore, a dumpy one pushing eighty who relishes gossip and is given to flatulence. That isn't unusual amongst the elderly but Mrs. Moore goes public too often for my taste. She has been known to lay one at the gates at suppertime and in the sitting room while strolling about, bweep-bweep gronch-gronch, and she smiles coquettishly as if farting is a privilege reserved for her.

All was quiet at the gasworks this morning. "Catching up on the news, I see," said Mrs. Moore. "Anything in there worth reading?" She pointed to the *Times* in my hands.

"Big riots in Miami," I answered. "Several killed."

"Oh, pshaw," she said, using a word not often heard anymore, one we are called upon to spell only infrequently, "who needs that kind of news?"

"Not much gossip today," I told her, trying for a sardonic laugh. Mrs. Moore prefers the tabs. You know, boys barbecuing their mothers, girls got pregnant by chimps. We've all read about the elderly being arbiters of taste, wise and inscrutable. Malarkey. Old folks are like every-body else except they've had their bad habits longer.

Mrs. Moore alighted beside me, wafting up an odor of stale cabbage, and Mrs. Walrod settled into a green wing chair with yesterday's *Mail*. She held it at arm's length and squinted at the heads.

"Oughta try specs, Emily," said Mrs. Moore.

Mrs. Walrod laughed easily. "I do have reading glasses, Mabel, but I keep forgetting them." On purpose, I thought to myself; girls who wear glasses and all that.

"Couldn't see a bear sitting on my lap without specs," said Mrs. Moore.

"I've been missing them myself lately," I said. "Maybe I'd best get a pair of specs too, Mrs. Moore. Tell me, what's the latest gossip?" I couldn't resist the tease.

"Nobody ever tells me anything, Mr. Carpenter," she answered. "I saw something though: Chef Michel walking out with that little Margie chippie."

"You did?" said Mrs. Walrod. "What do you suppose they had in mind, Mabel?"

"Maybe going home after work," I said.

"You're such a tease, Mr. Carpenter," she said, laughing and showing her dimples. An appealing picture, she was.

Our library offers books and magazines and the papers. There's a big fireplace and I hear they lay fires in winter. Now, in July, with the air on at full blast, you could flash-freeze a goose in there. I'd gone in to read but got myself involved in socializing.

"I hear you still own an old farm in the Midwest," Mrs. Moore said next. "Why don't you sell it?" That's her way; she'll ask you anything, including the condition of your bowels.

"I guess because it's home," I answered, wondering myself.

"Where is it, Mr. Carpenter?" This from Mrs. Walrod.

"In Illinois, just outside Magellan. You know, out east of St. Louis. It's only forty acres, known around there as Old Farm."

"Whatever for?" asked Mrs. Moore.

"A long story, Mrs. Moore. Once an elderly man lived there and people got to calling him Old Man and his place Old Farm. Even his house was Old House."

"Well I never," clucked Mrs. Moore, "strange people out west."

"Present company excepted," added Mrs. Walrod. "Come on, Mabel, let's go on up and stop disturbing Mr. Carpenter."

They went along then, despite my protests and before I could tell them about my part in the naming of Old Farm.

Old Man, whose name was all but forgotten, was up in his eighties and living alone with his dog and a team of horses that he used to till the truck garden across the highway from his house. Since the last century his family had raised truck for the St. Louis market, but now he found it impossible to cope with the high-speed cars and trucks that had come to the highway in the '30s. After several incidents of being nearly run down, he wrote to the Governor and demanded an electric stop signal.

Word of the letter soon trickled down from Springfield and Mr. Bradly, who had a nose for good stories, sent me out to write a series on this lone man's struggle in an increasingly mechanized world. My copy was strewn with references to Old Man, Old Farm, Old House, even Old Black Dog. People who knew him had given him the Old Man name; I added the farm and the rest for easy reference. Two years later Old Man died and I bought the place from the courts, thinking one day to retire there with Dorothy. When I did finally go to Old Farm to live she was dead, our kids were gone and I was getting on toward being an Old Man myself.

Old Farm is adorned by willows along a brook that flows too sluggishly to babble. The garden over the road, where Old Man and his ancestors grew tomatoes and cabbage, is capable still of producing vegetables for a family of forty, were anybody to tend it.

A fancy country retreat Old House is not. There is a big eat-in kitchen with fieldstone fireplace where I warmed myself in winter, a small living room, bedrooms at front and side, a bathroom behind, a sizable screened porch. They once cooked in the fireplace and carried water from a spring, but by the time I moved in, Old House presided over a new pressure pump and an oil furnace.

The kitchen was my favorite, large enough for an upholstered chair and a good reading lamp, but last May it was also the scene of some bad luck. Norma paid me a surprise visit while Rodney was off with some school group and Clyde was God knows where. She saw chars on my kitchen walls, big ones.

"You trying for insurance, Papa?" she asked, sniffing like a coon hound.

"A few pieces of bacon flared up," I answered, not being inclined to describe the frenzied arrival of our Rural Volunteer Fire Department, nor the other conflagrations I'd created. They could be laid, I suppose, to a short attention span. I kept putting things on, getting bored waiting for them to heat and wandering away. My returns ran to feverish dashes toward leaping flames.

Norma soon ferreted out the truth. "Papa, you just can't live alone any longer," she said, hands on hips, "not with these fires and all. You're going to kill yourself at this rate."

"I'm thinking of a really big one next," I said petulantly, "something in the cremation range to save you the expense of burial."

She laughed, but that didn't change the results.

"I'm taking you back to Connecticut," she announced

in a way that made debate seem unlikely. "We have a nice new place in Marlow that they call a 'Retirement Home.' You can have your own apartment there and lead a normal life, not like one of those places where they have three or four in a room just waiting to die."

How could I know it was Eagle Arms she had in mind?

She returned for me in June and in two days I was sipping a TWA Bloody Mary over Pittsburgh, a migrant after all those years in Magellan. In the old days you followed in your father's footsteps and tended his farm when he was gone and lived in his house. Now they come to get us when the sand is running out and we go into migration as if searching for some elephant graveyard.

A day of sorting and tossing, an hour of packing by two men in an orange truck and Old House stood vacant. Departing was sad indeed; Old Farm had been my retreat and my shelter against the world.

There is a double-headed eagle over the door of my retreat in the East, and inside are twelve stories of people shunted off into the backwaters. Charred walls or not, I'd return to Old Farm in an instant. If Norma would let me. How strange, she now the stern parent, I the child.

7

There comes a time, in the higher age numbers, when the human body begins to slough off its light-reflecting properties, a phenomenon especially noticeable in retail establishments. A couple of middle age has no trouble being seen; if nattily dressed and exuding money, their luminosity cannot be dimmed even by the explosion of a terrorist bomb in the street outside. And clerks zero in on kids fast enough ("What's the little creep going to steal today?").

But alas, we grizzled veterans of life, our personages eroded by a drizzle of Social Security checks, simply do not get seen, or waited on either. I cannot explain what happens; I only observe that it does. There is no evidence of ill will by the salespeople. They really do not see us. Consequently, to get waited on in the flossy establishments, you sometimes resort to dramatic means.

Fletch got this hankering for a sterling silver teapot; why, I don't know, but we're all subject to idiotic urges sometimes, and I could see problems ahead for my friend. Silver of the kind he had in mind is found at only one place in town, Teasdale & Son Ltd, specialists in fine jewelry, silver and china since 1841. Teasdale's is bridal country, overflowing with mommies and grannies flocking in with the betrothed to arrange the Bridal Register and pick out patterns. A little guy like Fletch would come nearer swimming the Sound than getting waited on at Teasdale's.

You help a friend when you can, and so was born my Old Fart Costume, consisting of a tired old red jacket three sizes too big, baggy pants and an orchid-splattered tie off under my ear. On my head went a hat I bought in forty, the brim turned up in Harry Truman style, and I left my fly at half-mast, the hallmark of a geezer playing with a short deck.

Fletch and I met at the front desk, and he was ready to back out. One look at me and he said, "Why, Ben, you're gonna have the guys with the bug nets after us if you go in that store looking like that."

"Nonsense, Fletch. It's the only way we'll ever get noticed. We go in looking decent and we'll still be standing there on Christmas Eve."

Lucy, who presides over the front desk, burst into laughter, and soon we'd collected a small crowd of Residents, come to enjoy the sight.

"You see?" I said to Fletch. "People are naturally attracted to somebody dressed up like an Old Fart. We'll knock em dead at Teasdale's."

Fletch found new interest in our expedition then; wanted to share in the attention is more like it. Lucy called us a hack and we went to sit on the bench by the door. Outside, we could see rain coming down as if the dam of the heavens had split.

"I was thinking about driving us," he said, "but not in this rain, I can't."

"Then you weren't kidding about having a car?" Until then I had been uncertain. You know how old people are, in their minds equipping themselves with possessions they sold off twenty years ago.

"No no, Ben, she's there, all right, in the PG. Maudie, I call her."

By his account, Maudie is a little black British car, a Morris Minor 1000.

"Hardly a fit day to take up driving again," I said.

"One of these times we'll do it though. You and me'll go for a nice drive and then I'll get rid of her, have to. They wouldn't renew my license, said I was too old."

Uh oh. I was left wondering what they'll say about mine. Not that I need it, having no motorcar, but it's one of life's possessions, like a fly rod or a plug that used to pull in creels of bass, that you hate to give up even after its usefulness is gone.

Heavy gray clouds hung around the Arms like shrouds and our driver went down the hill at a creep, his eyes sizing me up in his mirror. His first genuine loony in a week.

Horrid weather or not, Teasdale's was jammed with expensive dresses and tailored suits. They stared into the cases with such concentration as scarcely to notice if you gnawed an ankle or yahooed up their skirts. It might have been a discouraging sight for a couple of old clucks who looked good for no more than a plated porridge spoon, thrown as we were into the major money leagues, but by that time Fletch had gone too far to turn back and I was enjoying my role.

We hobbled around shouting at each other as if we couldn't hear dynamite go off; Fletch began slobbering when he talked and I took to pointing dramatically with my walking stick. Most of the attention we were attracting at that point came from our fellow shoppers but when I began rapping my stick on their nice glass cases a mortician type showed up quickly. Black suit, black tie, black mustache, a black toupee probably secured with Crazy Glue and a fake British accent. I felt upstaged by his rig and feared he might suspect a practical joke. No such thought seemed to enter his mind. Old folks doing something in jest is beyond imagining.

"Please, gentlemen, you must be careful," he said with scant civility. "Our cases are delicate."

"I want a good sterling teapot," Fletch told him straight out.

"A gift perhaps?"

Fletch's thoughts evidently mirrored my own in wondering what business it was of his. "No," he said. "I want to wash my hair in it."

I think Black Mustache was at the point of telling us to bug off when the size of the sale stopped him. Later, as Fletch counted out six hundred and eighty dollars in tens and twenties, he was the recipient of a smile, no less, from Black Mustache.

The teapot is a graceful thing with a curving spout and little acorns around the middle.

At supper we sat two tables apart but I could hear Fletch laying it on thick. And making himself out to be the star of the show. A fine friend he is; I do him a favor and he steals my act. Maybe Norma is right. Eagle Arms really is a kindergarten where the pupils are got up to look old.

8

He came to me on the early bus and presented himself at the front desk while I was at breakfast. Lucy, her glasses in her hand, leaned over me and half whispered, "It's your grandson, Mr. Carpenter, waiting outside to see you. My, he must be an early riser."

"Takes after his grandpa," I said, and laughed with her while wondering whether there might be some truth in her jest. Rising early and breakfasting while the house sleeps on. You keep looking hopefully for traces of yourself that might survive you.

He extended his hand, formal as a salesman recalled to the home office. "Good morning, sir."

I shook his hand but added a kiss on the forehead. He *is* my grandson. "What's with the handshake?" I asked. "Something your father taught you?"

Rodney chuckled gleefully, unused, I suppose, to an adult who teases. "No, Grandpa, Dad's go more like this." A fine rendition of a *heil*.

"Come on," I said, "let's go on up before we get into trouble."

He was clad in the standard dress for his age, gym shoes, faded jeans and a tee shirt. Kiss Me I'm Horny, it said across the front. No wonder Lucy was smiling. On the way up in the elevator my sails lost most of their wind. In the years at Old Farm I was hardly more active socially than a monk sworn to silence, taking an occasional meal at a neighbor's house, having a friend in to sample my chili, pretty poor preparation for entertaining a sixteen-year-old.

He sprinted for the love seat as soon as I had the door open. "Boy, my favorite seat," he said excitedly, "best place to sit there is." He flopped down and spread himself ostentatiously. I'd not been aware that he knew one seat from another, let alone was able to make a value judgment. Maybe the kids are brighter than we think.

I offered juice but he declined. "Just had breakfast," he said, seeming to find difficulty in suppressing giggles.

"Well what brings you here, son?" I asked, knowing the answer full well. You get the bad over with first.

"Mom said you wanted to see me." An outright giggle this time. So that was how she had prepared him. Grandpa wants to see you. It seemed to me that I had on my hands a boy with exquisite expectations: a shopping bag filled with tens and twenties, a trust fund set up for his benefit, a rewriting of my will in his favor.

"No hint about why you should rush down on the early bus?" I was stalling for time.

"Nothing about early, Grandpa, just said come see you. I took the early bus because I was in a hurry to see you." More giggles, a boy eager to open his presents.

Considering what I was supposed to say to him, I felt lower than Simon Legree on Judgment Day. "What do you *think* you're here for, Rodney?"

"Oh, gee, I dunno. 'Cause I'm your grandson, I guess. I thought maybe you wanted to take me someplace." He crossed his arms one way, his legs another. "To tell you the truth, I was hoping you would want me to go down to Ticketron with you to get us tickets to a baseball game. You know the Cardinals are coming next week, don't you?"

His dreams were hardly of estate shares or cash money; going with me to Shea is his fondest wish. I felt mean and narrow, and certain then that I could not do

Norma's bidding. Let her parent as she wishes; I'll handle the grandparenting. "I haven't thought about that," I said, "but maybe we can take in a game later. Can't we just pay at the gate?" At Sportsman's Park I used to get a grandstand seat for eighty-five cents, a bottle of beer for a dime.

"No, Grandpa, we go over to Ticketron on State now."

He had to explain that one to me, Ticketron not being a big deal at Old Farm. We did not get baseball tickets, didn't go anywhere. I pulled some ancient junk out of my walk-in as if it had been my intention all along, and he was enthralled. Modern kids are past understanding, fascinated with these electronic gadgets, but you show them a box of fifty-year-old trash and they go through it like a blind man examining a sculpture.

I gave him my slate from grammar school and a wooden pencil box, and he wanted to know who the people were in my Kodak pictures. The one with the pretty girl's face, dressed in the baggy finery of the twenties, turned out to be his grandmother, and he was delighted.

Once I asked how he's doing this summer at home.

"Fine," he said happily. "Mom leans on me sometimes but she don't mean it. I just stay out of Dad's way. I've read two books and busted the pee out of the lawnmower on a rock."

"Your mother used to write us what a fine little scholar you were."

"Yeah, but Mom don't know hardly nuthin."

I had to laugh at his grownup-style humor. Those who are only children, without siblings, seem to take steps into adulthood before they've rightly finished being a child.

At noon we went down to the dining room after everybody was seated and my grandson's tee shirt brought on some indulgent titters but no growling disapproval such as I had anticipated. Old folks seldom live up to the harsh images they get stuck with. Margie howled when she read his tee shirt, tweaked his ear and told him he was groovy.

Jackie later brought over Ruby Switzer, a quiet lady, widow of a corn farmer up around Cherokee in Iowa. She looks work-worn, still has the pale skin and freckles of a redhead.

Rodney, learning of her past life, announced, "Grandpa still owns a farm in Illinois, don't you, Grandpa?"

"A small one. What Mrs. Switzer is talking about is a big farm, hundreds of acres."

"We used to farm it all with horses," she told Rodney. "I don't suppose you can picture that at your age, but we always had six teams, sometimes eight or ten." She went on to remember the horses by name and color and idiosyncrasies. So far as I could see, she never noticed Rodney's tee shirt, a colorless person but agreeable and sincere, and Rodney liked her.

My grandson saw more than I thought. As I walked to the flagpole with him to see him on his way down the hill to the bus he said, "It was Mom's idea, wasn't it, Grandpa?"

"What?"

"This visit by me. She wanted you to read me the riot act, right?"

"Well . . ."

"Don't worry, Grandpa, I'll cover for you."

Evidently he did, in spades. In the evening Norma called and sounded as if she'd discovered the fountain of youth. "He's been just grand ever since he got home, Papa," she told me ecstatically. "Do you know what that boy did? He took everything out of the pantry and cleaned the shelves and then put it all back in neat rows. I don't know what you told him, Papa, but it worked like a charm."

9

Fletch came by after breakfast and read my Teasdale's account. "Sounds exaggerated to me," he said.

"Might be, Fletch, but that's the way writing is. You leave out all but the bare details and what's left can appear exaggerated."

"You sound like a dentist that got caught pulling the wrong tooth. What's this here about me stealing your act?" He pointed to the last sheet.

"I heard you at supper, you old goat, making yourself out to be the star of the day."

He cackled, his eyes sparking. "Have to do that, Ben, when you're entertaining the ladies. What you going to do with all this stuff?" He tapped my box lid, now beginning to fill with copy paper.

"When it gets full I'll throw it out and start over," I told him. "It's only to entertain myself, you know. I've been writing so long I can't stop now."

"Sounds nuts to me. Whyn't you write a book about that town of yours like that feller Lewis? Shocked hell out of everybody." He ambled out saying he was going for a swim. I've heard about his swims. In our pool, a little thing on PG level that Rufe keeps hot enough to parboil a steer, he sits at the shallow end and splashes himself. That's swimming, eighty-six-year-old style.

I'd go walking except for the infernal rain, the tail end of a hurricane, they say. I always thought hurricanes stayed down in Florida. Fact is, I don't know much about my new state; I walk in the streets and wonder what is going on around me. If I were to be reborn as a reporter down at the *Mail* I'd find out soon enough. I can imagine what they'd say at the *Mail* if I asked for a job, and what Norma would say if they gave me one.

My daughter has this image of Papa at Eagle Arms and I'd better match it or else. Take the card table and folding chairs in my walk-in, bought not because I wanted them but because they were on her list, put there by a girl with visions of her father playing poker and drinking beer with his cronies. Sometimes I want to tell her, "Ah, have a heart, child; I only want to live till I die. I don't care about setting styles." But I keep my mouth shut; she's trying very hard for me.

This flat, which Norma insists on calling my "apartment," is pleasing to her and she likes to open the double doors in the corner and admire my sink, the size of a soup bowl, the fridge, the cupboard above and counter to the left. The only appliance I seem to use is the electric kettle, for tea. I've toasted nothing, nor saucepanned, nor skilleted. Norma will come into some dandy gimcracks one of these days.

Despite my grumping, the place is comfortable enough. Inside my door is a short hall with bath to the right, walk-in closet to the left, a tiny linen closet hanging onto its edge. You come through into the living room and there's a door on the right to my bedroom. Double windows look out over rooftops and past factory stacks to the steel gray of the Sound. My work table is an old cherry thing from the home place, where it held this self-same typing machine. I bought it for seven dollars from the *Times* when Mr. Bradly, years and years ago, decided the new noiselesses more suited to his News Room. Until he got the bill. Mr. Bradly threw fits then, called us ingrates for wanting new machines. He had a way of forgetting the origin of ideas that went bad.

Places like this have one feature new to us all, the

Help switch with its lighted toggle and white cord dangling. There's one in my hall, another over the tub, a third in my bedroom. They come running when you pull.

My flat is a One Bedroom. The Arms also offers a Studio and the Alcove model Fletch took. He says it's so small that when he retires the doorknob gets in bed with him. There's a Two Bedroom too but I've never seen a sample. Mrs. Walrod has one on six, and last evening I met a fellow retired journalist who occupies a Two way up on ten.

Now we have as many drab and ordinary Residents as you'll find outside but I seem, like a compass needle, to gravitate toward those not so commonplace. Maybe journalists as a breed have a weakness for the bizarre, and it could be that one resident journalist here at the Arms is as barmy as the other.

I was coming out from supper, walking with Ed Cobb, our own Kentucky Colonel, and there stood Lucy with a woman hitched to her hand like a haltered mare brought to a stud farm.

"I want you to meet another writer like yourself," Lucy said, smiling sweetly. "Ben Carpenter, Ruth Kirkbride."

"Howja do, Ben," said Mrs. Kirkbride, extending a hand. She's new here in the last week, a skinny one in her late sixties, her shortish gray hair pointing straight back like a pike. Her voice is all growly, wonderfully suited to an Alpo commercial.

"Welcome to Little Sing-Sing," I said and, at Lucy's urging, we went to the sitting room to compare notes.

"What publications did you write for, Ben?" she asked.

"Only one, the *Times* in Magellan, Illinois."

"Oh, I've heard of that. They have a steel mill there, don't they, Ben?" It seemed to me that she was picking up on my first name a bit fast, even for a journalist.

"Three mills, Mrs. Kirkbride, we have three steel mills."

"Call me Ruthie," she said. "Everybody does." I was trying not to look at her mouth, scene of some unusual activity. Two of her upper incisors, as Fletch might put it, are on wires and the damned things jump up and down when she talks.

"You what they call a newshen?" I asked, throwing in a friendly chuckle. It's in my nature to tease.

"News what? Oh. No, I was a columnist, did a cooking column for years and years."

"That's impressive, Ruthie. What paper were you on?"

"Several; I had six in New Jersey and there were two in Pennsylvania for a while. 'Cooking with Ruthie' ran every Thursday in all of them. Thursday was grocery day in all the papers."

"So your column was syndicated, was it?"

"Sort of. My husband owned the papers, you see. You've heard of the Kirkbride Enterprises newspapers, haven't you?"

"Well, no, I haven't. I'm from the Midwest."

"My husband's father founded the chain," she explained, her teeth tossing about like chips in a roiling sea, "and my husband kept it going until we sold to Gannett."

"When they bought you out, is that when your column ended?"

"Oh, no, long before that. My cook did all the dishes for the column anyway, so I said one day, 'Lillie, you already do the cooking so why don't you do the writing too?' So she did, took it off my hands."

I was dumbfounded. "And it worked out all right?" I asked, thinking that perhaps journalism school is more of a waste of time than we realize.

"Oh, sure, better than ever."

Every one of our Residents has a different story to tell, but few I've heard are as strange as Ruthie Kirkbride's.

Fletch with his tale of indentured dentistry, Mrs. Switzer and her draft horses, Mrs. Cardoza and old-time Cuba, I and my days as a reporter—none of us can match Mrs. Kirkbride in unexpected twists.

🦆10

Geologic readings in the earth's mantle speak of a tropical South Pole and glaciers in the desert, and to them now can be added the migration of the monsoon belt to Connecticut. I called Norma this morning to inform her of my discovery.

"The monsoon belt?" she said, shrieking with laughter. "Wherever did you get that idea, Papa? We don't have more rain here than back home, except lately, with the hurricane and all."

"Rats. My first season here and you people order up a deluge for me. Whyn't you come and have lunch with me, and bring the tyke too? I'll pay." Old Ben pandering again.

"Can't today, Papa; some people coming from Altman's to measure for slipcovers."

"They must travel in rubber boats," I said.

"Why don't you write something, Papa? Maybe something about Magellan."

I think the town has hired a PR agent.

🦆

My part of Illinois in midsummer is an unending carpet of green. Corn covers the countryside as if it were a native flora never violated by plow. Highways make dark veins through the greenery and sluggish rivers meander like tired salamanders. It was the primordial ancestors of these streams that dropped their silt until a deep rich loam formed. Not until millions of years later did agriculture arrive.

Corn has fed the hungry since before history began, but corn did not build Magellan. From ten miles away, when the wind is in your face, you can scent the acrid smoke flowing from Magellan's vitals. In town, fly ash turns white curtains gray in two days and reddens the eyes of the uninitiated. The town's skyline is spiked by seven tall stacks, and when business is good all of them belch clouds into the pollution-paled sky. Magellan is no American Beauty amongst cities, but smoke and fly ash put food on your table and clothes on your kids.

Steel mills, in my mind, were what they had in Pittsburgh when I went to Magellan, a farm boy newly diplomaed in journalism by the University of Missouri. My schooling had cost my parents forty good acres, and now it was obligatory that I prove their investment worthwhile. The J School bulletin board told of a staff opening at *The Magellan Times* and to Illinois I went. Learning of life in a steel town was a mere accompaniment to a job.

Magellan received me and Magellan kept me until the day Norma jetted out to collect what was left. Here I have staff to bring meals and a maid to clean my flat. My life has not always been this way; once, it was better, a wife to cook my meals and a bus that, for ten cents, took me to work at the only thing I ever wanted to do.

Deadline madness and Clint Bradly notwithstanding, being a reporter meant more to me than medals or gold doubloons. Doubloons for sure; riches do not come to those on a reportorial staff. I made enough however to get us through, and to see me to the end unless I go for a hundred.

Newspapermen when I came along were a rough lot,

seldom sober half an hour after their last copy fell into the wire basket on the City Desk. If a piece was especially long, a midpoint refueling at Hagerty's might be necessary. Hard drinkers though they were, they wrote with fierce independence, putting down what they saw and believed. Their copy was rife with gritty opinion, and you never caught them hiding behind quotes from officials such as you see so often these days. They dug and they wrote, and it was partly due to them that we said Stateville had more politicians than Springfield.

I tried to pattern my career after those old-timers in the way I wrote, though in conduct I was never as brazen and, after a singular Friday evening's swilling with my colleagues at Hagerty's, and requiring the assistance of two of them to get home, I never tried to equal them in alcohol intake. One series I wrote got our new City Manager started on his way to the rock pile. Kansas City claims to have pioneered the city manager form of government. Fiddlesticks. Our City Manager was hired, fired and at Stateville before they ever heard of the idea.

The way to get ahead in newspapering is to go from reporter to the rim of the City Desk, into its slot as city editor and on up the ladder of management. One February I spent a year on the Wire Desk, and later two weeks on the City Desk seemed an eternity. The American ethic of slogging your way to the top did not take in my case. I had no stomach for copy-slashing or the counting of heads; God meant me to be a reporter.

My degree, making me the first college graduate ever at the *Times*, including Mr. Bradly, who considered two years at junior college sufficient education, was supposed to be a guarantee of success and sure wealth. When it became obvious that my parents had put their money on a sweepstakes ticket and lost, they were as understanding as saints and remained as proud of me as if I'd bought out J. P. Morgan.

Harry Cassidy did not understand, as city editors often don't. "Carpenter," he said, "you, a college graduate, why in hell do you keep poundin that damned typewriter? You'll never get rich that way." He needed a man on the rim at the time, making his advice suspect. Mr. Cassidy chewed tobacco and kept spitoons both left and right. When you approached from behind you learned, like passing ships, to make a signal for port or starboard. Otherwise, as many a cub found out, your copy might pick up a large brown splot.

At unexpected moments our City Editor showed streaks of kindness. When Norma was born, a Tuesday's child full of grace, he let me off until Saturday half-day, a generosity that got him a rebuke from Clint Bradly.

A basic tenet of journalism I learned from the itinerant drunks who passed through our City Room was this: when the fun is gone, move on. Dozens of them did. I stayed; Magellan and the *Times* were fun enough for me.

Most people have heard of Magellan, though not much, its star dimmed by the large shadow of St. Louis. In the census of sixty, when I was still on staff, we counted fifty thousand, almost. No small town by any stretch, and Magellanites resent being ignored while St. Louis is known round the world, though not lately for football. That's a local joke.

When my wife was alive we had a good house out east, on Reed Street, and in spring there were peonies in the front borders. I kept a garden in back to supply our table, and the bus stopped half a block up. I remember the bad times of the thirties, but Dorothy said that, together, we could beat anything. A remarkable woman.

In Connecticut we have no factory fumes and no fly ash, and I live in a place of luxury. But in an instant I'd trade it all for the little I used to have.

11

There was a major improvement last evening in my social season. At supper I sat with Lloyd Axelrod and Jackie brought over Mrs. Cardoza, who this time was silent and introspective, looking every bit her age. Lloyd was quick to fill the conversational gap.

"When I started at GE we were all just electrical engineers, EEs," he said. "Nobody'd heard of electronics yet."

"Newspapers had hot type when I started," I said, matching him step for step. "There were chases to hold the slugs, and lead shells came from the Stereotype Room. Now it's all computers."

"Is that so?"

"Well, not at the *Times* of course. The cost of changing over could give Mr. Bradly a seizure."

He came back with more tales from GE and I learned his daughter died of whooping cough at ten, his wife a year ago. He has a son in Stamford and hates Eagle Arms. "Boy, I wish I was back in Rochester," he said. Don't we all! Even Rochester.

I was out by the elevators when along came Mrs. Walrod and Mrs. Kirkbride. "Have you met Mr. Carpenter?" asked Mrs. Walrod.

"Yes yes, Ben and I've met," said Mrs. Kirkbride, smiling and wiggling her teeth.

"Lucy introduced us," I offered.

"Ben's from one of these steel towns in Illinois," said Mrs. Kirkbride. "Granite City, is it?" The bandying-about of my first name brought a look of surprise to Mrs. Walrod's finely featured face, I noted with a remarkably pleasurable feeling.

"I'm afraid it's Magellan, my dear," Mrs. Walrod said with a tinkling laugh. "We've all heard about the glories of Magellan, and Mr. Carpenter would love to be there right now." She smiled at me impudently.

"Is that true?" Mrs. Kirkbride asked me in disbelief. There are some towns you can't imagine anyone calling "home."

"Mrs. Walrod is right," I told her. "I'd give half a year of what I've got left to be back in Magellan."

"But it's so smoky and dirty."

"That's true," I answered. "You can see what you're breathing, all right."

"Your lungs must be black as stump water, Ben, and here it's so clean and clear."

"I know it sounds strange," I said, thinking of the sooty bags hanging in my rib cage, "but, dirty or not, Magellan is home to me."

I wandered off to the sitting room, thinking to find Fletch and get up a game, but he'd gone on, and I'd decided to go up when I felt ever so light a tap on my elbow. "You and Mrs. Kirkbride are hitting it off famously," said a low teasing voice. "She calls you Ben already." Mrs. Walrod, laugh wrinkles at her eyes, a sparkling smile.

"Well, she's a retired journalist, you know," I said with a near giggle, "and we had a lot to talk about."

She produced a blush, very becoming to her clear face. "I'm about to go up and make myself some tea, Mr. Carpenter. Care to join me?"

"Tea? Didn't Margie give you tea?" I'm afraid I'll never be known as a big operator.

"Good tea, I mean. I never take it in the dining room. Terrible brew. I think they make it with eagle feathers."

Mmmm, my kind of humor. "Let's go before you change your mind," I said.

By now I suppose the whole building knows; gossip runs through the Arms like fleas in a dog's hair. Norma once said, "Poor dears, what else have they got to do?" She's probably right, but I'm damned if I really care whether they talk or not.

She made good English tea, with milk and two lumps, and her flat is something, a huge place with a terrace off the living room. The sliding door was open and a smell of the sea was evident. "We're getting an onshore breeze," she said, and I guess she knows. We sat on velvet armchairs of gray with some color overcast. Taupe, she said, and was pleased by my compliment.

I was not unaware of the game in progress; only, time has eroded my abilities. She, sipping her tea and smiling winningly, knows every one of the rules by heart. Cute, I told myself, and she was.

"I was tickled that you and Dr. Pepper had so much fun getting his teapot," she said.

"Couple of geezers pretending to be schoolboys," I said, "but we enjoyed it, the hunt and the conquest and all."

"So wonderful for Dr. Pepper. He has a very bright mind, Ben, and so little to occupy it. Such a nice man."

It was her first use of my Christian name, which pleased me inordinately, though her opinion of Fletch seemed too forgiving for her own good. "Oh, he's quite nice," I said, "but the old rascal almost gave you the up-chucks the other night with his gory story." Setting the record straight, I told myself.

Emily giggled. "Wasn't that funny, Ben? Oh, he can sure be a tease when he wants to."

"Sure can."

"His problem is his lack of interests, I think. You have so many, of course."

"I do?" It was news to me.

"So I hear," she said, scooting around in her chair and

showing a nice set of dimples. "They say you're a writer, and I think that's wonderful, Ben."

"Was," I told her, "I was a writer of sorts, a journalist on a newspaper. I'm retired now, Emily."

"Oh, but you writers don't have to stop, like clerks and factory hands; you keep right on writing. We were chicken farmers, my husband and I, but I'm sure out of it now."

"So am I, out of writing. I pound my Remington occasionally for old time's sake, but nobody wants my stuff." The unfortunate truth.

"Dr. Pepper said you are writing a book."

"A *book?*" I gulped. Fletch has put me in there with Faulkner and Fitzgerald. "It's only some sketches for my own enjoyment. Nobody's ever going to read them except me."

Emily adjusted her bodice and laughed coquettishly. Don't ask me what a coquettish laugh is, but this was one. I'm out of practice, but not that far out. "You wouldn't mind letting me read a little of it, would you, Ben? I've never actually known a book author. Maybe you could have me down for tea, or a real drink. It's been a long time since I've tasted anything but wine."

Oi vey, as they say on television. She'll come if I ask. Wonderful. But having her read these pages, in which she and a lot of other Residents appear, is something else. I can imagine what some of them would do if they found out. Those things haven't been in prominent use since the Middle Ages.

The doorbell's dong-ding saved me from answering.

"Who could that be?" Emily said, vexed, I hoped.

There was a voice in the hall. "Oh, I'm sorry; didn't know you had company." In she came, Mrs. Moore in person, her eyes darting like a weasel's in a henhouse.

"We're having tea," said Emily. "Come in and join us, Mabel."

"Hello, Mrs. Moore," I said, a sigh slipping out.

Mrs. Moore swept over from the hall emanating a faint odor of Bismol, her eyes checking the level of the tea in our cups. "Good evening, Mr. Carpenter. I hope I haven't disturbed you two."

"You want tea or not?" Emily asked. "Make up your mind, Mabel."

"Not this time, thanks. Tea comes back on me sometimes, causes trouble in my entrails."

She'd seen us go off to the elevator together, I suppose, and now had arrived to check our progress.

"At least sit and chat a minute, Mabel," said Emily.

"Oh, three's a crowd, you know, and besides, I have to go up and take one of those awful enemas. What's that sweetish smell?"

"A sweetish smell? Why, I don't know, Mabel. My cologne maybe, but it's not sweet. Do you smell anything, Mr. Carpenter?" I had to admire the subtleties of her play, returning to my surname in the presence of an outsider.

"No, I don't smell anything," I said, "but then, my nose gave up years ago." There was some observed truth in what I said; the sense of smell goes first.

I next witnessed this incredible thing with Mrs. Moore's proboscis. It wiggled, so help me, like a rabbit's, and I could see her trying to home in on a scent. "It's coming from your bedroom, Emily," she announced.

Then I remembered a piece of gossip I'd heard. Mrs. Moore claims she can detect an odor when people have been fooling around, has this incredible ability to smell sex. I very nearly burst into laughter when I realized what was happening. Mrs. Moore was doing a scent recon in Emily's woods, and probably checking the spread for heel and toe imprints as well. She evidently confused us with a pair of rabbits, and young ones at that.

"A perfume bottle. That's what it was," said Mrs. Moore, emerging triumphantly from the bedroom. "Maybe I will take that cup of tea after all, Emily."

And she did, was still sipping it when I left.

12

I wish I knew what my daughter is up to. She called this morning to warn of an impending visit; like get yourself ready, the Queen is coming. Which I thought, but what I said was, "Good news, my child! Whyn't you come Monday, say about eleven, and we can visit and go down to lunch. I haven't had much chance to show you off." In a place like this you like to exhibit your relations, unless they show creases left by handcuffs or wear a coat riddled by buckshot. Maybe even then.

"Oh, I'm not sure about the day, Papa, and I can't spend that much time. I just want to ask you about some family things, make some arrangements."

"Norma, arrangements are exactly what are made over lunch here in the East. I've seen it on television, and in movies too."

"Well, I just won't have the time, I'm afraid, but I'll call you right before I leave home. Got to run. Bye now."

They never have quite enough time for you. I'll bet Clyde thinks nothing of spending two hours over Martinis and roast beef, extra well, please, with some client. Or Norma with her bridge club or Clyde's boss's wife. But forty-five minutes to sup with the old man? Not today, no. My kids did not invent this shortage of time by any stretch. I can remember myself when twenty minutes visiting in some nursing home seemed like hours. It has to do, I think, with not wanting to be reminded of how you'll look one day.

Maybe she wants some more of her mother's dwindling possessions, or to talk about Old Farm, make sure her name is spelled right in my will. They always get around to wills if your hair is white or your company gives you the retirement boot and lays it on heavy about the Golden Years, an expression that rates on my popularity list just below Balance Due and Stagflation. Next time you hear somebody spraying rose-scented words on the Golden Years sneak up and kick him in the ass and say Ben sent you.

I was writing good stuff at sixty-four, though no longer first-line news, and on my sixty-fifth birthday Clint Bradly called me over to his desk in the corner of the City Room. I'd taken two obits and the weather and done a column on a Chinese first-haircut party, and now, I was sure, he would ask me to stay on.

"Ben, you've had a long career here at the *Times,*" Mr. Bradly began. "Know how long it's been?"

Of course I knew. A man keeps some track of his life. "Something over forty," I answered.

His smile suggested I was amusing but he knew better. "Forty-three to be exact, Ben. I researched it for the watch."

"The watch?" I should have known, but didn't yet, perhaps because I didn't want to.

"Ben, you've had a long career here at the *Times,*" he began again, as if he had to start at the top to get it right, "and now I hope you have a happy and fruitful retirement of equal length."

"That'll get me to a hundred and eight," I said, "but what'll I do after that?"

His middle drawer yielded up a thin box of cream plastic. "A small token of our esteem, Ben."

"A Timex, Mr. Bradly?" I wasn't letting things go quite the way he'd planned.

He gave a dry laugh to show he knew a joke when he heard one, though not well. "I think you'll find this watch to be a pretty swell timepiece, Ben." He handed it to me with his left while shaking with his right. Dale Carnegie has a chapter on that.

The watch said Bulova on its face and the back showed my name with starting and retirement dates. It was like receiving a summons to the gallows, and as unexpected. I'd been sure he would keep me on.

"Ben, you've been so faithful all these years, just exemplary"—he'd been digging into *Roget's* as well—"so now I want you to take off early today. Just go home and enjoy your new freedom."

It was going on eleven, and a Saturday. We knocked off at noon on Saturdays and the presses already had had a trial start-up, with the usual back-shop yelling. One of the webs had torn but they'd be rolling soon. Big deal.

And so it ended with neither banquet nor speech. In a single morning, after forty-three years, ten months and six days, my career ran down and stopped, and I got off an hour early. I was never fond of fanfare, would have rejected a banquet and encomiums, but he might at least have given me the opportunity to say no. The Falcon waited in the parking lot and on the way home I decided to sell out immediately and move to Old Farm. Dorothy had been dead two months then, cancer of the stomach killing her in a scant three weeks. The kids were gone too, and so at last it was time for me to get out.

The money part went down all right, as they say. I'd paid twenty-three hundred, sold for forty-two thousand. We never lived high off the hog and now, with savings and my retirement pay and Social Security, I'd probably have enough to see me through. Sometimes though when I awaken at three in the morning I fret about running out and having to eat Alpo and exist on welfare. What still galls me about those days was being torn from my job like a chimp stripped from its mother's arms.

Forced retirement did not befall Mr. Bradly of course,

for he is the Owner. On my first day at the *Times* I took him to be much older than myself. Now I know he was only twenty-eight, but I was twenty-one. Seven years can be a thick proposition if you look like Clint Bradly, steel-rim glasses grappling at his ears, a scowl illuminating his features as he looked over the ads and toted up his profits.

They were still peddling tales about Clint's daddy, Roy, when I got to town, a huge man with gargantuan appetites who at sixty discovered the motorcar and set out to make up for lost time. He took a Cadillac sedan, had it repainted flaming red and roared around with visions of Barney Oldfield in his head. Drank like a fish, drove like a maniac, they said.

One autumn evening on the rise at the south end of Madison he met a trolley head-on. It was old, and mostly of wood, and the avenue was left filled with a haystack of splintered planks covering tortured red metal shards. Roy Bradly took the motorman and five passengers with him on his last ride.

I spent years watching hopefully for hints of manias in Roy's son but none appeared. His appetite lay in the cashbox. He is there yet, reaching now for eighty, still a much older man. You have to feel younger than somebody.

The worst part of being a retired journalist is knowing your copy has lost all worth. The little envelopes at the *Times*, filled every Friday with greenbacks and silver, put a value on my work. At Old Farm I tried novels but got nothing down worthwhile. I had other work there: gardening in summer, hacking on my woodpile in winter.

There are no woodpiles here, or any gardens. I do find one tiny sample of journalism, a little monthly called *Notes from the Eyrie* put out by none other than Mr. Harmon. One can see he's desperate for help so I've decided to offer my talents. For free. How can he refuse?

Notes appears to have been concocted by a junior-high class in remedial journalism; you know, all the kids that failed last year. On p. 1 of this issue, under "Stwum Fun," it tells about the "relaxing and rejuvenating exercises" led beside our pool by, of all people, Mr. George Harmon. He gets his name in a lot, I've noticed.

On p. 3 we read that Residents were charmed by a picnic in the sun room, swarmed to mezz for a slide show on Nepal, and happy birthday to Becky Fisher and Ruby Switzer. In truth, the picnic was as dull as a teetotaler's wake and at the slide show Residents outtalked the narrator.

"Romance?" says the boldface intro. "What beauteous Resident over eighty years young is being courted by a Dapper Townsman who is—get this!!—too young to move in but wants to?? Just wait folks and see, love will find a way!"

A decent journalist could no more let malarkey like that go by unprotested than Carry Nation could ignore drunken haloos from a saloon. Hang on, Mr. Harmon, help is coming.

13

Ben, you numskull, when will you learn that Tuesdays are for staying in bed and having trays sent up?

Importuned in the morning by my daughter, scorned in the afternoon by Mr. Harmon, in the evening given a talking-to by my grandson—what more could go wrong?

Norma's promised call to warn of her visit came from downstairs. "Papa? It's me. I'm coming to see you, okay?"

"Come ahead."

I hadn't got the spread on my bed before the doorbell

went off. "You just set a new world record," I told her. "Two minutes from your house to here must be near a thousand miles an hour."

"I was only downstairs, Papa." She settled on the love seat with an indulgent smile.

"Some warning you gave me."

"I was going to call from home but didn't have time. I was so rushed."

I would have taken her to task for the time required to call from home versus downstairs, which seemed like something out of cuckoo-land, but the way she sat with her purse clutched in her lap as if it held the crown jewels told me it was no time to jest. The kettle was full and plugged in when I took the red chair.

"You're always so rushed, my dear," I said kindly. "You and Clyde too. In fact, everybody in the East. What's wrong with you people, Norma? Got permanent wasps up your behinds?" People on the outside here do seem to have their governors stuck on Trot.

"Always so much to do and not enough time to do it, Papa."

I used to feel that way myself but I know better now. "Do what you can and skip the rest, Norma. Going through life with white knuckles is scarcely living at all."

The kettle whistled and I made tea, two lumps and milk for me, plain for her. She drinks her coffee black too, I notice, and has a husband who takes his gin straight, almost. They are people of severe tastes; none of your sweet touches for them. It's like, almost twenty-five years later, finding your daughter living grimly and self-righteously amongst the Amish or the Hutterites. I think Norma and Clyde are fast making up for my own miserable failure to accumulate great wealth.

We'd taken maybe two sips when she came to the point in a rush. "Rod," she said. "We're having trouble with him again, Papa."

Like a broken record. "What this time?"

"He went down the other day and did pre-enrollment without even asking us. Put himself in all easy courses, Appreciation of Art, Village Life in Pre-History New England, things like that." She named off more but I've forgotten.

"They sound good enough to me," I told her, which was true. "If schoolwork is anything like it used to be, that Village Life one is no snap."

"But they're all so useless, Papa, don't you see? How can anybody make a living out of Appreciation of Art? That's what Clyde said, and that Rod has no business sense at all."

"Your husband is involved now, is he? That's wonderful, Norma. Sometimes I worry that he has no time for anything but his job."

"I read him Rod's schedule on the phone and that's what he said. Clyde's in Detroit."

"What does he want the boy to take? Basic Bartending? Toll Collecting for Beginners? Now there's a couple that could turn money."

"Clyde says he should take some business courses, maybe one of those in executive development, that kind. And he's a man, he should know."

"I'll just bet that's what Clyde wants, but everybody does not swing the same way, my dear. I never studied business but I did manage to keep food on our table. What do you want of me?"

I didn't have to ask. Talk to the boy again, she says, like last time, little suspecting the truth about last time. Get him to thinking right, she says, like Clyde does, and get him to make changes in his school schedule. I have such a way with my grandson, and she knows I wouldn't mind.

"I'll talk to him, sure," I said, "but I warn you that I'll give him what I think is good advice, not necessarily what Clyde wants."

She went away looking dubious.

My interview with Mr. Harmon, if anything, was less rewarding yet. He fired me before I ever got the job, consigning me forever, it appears, to writing for my box lid.

Now George Harmon has admirers. Some of our ladies very nearly swoon when he passes and throws them a smile. I'm simply not in that group. Even God doesn't demand such a title. God is only God. Mr. Harmon is Executive Director. If staff wore uniforms he'd be sewing eight stars a shoulder like Latin dictators. We Residents only pay his salary and, in exchange, get to wtach him move easily amongst us like Jesus Christ in elevator shoes, his green-tinted glasses with pop-up lenses clamped securely to his face, his salt-and-pepper toupee cropped close in GI fashion. George Harmon sees an imposing figure in our wall mirrors, I'm sure, but the elevator shoes are a mystery on a man who must stand six feet in socks. Maybe he met a man of six two and got a fright.

The ladies are by no means universally admiring. You hear them talk about his Prussian blood, and they laugh, and about the anglicizing of his name. Ellie Longo, who lives between me and the corner, favors little *heil* salutes behind his back, and once when he was lecturing Rufe on vacuuming, Jenny Biggs put two fingers beneath her nose for a mustache. Mr. Harmon commanded Rufe to vacuum both up and down and back and forth, which even I knew was unnecessary, the machine having sufficient lung power to suck up a billy goat.

I have sought a sweet reasonable side to Mr. Harmon, but in vain. What you see is what you get; there is no more. Lucy announced me this afternoon and Mr. Harmon himself opened the door and gave me a gorilla handshake. His lenses were flipped up in gull-wing fashion.

"Well, Ben, come right in," he said jovially. "I don't get to talk to you often." True, but hardly my fault since I'm not on the road much these days.

"I want to talk to you about this," I said, holding up a

copy of *Notes*. "I think I could help you, being a professional journalist with a lot of experience."

He flipped down his lenses one by one, snap snap, and sat in his monster black chair, motioning me to a spindly wooden thing of French design. He has to have the upper hand even in furniture. "A journalist, huh?" he mused, running knobby fingers through his toup. "I knew you worked on newspapers, Ben, but I didn't realize you were a journalist too."

"Same thing, Mr. Harmon. Reporters and deskmen are called 'journalists.' "

"Oh?" he said, looking puzzled. "What does this have to do with our in-house publication?" Now there's a journalistic term he knows, a man of many talents, deficient in all.

"I could give it a more professional tone," I answered.

Mr. Harmon was becoming noticeably leery, my reputation for leg-pulling having spread around the Arms, enhanced by the Old Fart Costume drama. It seemed to me that he expected something on the order of a stink bomb left in the pocket of his golden blazer, which hung on a coat tree at the door. "Oh?" he said, and that was all.

"I'd donate my services, Mr. Harmon," I added. "Wouldn't cost you a cent."

He removed his glasses, bit the earpiece and tilted back and forth. "Well, Ben," he hemmed, "I'm afraid that just isn't possible."

His bald rejection, before he's heard a single detail, made my ears smoke. "And why the hell not, Mr. Harmon?"

Suddenly tense and uncomfortable in the presence of a Resident who used foul language right in front of the Executive Director, he was trying yet to sound reasonable. "It's like this, Ben. We find it's best if Management produces the contents of any newsletter for Residents. Everybody in the field knows that."

I didn't give up easily. "How can it be a Residents'

newsletter if they have nothing to say about what goes into it? All I want is to contribute a few pieces."

"We can appreciate that," he said, replacing his glasses, "but you must understand that we are experienced professionals when it comes to communicating with Residents."

Oh, yes, the fears of Management of anything that might be the least threat to their Investment. Moscow is hardly up to the kind of press control we have right here in Marlow. It was clear I'd never get anywhere, but the urge to devil came upon me. "Maybe there's room for a competitive newsletter, Mr. Harmon. Competition always improves journalism, they say."

"*What?*" His eyebrows shot up and his expression suggested he'd just swallowed a toad. "What do you mean by that?"

"My own newsletter, Mr. Harmon, one with the real news. Let's see, I might call it *Droppings from the Nest.* Clever, huh?"

He looked at me with blank Orphan Annies then, a tiny ho-ha falling from his mouth, unsure what to make of me.

Late in the day as I passed by the mailboxes, he came across from the sitting room and, spying me, hurried into his office and closed the door. Evidently he expects me to lob something that emits smoke in his direction and he wants a head start.

I was putting on my tie for supper when the phone rang. "Hello, Grandpa, this is Rodney."

"How nice of you to call. You've never called me before, you know."

"You can save your breath about what I'm gonna take in school." Just like that.

"How can you judge my advice without hearing it, Rodney? I might say something you'd like."

"Fat chance, Grandpa. Are you and Mom and Dad all in cahoots now? Coming down on me like a ton of shit."

I got off soon, saying I had to go to supper. Imagine a grandchild saying things like that. Now I have a mind to call him down here so I can tell him how grandsons are supposed to treat grandpas.

It seems to me that the more I get mixed up with this family of mine, the worse it gets. The idea of living in a cave in the Outback has some appeal, but only when I'm piqued. When you have as few loved ones as I do, you hang onto them even if they do sock you in the nose sometimes.

14

Monday morning, a little after ten, and it looks like rain. Puffy grayish-white clouds sail across the Sound like ghostly storm birds. It smells of rain too, and there's an early-autumn nip in the air already; September is two days off. I could feel something coming on when I was out walking after breakfast, though the sun was then as shiny as high noon on Midsummer's Day and the cold front nothing but a thin eyebrow of gray to the southwest.

While I watched, a dark speck emerged from the cloud bank, slowly voiced a drone as it grew in size, and passed overhead, a toylike thing with stripes fanning its wings. I was reminded of another aircraft, long ago, which brought serious romance into my life. Today's plane was quite visible; the other remained forever a mere light in the night sky.

Rain dribbled down that Sunday while I was out east on the Collinsville road, dispatched to look for wreckage. Some farmers had rousted Clint Bradly out around midnight to tell him of a craft that had flown in circles but now had gone down in flames. I had been off at dawn to drive around and tramp in the dripping woods.

The Sheriff eventually called it a hoax; I figured too much home brew, though the farmers saw something, I was certain. Pilots lost in the dark were known to drop flares in hopes of illuminating some recognizable landmark or to light a highway for landing. This one, from the evidence, did so but, finding nothing, flew on to safety. Gravity-defying machines were new and mystical in those days and were expected to fall from the sky regularly like meteorites.

On my way into town at dusk a mammoth Pierce-Arrow came out of a side street and stopped across my way. My T-Model coupe was skidding wildly when it struck the spare tire sunk into the front fender. Magellan had no signals as yet and few stop signs, and neither at this intersection. But stopping dead in front had been frowned on even in buggy days.

Much unreasoned yelling followed, mostly by me, but enough was said also by this rich-looking kid in a fedora of soft velour and expensive driving gloves. I demanded to know why Daddy hadn't taught him to drive before giving him his fancy gig. Things of that nature. I was twenty-three, a big-time reporter, driver of a rawboned car, a tough bunch of owl feathers, by my own reckoning.

An engine approached with a metallic bonk-bonk which told me it was a Chevrolet, and I worried that it might not see us in time. Street lamps then were bare bulbs under scalloped reflectors, weak and spaced far apart. I was waving and yelling when the Chevy halted just short of my Ford. Out stepped a figure in a new kind of short wrap, a blue thing they now call a "car coat." There was a smart cloche hat, bobbed hair, a chic girl with sporty-spoiled looks and white kid gloves.

"You chaps all right?" inquired a hearty voice that would have been at home shouting at a polo match. "Anybody hurt?" Sweet Jesus, another rich kid. She had that air about her and my bent-back radiator seemed tawdry in her presence.

"Nothing wrong that couldn't be cured by some sympathy from you," said an oily voice, and I could see a sparkling smile beneath his neat mustache. I've always taken a dislike to people with excessive panache and the idea of poking him in the nose appealed mightily.

The girl had a pretty face, I could see even by street lamps that you'd scarcely trust to illuminate your refrigerator today, with pale cheeks now probably tinted by a becoming blush. "Oh," she said, and that was all.

"Both fine, miss," I told her. "Fauntleroy here parked in the wrong place, that's all." Nasty takes little learning, but to be snide with style requires seasoning, of which I had little.

"Look, you beggar," Velour Hat shot back, "any more nonsense out of you and you'll have real trouble on your hands."

I readied myself for a shove to the shoulder to find out bluff or guts when the girl gasped and exclaimed, "Why you're Mr. Carpenter from the *Times*, aren't you?"

She looked a total stranger to me. "I work there, yes; I'm a reporter."

"I thought so," she said with booming laugh. "I've seen you going up to the City Room, and your by-line too."

Velour Hat's temper had cooled by then, and he looked from one to the other of us.

"Do we know each other?" I asked, certain I wouldn't have forgotten such a lovely creature.

"Oh, I work at the *Times* too, but in Advertising and we don't get noticed like the news people. If you want to leave your motor here, I can take you to your place."

Custom required a momentary demurral. "I can walk to the trolley, thanks," I said.

"Oh, but the cars are way over on Madison," she announced in a flat statement suggesting the issue was settled, as indeed it was.

With the help of the girl and Velour Hat, I draped the hood over the engine. The slanting radiator suggested more damage than really existed. Together, we pushed Lizzie off the bricks and put up the side curtains in case of more rain. I had confidence my coupe would recover, for Ts were tough. The Pierce had sustained one small dent. It was tougher.

Visualizing the scene today, one might wonder about the massive traffic jam and the blare of horns. Besides the girl's Chevrolet, one car came along, an old Essex that squeezed past, its driver leaning out to gawk and shout, "Anybody hurt?" Our motor population was still minuscule at that time and on a rainy Sunday evening such as that you could sit in the middle of Madison Avenue with scant danger of being hit.

Velour Hat's wrath turned to puppy friendliness and he offered to pay for my car. All my life I've observed an unnatural awe of journalists, a willingness of others to see us as infinitely more than the underpaid wretches we are, two pencils and a fold of copy paper in our pockets.

"Don't worry," I told him. "I'll hammer her out myself in the morning. He started his Pierce and waved goodbye without my ever learning his name. There was no police report, no exchange of licenses, no insurance discussion. Life was simpler then, and you took care of your own wrecks.

In the Chevrolet, close to the girl, I was both drawn to and frightened by her beauty and the scent of alluring perfume. At times I could be brash as an act but by nature I was and am shy, and riding around with a beautiful girl was deep water for me. She showed blond hair, an upturned delicate nose and, as I was to learn, pale green eyes, an Irish cast right down to a sprinkling of freckles.

"I think I need glasses," I said.

"You lose yours?"

"No no. I don't wear them, but maybe I should if I can miss somebody like you at the *Times*." Brash enough, I suppose.

The hearty big laugh came again, and her teeth were even and white. "Thanks for the comp, Mr. Carpenter. I'm Connie—Constance Livingston, and I do want ads."

"Call me Ben."

Between shifts, for we were moving by then, she stuck out a hand and gave me a grip as strong as any man's. Shaking hands was very forward for women, as whistling at men may be now, though it is difficult to conceive of anything a girl could do today to get herself considered fast. Clearly, Constance Livingston was no shrinking violet.

"You haven't told me where we're going yet," she said. "Where do you live?"

"I have rooms on Eighteenth right off Delmar," I answered, pluralizing the singular to make it sound commodious.

"Smack downtown, huh?"

"Close to the office." My room was also cheap, but four dollars a week was about right when I earned only fifteen.

"I live out on the Belt Park," she said, referring to a green band that ran across town from west to east. In the prosperous eighties it had been Magellan's northern boundary but, after growth, it lay halfway to downtown when I arrived. The Belt had once been posh and still was in some places, but by the twenties decay was evident, the old mansions turning into rooming houses or flats.

"Ritzy out there," I said.

"Sure, Ben, some houses are, but mine has been cut up into four flats. Say, you want to see my place? I have some boughten gin and Italian. A drink might be good for you after your ordeal."

I wondered what kind of girl I'd fallen in with. Ladies did not invite men to their lodgings, in fear of becoming known as Loose Women. Could this lovely creature be a Loose Woman? I was torn between hoping yes and hoping no.

"I haven't had real gin for months," I said. "A gin-and-It would hit the spot." In truth, I detested the taste of gin, but that evening hemlock would have been fine if served up by Connie Livingston.

ᴌ15

Schools are open again and when I'm out walking, the streets rumble with yellow buses. Piping voices are strewn from the windows like flower petals and miniature hands wave to me. I flourish my stick and they giggle at the funny old man.

My own academic report is unfavorable: Grandpa flunked his assignment. There were no pointed suggestions about courses that make money, or helpful hints on how to treat grandfathers either.

Day before yesterday it was getting on four when the phone rang. "Your grandson and a friend," Lucy announced. "Should I send them on up?" Marlow High is only four blocks away and I guessed they'd walked over after classes. Rodney and a friend. The boy can't be all that bad, I thought, if he wants to show off Grandpa to a peer. Either he's a born politician or suffers a dismal lack of after-school activities.

Two pretty grins came around the corner as I waited at my door. "Grandpa!" Rodney called out, running up to hug me.

"This is a nice surprise, Rodney. Who's your friend?"

"Judy," he said. "Judy meet my grandpa Carpenter."

She stuck out a hand. "Hello, Grandpa Carpenter," she said, her eyes sparkling. I hadn't considered a girl-type friend, with Rodney so young. But a junior and going on seventeen. I suppose so.

Judy is a cute skeeter, her brown eyes mischievous, her black hair streaming down over her shoulders. I brought them in and fetched pops.

"Got any beer, Grandpa?" Rodney asked, all grins.

"A few, but I'm saving them for when the water goes out." The two of them, sitting together on the love seat, had a giggling fit.

"Mom won't let me drink beer if she knows," Judy announced.

"Shouldn't tell her goopy things like that," Rodney said. They all glug beer and smoke pot, according to what you hear. I imagine Rodney sneaks some beers but I don't think he's into reefers or I'd have heard. Norma is not one to keep her troubles to herself.

"So what brings you here?" I asked, sipping my cream pop. Rodney had taken Dr Pepper, Judy a grape. My bar is well stocked but not exactly exciting.

"To see you," Rodney answered. "First time I've had a grandparent this close."

I think he means it.

"My grandparents live down on the water," Judy said. "Mom's parents. Dad's are in Oklahoma."

"Your father came east, eh?"

"Oooo, a long time ago, the year before I was born, and I'm fifteen." Sixteen years is a long time? If it's more than your lifetime, I suppose so. The year before I was born people kept horses and laughed at Teddy's antics. In Judy's time they kept Fords and delighted at the young Irishman in the White House.

"Grandpa's a journalist," Rodney announced proudly,

going over to my writing table. "See his typewriter here? It's real old." He and Judy peered down at this Remington as if it were a rare treasure.

"A retired journalist," I said, not without pride. Having anyone bring up your past, when you were successful at something, is pleasing. Most see us only as we are, old and no longer good for anything.

"Wish I had a typewriter like that, Mr. Carpenter," Judy said. "Neat."

"They have nice light portables now," I told her. "That's what you should wish for, not an old wreck like mine."

"But this one is so *interesting*, and the new ones are so simple-looking."

"He types all the time," Rodney said. "Don't you, Grandpa?" He took a sheet out of the box lid and started reading it.

"Uh, don't bother reading," I said quickly. "It's only drivel." Better to have Clint Bradly scowl through my copy than be reviewed by teen-agers.

"You're writing a book, huh?" Judy said, just like that. They don't mind asking these days, even the kids.

"It really is only drivel," I said, "stuff for my own amusement. I'm like an old fighter who puts up his dukes when he hears a bell. I can't stop typing, even if it is only for the purpose of covering copy paper."

"Copy paper? What's that, Mr. Carpenter?"

"The name they give to typing paper on news staffs," I answered.

"Oh, that's interesting. I never heard of that."

By then it was after four-thirty and the gates would open soon.

"Look," I said, "how are you kids going to get home? Your buses must have gone long since."

"The Connbus, Grandpa. Judy lives right down the road from us."

"Your parents know you're here?"

"My mom doesn't get home till six and Dad later," Judy said. "I'll be there way before." She has life's little arrangements all worked out.

"Mom don't worry if I'm late," Rodney announced.

Norma not worry? Horse feathers. I know her better than that. And here was I, detaining these kids. What would she say? Plenty, no doubt.

"You call your mother right now," I commanded, shaking a finger.

Rodney was embarrassed, being bossed around by Grandpa in front of his girl friend, and wanted to argue. "I'm not kidding, Grandpa. She don't care at all."

I'd forgotten how tricky it is to deal with teen-agers, even charming ones like these, both clad in jeans that appeared to have been scrubbed on rocks beside some stream in India.

"Well," I said, "if you two like, you could stay and have supper with me. Then I'll send you home in a hack."

"Great!" exclaimed Rodney. "Come on, Judy, let's do it up." They talk like that these days, and their grammar could be improved.

"What's a hack?" Judy wanted to know.

"What Grandpa calls a 'taxi,' dopey," Rodney answered with a laugh.

"They called them that when I got to Illinois," I explained, "and it's hard to break old habits."

"And he's never heard about apartments. He calls this his flat."

"Gee, you do have different words, Mr. Carpenter," Judy said, with some admiration, I thought. But then, you always want to think so.

"What about it, Judy?" Rodney asked her. "It'll be loads of fun. They have pitchers of wine right on the table."

"Oh, sure, I want to, and thank you for asking me, Mr. Carpenter. But I have to call Mom exactly at six so she won't worry." Who says kids today have no manners?

"Well good. And now I'll call your mother and tell her," I said to Rodney.

She came on after one ring.

"Norma," I said, "Rodney dropped in after school."

"Oh? Then how'll he get home?" Practical Norma.

"Has a friend with him." Let her wait a minute. "Her name is Judy."

"Judy who?"

I asked the girl. "Kaplan," I said, "Judy Kaplan."

"Oh, the Kaplan girl. She's a wild one."

"I was thinking, Norma, they could have supper with me and then I'd send them out in a hack."

"You spoil him so much, Papa," she whined. "He should be home studying this minute."

"He *will* be, Norma, only a little later. You think we have midnight suppers here?" Her tone annoyed me.

A crafty new thought at her end. "Oh, all right, Papa, if you'll have a talk with Rod and get him to transfer out of these snap courses he's taking and get into some that are useful."

I felt at a serious disadvantage, not wanting to discuss the boy on the phone with him listening. "We'll see," I said, "but I think that argument is over with." And indeed I do, with my grandson exhibiting enough spunk and independence to win. Good for him. They can't decide everything in the life of a boy almost seventeen.

Norma did not seem to react to what I said, or more likely she hadn't bothered to listen. They do that to you a lot. "And watch that Kaplan girl," she said. "She's a heller."

Now having supper with your grandson and a young lady hellion is an event of note when you're doing life at the Arms, even if he is taking the wrong courses. I watched expectantly for some fascinating act of degeneracy by Judy but she was as ladylike as Bess Truman. That Norma is a nut on some subjects.

I arranged with Emily to sit with us, and she took a liking to them. Showing off my kids to impress Emily; well, you play with the cards you've got.

Rodney turned a glass up and before I knew what was happening Judy had poured it full of white.

"Hey," I protested, "you'll get us in trouble. You are not of age yet, young man."

"Close enough, Grandpa."

Emily tinkled with laughter. "Not all that close, are you, Mr. Kemp?"

"Pretty close," he answered with a winning smile.

"Pretty far, if you ask me," said Judy, and they giggled together anyway. "I like red wine, Mr. Carpenter, but not if they put you in jail."

In the end they both got sips. "Naughty, naughty," said Margie, coming past with salads. She winked at them conspiratorially. The ladies gawked and commented on my guests to each other, which made my chest swell like a steer with blackleg fever. On the way out several came by to say hello, Rodney each time standing straight as a West Point cadet.

"It's the voices," Emily whispered.

"What?"

"The sound of young voices draws them like the ocean is attracted by the moon." I hadn't thought of it, but she was right of course.

Lucy got them a hack and I gave the driver seven dollars and they were gone.

On the way to the elevators I saw Mrs. Moore coming along from the dining room and decided to check my mailbox for eviction notices, chain letters from God, whatever. I was not anxious to hear her review of the evening, but she waited and waited, and I gave up.

She wanted to tell me how handsome my grandson is, she said, and I felt mean as a jay bird. I thanked her and we came on up.

As the elevator opened on four, she said, "His girl friend, a Jew, isn't she?"

"Looked white to me," I answered and went off to my door.

I heard a comedian say that on television. Mrs. Moore's question is not unusual for this place. You hear a lot about people being Jews or not, and "dago" and "nigger" are not words that seldom are heard. Mrs. Moore would deny she is prejudiced. It's just that she comes from a time when our ideas of prejudice were different. To some people, being unprejudiced used to mean not beating your houseboy when he broke a glass, even though he was nothing but a "chink."

ᕦ16

Deep in Canada the boreal bleakness bides its time while here on the Sound gentle zephyrs, perhaps after brushing Old Farm itself, waft out of the southwest, and Indian summer goes on. Norma, on the phone, says no, it can't be; you've got to have freezing, and the thermometer way down, before anybody can claim Indian summer. I asked when she'd become such an expert on Indian summer.

"In my blood, Papa. I have Indian blood and you don't. We Indians know."

She had me there, though one-eighth Cherokee wouldn't get you many feathers on the reservation. She'd rung up early to ask how I am. Christ, you can't get a sore throat in this place but they summon your kin and tell the undertaker to stay on the line.

Some bug keeps me away from the nice sunshine.

Nursey came at eight and I said I felt like I'd been mauled by sled dogs. She took my temperature and looked down my throat with her pocket light.

"I'm sorry to tell you," she said, "but you are going to live."

Just when I had a big funeral planned.

A sense of humor helps Nursey survive. We have enough complaints to strain Walter Reed but she copes. There's a name on her door, Carolyn something RN, but we call her Nursey and she smiles indulgently. Nursey is a woman Norma's age, gone thick in the waist but she has this baby face that forgot to age. Wide innocent eyes, a delight in being teased by her time-worn charges. Hours are posted on her door on mezz but she seems always here in the day, arrives quickly if anybody needs her in the night. If her caring is an act she deserves her name in California sidewalks, even if she is the one that called Norma and said I'm ill.

"She thinks I may live," I told Norma, "but nurses make mistakes and I could be dying right now. Better rush on down." Pandering again.

It didn't work, of course, Norma having someplace else to go, a museum in Greenwich, I believe. She had to give me a little rap too, dying or not. Indians, like elephants, never forget.

"Why didn't you speak to Rod, Papa, about his courses?"

"I told you, Norma, told you on the phone. It's over and you and Clyde have lost. The kid has spunk, and he also has the right to choose his subjects. You're trying to make him into an ulcered millionaire before he's got his first job."

"You mean we're just supposed to let it go, let him ruin his life?"

"You've got to let loose, my child. Get your hook out of his nose and let him grow up."

"Oh, Papa!" Outraged.

"I'd have told him that too, except he had his girl with him."

"His girl? Oh, Papa, his girl!" Hoots of derisive laughter, and I suppose she thought I was farther over the edge than anyone has realized. "Judy Kaplan is not his girl. He's only a child, Papa, and doesn't have a girl, never has. That little twit is only a friend."

Twit indeed, a nice child like Judy. Norma had to run then, probably drawing up plans in her head to pad the walls of my flat. When I got the girl business wrong she evidently found it easy to dismiss everything I said. Sometimes I get the feeling that my daughter's family is living on a volcano that has already begun to rumble. But the intimations of trouble stay at the very periphery of vision, and even if they came rushing up demanding of solution, what could I do? Damned little, I'm afraid.

So here I am, sipping the beer Nursey forbade, and limbering my fingers on the keyboard and trying to keep my mind off somatic and familial considerations.

Constance Livingston's flat was a big clapboard dating from the lavish days of the last century. She parked in back and we clumped up wooden stairs to a porch that gave rear access to her place. Light rain had started again and it was cold, making a drink appealing, even gin. The presence of a sleek young body and a lovely face wouldn't hurt either.

The door glass cast a yellow rectangle on the porch floor, which should have told me something but didn't, nor did the fact that she used no key. Connie twisted the knob and in we went, stepping into the kitchen, which was customary in second-story make-overs, a smallish walk-through with gas range on the right, sink and brown icebox opposite. Through a door on the left I saw a tiny dining room; they were still demanded by anyone half in a position. A dining room meant you didn't eat in the kitchen like poor people.

What Connie said next brought moisture to my palms. "Yoo-hoo!" she shouted. "Where is everybody?"

For all I knew she could be married, and though in her unrestrained way she might feel easy about bringing another man home, I could imagine a husband with a different view.

"You married?" I panted, suddenly out of breath.

She smiled the smile of a wolf considering a lamb, or so it seemed, and slowly pulled off her elegant driving gloves. Not a word issued from her lips. Such a tease.

From down the hall came a shout. "That you, Connie?" The tones were throaty but definitely female.

"Your mother?" I asked.

Connie stuck out her tongue and made a face, enjoying my state of nerves. "Don't be so jumpy, Ben," she said easily. "I have a roommate, that's all. To look at you, you'd think I've brought you to a blind pig full of thieves and cutthroats."

"I'm shook up over wrecking my motor," I explained in a transparent lie.

"Dorothy, come meet our guest!" Connie shouted, slipping out of her fur-collared wrap. Underneath was a navy dress with a broad white collar and a string of large pale-pink beads. In the full light of the kitchen Constance Livingston's face was something to look at, and I stared and caught my breath. Audibly, it developed, for Connie tilted her head just so and gave me a smile sufficient to light up all St. Louis.

In through the hall came a hesitant figure, a book dangling from one hand. I was struck first by the gleaming blue-blackness of her hair, then by her figure, so slight as to make her a walking skeleton.

"Dorothy Simpson, meet Ben Carpenter," Connie said, waving a hand. "He's one of our reporters, you know. Bet you've seen his by-line oodles of times."

Dorothy came into the room cautiously, as if approaching a ticking bomb, a tiny smile showing, and nodded slightly in my direction. Her face was attractive but in a way very different from her roommate's, her skin dusky, the high cheekbones showing a reddening of rouge. There was a sparkle in her eyes but she remained silent as a statue. My tongue was paralyzed as well. What an inauspicious introduction to the girl who was to become my wife, though I had no inkling then, my interest being in Connie.

"Well, Christ amighty," roared Connie, "you both struck dumb? Say something, Dot. You know, 'Hello.' 'Howareya?' 'Boop boop a doop,' something." Her booming laughter filled the room.

Connie was enjoying herself, and later I was to see it again and again, this outrageously uninhibited girl seizing two shy people and verbally knocking their heads together, always with thundering laughter. It was not a trait to admire, but one found forgiveness easy for someone so full of good feelings.

"Hello, Mr. Carpenter," Dorothy said throatily. "Pleased to meet you."

Connie nodded curtly in approval and turned to me. I said something, though I've forgotten what, and we were introduced to Connie Livingston's satisfaction.

"He's had an accident with his motor and needs a drink bad," Connie boomed. "I'll get the goods and you get the glasses. Any ice left, Dot?"

"Part of that last fifty is still there," Dorothy said, rummaging for glasses.

Connie produced a bottle of Gordon's and another of Italian from some hiding place, then opened the icebox lid and began stabbing with an ice pick as if killing dinosaurs.

Dorothy and I smiled shyly at each other over Connie's chopping. She had on a plaid skirt and a lavender sweater that set off her eyes to a turn. Unique eyes, they were, quite the most unusual I have seen to this day, violet in color with tiny dark candle flames beneath the pupils, a gypsy sparkle when she was filled with happiness. I thought I detected an Italian strain, maybe Portuguese; in fact, her veins flowed with a large amount of Cherokee blood.

The girls led the way into the living room, past one bedroom that appeared to be inhabited by wild animals, a second that was neat as a nun's habit. I could guess who slept where but said not a word, for looking into a lady's bedroom was bad form, which young bachelors enjoyed whenever possible.

The tray of drinks went on the coffee table and we arranged ourselves across the corner, Dorothy and Connie on a worn davenport, I on a rattan chair that looked like something from the secondhand store. A gas heater bubbled in the corner, a warming sound in view of the spring chill and dampness outside. Our drinks rattled with shards of ice in the finest of jelly glasses.

"To drunkenness and debauchery," Connie said, taking a huge gulp.

"Oh, Connie!" Dorothy said in consternation. "You do say the awfullest things."

An involuntary shudder followed my first sip.

"Really good stuff, eh?" Connie said brightly.

"Smooth indeed," I answered in, I hoped, a nonchalant tone. The taste of raw gin remains at the top of my distaste list to this day, though Gordon's was better than bathtub.

As for Connie, she tossed it off like Nehi grape, and Dorothy drank with remarkable heartiness. I felt like a Baptist thrown in with lushes.

"A freshener?" Connie asked, draining her glass.

"Uh, still working on this one," I said, red-faced at my

backwardness in the principal sport of Prohibition days. "Your roommate could use one though."

She scooped up Dorothy's glass and headed for the kitchen. "Oh, her," she said over her shoulder. "Dot's having her sissy drink, near beer. Ugh."

"Well, I *like* near beer," Dorothy said to me with some passion. "Connie makes fun of me but I can't stand real liquor. It tastes awful."

I gave my man-of-the-world laugh. "Everybody to his own," I said. "To me, near beer is worse than none at all."

Dorothy's taste for near beer, from a company in St. Joseph, lasted all her life. She never smoked and could not abide whiskey. Her vice, if it be one, was near beer.

"Here we are, chaps," said Connie, breezing in with fresh drinks. "I see you're getting on famously. Have a fag?" She held out a flat tin of tailor-mades, new since the war, but I declined. Connie tapped a cigarette expertly and flicked a vase-size lighter. They were new then too, some fueled by gasoline. A flame of olympian proportions shot into the air and I had visions of the whole place going up.

"Well, have you two found out a lot about each other?" she demanded, puffing mightily.

"You didn't give us time," Dorothy said.

We found out a lot in a hurry with Connie supervising. No, Dorothy had not noticed me at the *Times*, though she too worked there, nor did she remember my by-line. For my part, Connie grilled until she determined, unbelievingly, that I had never heard Dorothy Simpson's name.

I was entranced with Connie and her cosmopolitan ways, someone so opposite myself but wonderfully appealing. With her, I imagined, the laughs and good times would go on forever, a delightful prospect for one so recently liberated from a bleak Kansas farm. And think of waking up to a face like that, not to mention pleasures of the body which I tried not to contemplate.

Connie eventually went on to a third gin-and-It while

the original issue, aided by the heat, made me feel dizzy. At one point she demanded of Dorothy: "Tell him what you do at the *Times*, Dot, and make it sound good."

"I'm in the Business Office," Dorothy said obediently.

"Not where you work, Dot; tell him what you *do*."

"I try to collect overdue accounts," Dorothy said with a shrug, "and I'm not very good at it. I suspect Mr. Bradly is going to fire me, because he says I'm not forceful enough."

"Wants you to go out and beat them up, no doubt," I said.

"Old Clinty'd like that, wouldn't he?" said Connie, guffawing.

"My trouble is I feel sorry for them and want to help," Dorothy said.

In my heart dwelt the same feeling, except I still felt compelled to play the role of a tough and worldly reporter whose game was catching bullets in his teeth. Fortunately, Dorothy, who was not fired but ultimately resigned from the *Times* with apparently genuine regrets expressed by Mr. Bradly, sensed my charade from the beginning.

Eventually, Connie, quite unaffected by the drinks, drove me to my digs somewhat in the manner of an Indy veteran. On the way I asked her to the pictures.

"What's playing, Ben?"

"Not sure, but I think it's something with Norma Shearer." Movies came to Magellan on Friday and Saturday nights but not during the week, certainly never on Sunday. Motion pictures, even before they had voices, were suspected of being the handiwork of the devil.

"Oh, goodie, I look something like her," Connie exclaimed. "Don't you think so?"

We laughed and the date was made.

17

Let me tell you about life on the far side of the hill. Yesterday I came in from the drugstore and put my new bottle of after-shave in the medicine cabinet. It has a nice smell, and I need all the help I can get.

The shadows were still doing a morning stretch amongst the firs by the yellow church when I shaved and reached for the bottle. What's this? Old Spice red has turned to brown, and the label says Coppertone. Some dastardly fiend, in the night, has slipped in and made a switch. He's been here before too, a regular visitor when you are up in years. Shelves of merchandise loom and, as has long been your custom, your eye picks out what you want, your hand reaches and you present yourself at the cash register. Much later, at home, you find the bag contains the wrong product. Eye and hand come to lose their accustomed teamwork somewhere along the line, and what the hand chooses may not be what you want, perhaps not even on the same shelf.

The lines connecting the organs fray late, much after the first hints of aging appear in the forties. Bursitis strikes a shoulder but lasts only a day; trouble with the eyes clears by noon.

Old age is like an unbidden companion who joins you on some dark path, touches and goes. You feel his presence but when you look he's gone. Then one day he arrives to stay and nothing you do can rid you of his presence. The leg you broke as a child goes gimpy, the pains in the joints and the impaired hearing refuse to go away. All the natural foods in the world, a bushel of rose hips, thirty dozen oysters—nothing stops the aging process.

Your view of old age, as Rodney might say, depends on where you're coming from. A mere lad, in his mind's eye, may picture some toothless geek with an eggplant where hair used to grow. My own vision for years took the lines of Frank Simmons. Frank's son Charlie married Dorothy's aunt and the three of them lived on a farm down in Missouri. Charlie dealt in cattle and native lumber and set up a one-pump Texaco station on the road for his father to operate.

On a blanket-covered white kitchen chair in the station, redolent of tobacco juice and lubricating oils, Frank sat and hummed and grunted and stoked his iron stove. Only occasionally was he called upon to pump up gasoline for a customer or to turn a quart of oil out of a spigot, and I sat with him and listened to his stories.

"They came across here from the north one day," he'd say, "Union boys in blue and right sharp pikes on their rifles. I's too young to go but I see em all right. Couple of days later they come back draggin their tails. Got theirselves whupped right good down about Springfield."

Old Frank, as they called him, had good food and a warm bed and vivid memories and that, I thought, is enough to make the last years happy. A little past ninety his mind relaxed until he gave up station-tending and Charlie put him in a nursing home. It was a fieldstone building on top of a hill and as we drove up I spotted Old Frank and three others in the yard, his eroded figure now crooked.

"What in the world are they doing?" Dorothy asked.

"I don't know," I said, parking. "Let's watch."

We saw their hands cup over their ears, a finger move to the elbow opposite, one foot lifted, which made them stagger and, in that single game of Simon Sez, my ideal of peaceful old age was shattered.

I last viewed Old Frank in their infirmary, his steel railings up, his eyes staring. There was no response when I spoke but at the sound of Dorothy's voice he rolled his eyes and tried to locate her. Amongst gurglings, there were mumbles from his chest. I made out three words, *this mortal coil*, and I understood. He was fearful of death.

Dorothy took his hand. "It's all right, Uncle Frank," she whispered. "You'll be up and about soon." That immemorial lie.

An angry sob came then and there was no mistaking what he said: "Why won't it *let go?*" He wanted out of it.

My first hint of mortality came when my meals went bland and I took a heavy spicing to help my taste buds. Slowly it dawned on me that the part of taste that is smell had been debased. Smoked fish came to differ less and less from chopped meat. My nose had passed into senility, and I was still short of fifty.

You expect the eyes and ears to degenerate, they being the aristocrats amongst our senses, but nobody foresees the mist that falls in the mind. You can see and hear satisfactorily but your mind perversely refuses to process the data. Suppose you are in a room with a dozen people and someone speaks your name. Swimming the Channel would be easier than locating the speaker. Or you go looking in a room full of people for Florence and Herbie, who may be your own kids, and what you see is a mass of faces as indistinguishable one from the other as cottontails.

The man with the stiff upper lip finds at seventy that what hangs beneath his nose is flabby and creased, and the eyelids no longer spring to fully awake. The unlucky ones discover one lid drooping more than the other like pop-up head lamps with one only half popped.

I see myself yet as a lithe young spirit in a body that has lost its sparkle, a turtle in long johns inside a wrinkled and scarred shell. It's a kind of joke by nature, no doubt. I can take a joke as well as the next man, and I only wish I could find one in what's happening to me.

People get the most gosh-awful misconception of the elderly. Passing in a car, they see an old codger hobbling with his stick, and they wave and smile. He grins and returns the greeting and they think my, what a cheerful old man, and feel good. It is not in their ability to think about how, long after they are out of sight, the old man is still going to be hobbling.

Back home there was a man named H. Bo Hartley, who, with booming voice backed by three hundredweight of flesh, made his living as a public speaker. He came to specialize in retirements, speaking garrulously, for his thousand-dollar fee, of the wonderful Golden Years, nothing to do but golf and flirt with the girls. Back sometime in the fifties Magellan Power & Light had him speak at the retirement dinner of their Treasurer and after the oration I caught H. Bo at the bar, a brandy in his hand. "How old are you and when are you going to retire?" I asked.

His look would have fried a chicken at fifty paces. "Never!" he spat, clamping down on his cigar before turning like an elephant pirouetting on one leg and ambling truculently away.

I find this an awkward age not unlike adolescence when, because of lack of experience, the world looks so frightening. In the late years you have the experience but you've lost your place in life's pages and there is no opportunity to show you can cope. In your teens there is hope but on the graveyard shift it takes powerful energy to keep alive any expectations for tomorrow.

Dorothy lives still in my mind, and sometimes I see her over there on the love seat, as real as the girl who drank near beer on that rainy evening. And childhood memories, lost for decades in the recesses of the mind, have moved again to the fore and the faces of Jimmy and Carl and Gick and Sue are as clear as when I was five.

The dreams you cannot forget, and that keep returning, are the nightmares. The one that has haunted me since college will, I am certain, recur on the last night of my life. It's a school morning and, books under my arm, I come down the little hill toward Jesse Hall and realize with horror that I do not know where my class is being held, or even what the subject is.

Dream arrangements for old codgers evidently are courtesy of someone with Jack the Ripper humor.

18

When darkness falls tonight, and before moonrise, I shall go to our roof garden and look overhead for a new star, a mark in the sky signifying miracles wrought right here at the Arms, soon to be known as the Lourdes of the New World.

My son-in-law, you see, is paying me a visit. The phone was ringing when I came in from breakfast: Norma, to announce her husband's arrival this afternoon. Divine intervention is the only explanation, though what he wants I haven't the faintest.

I'm wondering now where he is and why he did not make his own call. Maybe, like the Queen, he sends runners to warn of the approach of his coach. If Dorothy were around I can imagine what she'd say—that I ought to be more charitable. Of course she would have found something good to say about Judas Iscariot.

In the week after my wreck I was out on assignment day after day. It was spring-flood time on the Mississippi, a big story for us even though the river lies some miles west. On Wednesday I did manage late in the day to get to my typewriter—this one—for a new lead in the City Final on the piece I'd already called in to Rewrite.

My motor had got fixed with dispatch on Monday morning. Mr. Bradly saw to it, even paid the bill; though his purse was rife with fishhooks he would spend if there was a benefit to him. Having me on the river to cover sandbagging parties, breaches in the levee and the flooding of fields was to his benefit because, in a year, I'd become a veteran. A little experience went a long way in a shop where reporters and deskmen flocked through like black-birds in migration.

I did not see Connie during the week, but I heard about her. Our City Room was a gymnasium of a place where everybody was visible, including Mr. Bradly sitting in the corner with his feet in his bottom drawer. The leading observation of the week was this pretty blonde from Advertising who glided in twice, leaving a trail of heady scent, to ask for Ben Carpenter.

"Got a chickie on your griddle, eh, Ben?" Billy Parker asked from the next desk amidst guffaws.

"Looked plumb predaceous, like she means business," said Ed Early. He wrote a humor column and made up preposterous words.

I blushed deeply but managed a small smile of triumph; being preyed on by Connie Livingston was a very desirable fate. She was a looker, as they put it in wonderment. Their biggest wonder was at her interest in such a greenhorn as myself. There were many claims—false, I was sure—of carnal knowledge of Connie.

"Comes from a rich family, Ben," said Duane Thresher.

"Suppose he's heard about rich being better than poor?" This from Billy. I had heard, yes, and I'd seen a lot of being poor, though I said nothing. Let them talk, I thought, and went back to my typing when they began spinning tales of their rumble-seat exploits with Connie Livingston.

On my dash that evening from the parking lot through the gloom to the staff door I had almost crashed into a small figure in a lavender coat and pillbox hat. I'd already dodged past when I realized my near victim was Dorothy Simpson. "Oh, hi," I called. "Almost didn't recognize you." I had the idea of going back to inquire after her roommate but had no opportunity. Dorothy turned and smiled shyly before hurrying away.

By Friday the river was receding and I was off assignment in time to appear at Connie's door promptly at seven. She was there and ready. So was Dorothy Simpson. I'd had to grit my teeth to a thousand pounds an inch to muster the courage to face Connie, and now, confronted with two waiting dates, I entered a state of suspended animation in which nothing about me worked, especially my tongue.

Connie's was in fine condition of course. "Dot needs to get out more," she said breezily, "and she's a big fan of Norma Shearer besides."

"I hope you don't mind." From Dorothy, timidly.

"Of course he doesn't, goofy," Connie said with a chuckle. "Not with two beautiful babes like us. You don't, do you, Ben? We'll naturally pay our own way."

"Don't mind at all," I said with as much nonchalance as I could muster. "But I'm paying; the man always does on my dates."

"Not on this one," Connie answered firmly. "We go Dutch." All this forty years before women's lib was discovered.

In my T, it was Dorothy who sat in the middle, while Connie held down the far end like a captain at the helm, smoking, wisecracking, directing my driving.

The picture, I still remember, was called *The Demi-*

Bride, and it did indeed star Norma Shearer. But I haven't a clue as to what it was about. Two more of these threesome dates followed—to the pictures again and to supper at a restaurant in Venice, next to the McKinley Bridge. I came to enjoy the company of not one but two pretty girls, for Dorothy was no slouch in looks either, but I often wondered what was happening and how this strange episode would come out. I was determined to stick around and find out. No doubt I should have divined the truth, but even my mother used to tell me I was naïve. Dorothy explained the situation at the end of supper when Connie had gone to the ladies'.

"I guess you wonder about this, don't you?" she said.

"A little, yes, but as I see it we're just good buddies."

Dorothy clasped her hands together and blushed, an affliction we shared. "It is more complicated than that, Ben. You see, Connie brought you home to meet me, and thought you might take me out. Then you asked her."

The progress of the game became clear enough with Dorothy's scorecard, but I found nothing to say.

"Please don't be mad," she went on, painfully, "because Connie means well; she just overdoes sometimes."

I laughed and managed to find my tongue. "She sure does, but I am flattered by all this attention. I like both of you, especially you."

It was the truth, though Dorothy doubted me in a fetching way, knowing of Connie's powers over men. Even by that time I had come to realize that such opposites as Connie and I would not be happy together. It was Dorothy and I who were birds of a feather.

Later Connie was to marry a newly frocked dermatologist and go to live in St. Louis. She and Dorothy kept in touch by letter, and met sometimes in the city to shop together, but I was not to see Connie again until after Dorothy's death.

Dorothy and I began slipping up and down the stairs

at the *Times,* for Business was on one and News on two, to have clandestine meetings filled with the painful pleasures known but to lovers. We ate together at the greasy spoon huddled against the *Times'*s back wall, and kissed passionately, which was forward for those days, and I once squeezed her knee. We did not go to bed together. It was simply not done, especially not by two very shy people. At twenty-three I remained a virgin and knew instinctively that Dorothy was as well. I didn't ask; that was not done either. For a wonder, it still isn't.

As summer came on I asked Dorothy to marry me.

"I can't give you an answer until you see my people," she said. "Then I'll know." Her father farmed a spread a little south of St. Louis.

Parental approval as a precondition had gone out in her mother's time, if not before, and besides, we were living in the carefree twenties. But see them I must. Clearly, this was an old-fashioned girl I'd fallen in love with.

~19

Clyde came in on my coattails at noontime yesterday, stomped on my toes a while and took to his heels so he wouldn't be caught out at the office. After some of the things he said I felt like giving him a boot to assist him on his way, but I guess he means well.

I'd barely closed the door after coming up from lunch when I heard this rapping of knuckles on metal. Clyde does not bother with the subtleties of door buttons.

"Hello, Dad," he said, a smile on his face like he'd taken a swig of vinegar. Let's see, they've been married almost twenty-five years now and it's the first time he's ever called me that, or anything, as a matter of fact. Not Ben, not Mr. Carpenter, nothing. I've thought of telling him to call me anything he wanted, within reason, but he's never given a sign of needing suggestions. Now, after all these years, he comes out with "Dad."

"Nice to see you, Clyde," I said, and it was, Dad or not. "Come on in and I'll get you a beer or a bottle of pop, whatever you want."

"I'll just take a little juice," he said, moving over to extract the oj from my fridge. Making himself right at home, he poured a glass, offered me some and put the jug back. And why not? He *is* family, though I thought he might have taken his hat off.

In fact, I put my hand out and said, "Here, let me take your hat."

"No no. I'll only be staying a minute." He very nearly lived up to it.

We sat and Clyde began what looked like a business conference. "Fine weather," he said, stretching his lips to show a tooth or two.

"Like late summer back home," I answered, looking him over. The hat was dark, the brim mashed down in front in G-man fashion. I saw an alligator-scale tie of silver and blue snaking out of his severe charcoal vest. An Eastern business ensemble, I suppose, as unadorned as a mortician's umbrella. "I thought Norma might come with you," I added as he drank off the juice in one pour, as if its flow, like some gelatinous ribbon, could not be interrupted.

"No. I came straight from the office, and I have to be back before two." I thought it strange, a man in his position sounding like a boy messenger who gets flogged if he's late.

He pulled an envelope from his inside pocket. "Norm and I've been talking about this, Dad," he said, "and she thought I oughta come see you." Norm indeed. Nobody, so far as I know, ever called her that, not even Clyde, and now he was on a mission for Good Old Norm.

"What in the world have you got there?"

"Uh, your will," he answered, letting this accordion sheet unfold itself until it looked a yard long.

I had difficulty believing I was not a part of some Looney Tune and I half expected the Road Runner to appear at any moment. "My will? Why my will? You and Norma want to cash me in early?"

A couple of toneless husks of laughter came from his throat. "We got to reading this copy the other night and thought maybe it should be changed. Says now your estate goes to Mom or, if she is deceased, to Norma and Christopher or their heirs and assigns." He had it down by heart, and I barely noticed his name for Dorothy. He never called her anything either.

"That's right, Clyde. It's the way we made them out way back there in the forties."

"Have you changed the original? Where is it?"

"No changes at all, and Larry Knight has it in his safe in Magellan."

"Your lawyer?"

"Yep, still is."

As I say, a business meeting, and it seemed to me that he wanted a big hand in my affairs. "Don't you think it should be updated?" he asked next.

"Why? It's perfectly workable, Clyde."

It turned out that he thinks Dorothy's name should be removed, the estate going directly to Christopher and Norma, especially Norma, no doubt—and could Rodney be mentioned?

"Why?" My usual.

"He might need it for college," said this man with the big salary.

"You mean in case I drop off tonight?" My sarcastic tone seemed completely lost on him, I suppose because he's so used to people who speak without the nuances of family discussion.

"It'd be just in case, Dad. He may be pretty hard put to make it through."

"Well, Norma can give him as much of her share as she likes."

He never did get up nerve enough to tell me what he really desires, to have Rodney named as a primary beneficiary, thus cutting him in on Christopher's share. And Norma's too, though I imagine they'd shake the boy down for that quickly enough.

I keep thinking to myself that Clyde means well, and surely he does but, writing all this down appalls me again. I was nice as you please when he left though, told him I was sorry he couldn't stay longer and saw him to the front door. Then I stewed to myself in the sitting room until Lloyd Axelrod came along with some sad news.

It's been a while now since I've seen Mrs. Cardoza, the Cuban with the frank tongue and the neat mustache, that I used to call Mirandy sometimes, for she liked to be teased. "Why should I piff up like old hen?" she said once. "I yust take what left and not worry about nothing."

I hadn't thought much of not seeing her; people are always going off to visit their kids. But that is not the case with Miranda Cardoza. She is dead, been dead a week in fact, buried yesterday in Miami.

Lloyd's news shook me. Oh, we're all here on a mission whose only goal is death, but Mrs. Cardoza is the first Resident I've known to go, and it sets me thinking. From what they said at supper last night, Mirandy had it very hard at the end. A drug overdose would have been merciful, but they are all wasted on the young.

Mabel Moore, our queen of dark news, sat one table over and delivered the details, helped along by Inez Bowman, a chunky one with frizzy hair and a high pitch like Eleanor Roosevelt.

MRS. MOORE: I hear it was one of those cancers in the belly that went through her in no time at all. Why, they took out most of her entrails, they say, but it didn't do any good.

MRS. BOWMAN: Poor Miranda, she must have had awful pain.

MRS. MOORE: Oh, I'm sure she did. That kind of cancer is the worst.

ME (*muttering*) : Gruesome, and they seem to enjoy it.

FLETCH: Bloodier the better. Mrs. Moore may yet get around to the bucket of excised guts. Well, at least we know where she stands.

MRS. MOORE: Poor thing couldn't eat at all, had no entrails left. They fed her through a tube in her arm.

MRS. BOWMAN: My uncle had the same thing and they even took out his rectum and put a bag on his waist.

MRS. MOORE: A bag? What for?

MRS. BOWMAN: To catch things, you know.

Fletch and I skipped dessert and went off to the card room.

"Listening to talk about entrails gets my appetite," I said in the elevator.

"No use to keep it quiet though, like they always try to do here." He's known other deaths at the Arms.

"My wife died of abdominal cancer, Fletch, and there was nothing gory like that. They operated once but it didn't help."

"That Mabel Moore was gilding the lily, Ben."

"But you're always holding up for her. Why, Fletch?"

"Oh, I just think she's all right. You know, always herself, likes gossip and makes no bones about it. It's the hypocrites that get me, being scandalized by things they're dying to hear."

"You might have something there," I said.

We strolled along to the card room, Fletch a step ahead so we didn't lurch into each other. You have to walk that way after your legs lose their nimbleness. Nobody else was around so we played gin and Fletch took me for twenty cents.

So that is it then for Mrs. Cardoza, not a tear shed, dead and buried before we knew. That is the way things go here, by Fletch's account, and even when Residents learn somebody has been taken to the hospital, the executive-suite crew never seems to know which one. Once in the hospital, few come back.

For Mr. Harmon and the Owners, death does not even exist at the Arms. Passing on, they call it, as if you are traveling somewhere. They're quick enough about putting a steel spike in your door though, Fletch says. I went to look at Mrs. Cardoza's lock and it's there, all right, half a key that sticks out and makes entry impossible without the other half. Sealing the apartment, they call it, meaning they keep all furniture and valuables inside until they get what's coming to them.

Ed Cobb told me at breakfast that these retirement residences are all shy about death. "They worry something awful about their Investment," he said. "Here they're scared silly that Eagle Arms might become known as the Death House on Third Street. Bad for profits."

I hadn't thought of it that way. "Can you imagine," I said, "the look on Mr. Harmon's face if somebody called up and said, 'Hello, is this the Death House?' "

Ed is unusual in having lived in two retirement residences, which, like mausoleums, are usually dealt out only one to a customer. Once a farmer in Kentucky, then a tobacco auctioneer, he went to California to retire near his son and, when the boy was sent to Germany, he came here because a daughter lives in Stamford. "I never thought I'd be chasing cross-country after my kids," he said, "but at my age there's not much else to do. You just hope they stay put a while."

"Long enough for you to die, is that what you mean?"

"One way to put it, Ben."

"Well, I'm damned if I'm going to stay and die," I said, infuriated at the idea, my temper probably linked somehow to my son-in-law's visit. "I'm getting out, Ed."

How much better to die in your own home, I thought. You can't pick your birthplace but you sure as hell ought to be able to choose where you die. Old Farm is out of the question so long as Norma is in this world, but I might swing a flat for myself.

Ed was impressed. "Good luck if you can do it. When's your lease up?"

"I'm not talking about that. What I have in mind now is just getting out, period."

"You mean break out? Let me know when you do and I'll go along." He chuckled in that Southern way, indrawn breath at the end.

We sounded like inmates discussing an exit from Stateville. You hear talk here about breaking out, which means taking off without notice to Management, kids, anybody. Some wackos wander away occasionally and are led home by the police, who have come to know them by sight. But that's a different game. A breakout is done by someone with all his marbles, and it happens often enough that policemen on community relations give lectures in our chapel on mezz about the nasty things that can happen to well-dressed oldies who wander alone at night on the streets.

When there's a breakout the first place they look is Howard Johnson's in Stamford. For us, HoJo's is more practical as a goal than Rio or the South Seas. Like a convict, the escapee is brought back to serve out his term. Our rent is paid in advance, and they're going to give you your money's worth whether you want it or not.

But a breakout is not my game either, I told Ed, no siree. "I'm going in dignity, for everybody to see," I said. "And my daughter is going to be helping me."

So goes my new resolve, pushed no doubt from a vague, amorphous inkling into a determination by the death of Miranda Cardoza. I don't want to be just another one of the missing at Eagle Arms.

🐌20

Is there sex after seventy? Eighty? Ninety?

I can't answer for those big numbers but I can tell you that at seventy-three a man retains the same urges that deviled his life at sixteen. They don't rear up so often, and the fire that makes a young man cast lecherous looks at knotholes is banked, but fire is fire.

What does the single old man do for sex? I don't think those self-help authors have got around to this question yet, and I never heard of a geriatric singles bar or of old gaffers picking up women in parks either. It could make a dandy TV commercial though, these fuddy-duddies getting their canes mixed up, smiling brightly and then, at the fade-out, waving their sticks to hail a hack.

Sex for the septuagenarian is likely to arrive in the shoes of a friend, and later you remember the touching as much as the act. Our touching ration at the Arms is skimpy indeed. The shoes I'm thinking about are sensible low-heeled pumps, oxblood with a gold bow at the instep. Emily Walrod's.

I owed Emily, you see, because she had me to tea.

Outside the gates after supper I caught up with her. "Tea?" I asked. "Coffee? Something stronger? My turn, I believe."

She gave the quick smile of a girl getting her first puppy and looked around to see who was listening. That put an entirely different slant on the proceedings. My tired blood began zipping around as if I'd dined on a gross of oysters. In a near whisper she said, "Why Mr. Carpenter, that would be just divine. You go on up and I'll come later so nobody sees us. Remember what happened last time."

I was nervous as a boy on his first date, running around here straightening and dusting. The kettle was filled and its whistle and the doorbell went off simultaneously. I rushed to open the door and there stood Emily, obviously having stopped by her flat on six to freshen up with perfume and face powder and lipstick. She now wore a soft-blue dress with a light white sweater over her shoulders. Quite a picture.

"I'd guess the water's ready," she said, laughing. The whistle could be heard by boats on the Sound.

"Sounds that way," I said, dashing to switch off the kettle. She came in through the hall and I offered to take her sweater.

"I'll keep it, thanks. Frightfully nice of you to have everything ready, Ben. But I do believe you mentioned something stronger. To tell you the truth, I feel like a real drink for a change."

Good for Emily. At the Arms people take wine but few admit to the hard stuff. I fear we have a fair-sized hypocrite population, once the door is chain-locked. I'd rather be open about it.

Emily and I sipped our brandies-and-water and talked about our deceased spouses, a favorite subject when you're up in years and alone, and about life at the Arms. I've never been fast on the uptake but reading Emily was no trouble at all. Even a cluck knows a winsome look when he sees one, and she puckered her mouth to show her white teeth and lovely deep dimples.

Ben Carpenter, that rascal, was taking it all in with open mouth and big double Os, struggling fiercely to play the oldest of games after a long off-season.

After starting on second half-drinks we fell silent and stared at each other.

"A penny for your thoughts, Ben."

"To tell you the truth," I said, "I was wondering whether a man of my years is still able."

A fine warm smile. "To tell you the truth, I was thinking of the same thing, except without the doubts."

Describing erotic doings amongst old folks is not my style. Let it be said merely that we were successful. The act takes more time these days, and is the more pleasurable for it.

Later, as they say, we lay together and held each other, which was awfully nice. Emily is a neat bundle of woman, lovely pale body, youthful figure.

"Well, Benjamin," she said, twinking my nose, "what do you suppose is the next step?"

"The next step? You mean putting our clothes on?"

"No. I mean now that you've had your way with me, when are we going to set the date?"

My smile decamped like a meteorite in flight. I had not heard that expression in forty years. "Ummm, well," I said, swinging my legs out and grabbing my pants.

"Why, Ben, where are you going?" I imagined a feline look.

"Home," I muttered, standing to draw on my trousers. Next thing I knew, I was on my back on my braided throw rug.

Emily stopped laughing and came to put a hand on my arm. "Oh, Ben, are you hurt?"

I wiggled my arms. "Apparently not. I forgot to sit down to put on my pants."

"So I see. Were you joking, Ben? I mean, I was, only funning."

"Me too, Emily."

"Let me tell you something then, dear. You *are* home; you live here, remember?"

21

C. C. was here last week—my son, who remains forever Christopher in my heart. I've wondered how I can get something down that will seem right if I read it again in a month before putting it down the incinerator.

He stayed two hours—that is one of your basic facts in the case—and went back to New York to have supper with a noted Broadway angel. A famous man, Christopher said, though I never heard of him. I have a feeling his fame is found mainly in the minds of his acolytes. My son is lining up cash for a new picture. "I'll be *the* producer this time, Pop," he told me.

Christopher showed me a photo of my only granddaughter. "That's Meghan," he said, pulling a piece of plastic out of his wallet. I've seen Meghan only once, when she was four and they came by Magellan on a summer afternoon and left before dark. You could sense trouble even then, but their daughter was beautiful.

The picture showed it too, the raven hair in cascading waves, the animated eyes; shades of Dorothy. That woman could throw her looks, but the drama in her genes went to our grandkids. I was pleased that Meghan had held her beauty as she grew and told Christopher so.

"She's twenty-one now," he said. "All grown up."

I hadn't realized. "Looks a little young for her age in that case," I said, the girl in the picture being tennish, maybe eleven.

"That was taken a while back, Pop."

"So what does she look like now? You got anything recent?"

"No. It's the last I took, and I haven't seen her since. I have no idea what she looks like now."

His casualness horrified me, which, being the old devil I am, I told him.

"It's what Rosamond wants, Pop, wants me to leave both of them alone, alone, alone."

"But my God, man, she *is* your daughter. You do have some rights, Christopher."

"C.C.," he said, "everybody calls me C.C. now, and I don't worry about my ex and the girl. They're able to take care of themselves."

Taking care of themselves is hardly what I had in mind but I let it go. C.C. has become a man unused to taking advice, especially from Pop, who can't even get his name right. He must have corrected me five times but it almost always came out Christopher. Old habits die hard in old coots. I did manage a couple of C.C.s to please him but as he drove away in his hired limousine (oh, yes, a limo) my last words were, "Good-bye, Christopher!" Stubborn, you know.

By the way he does things, I may not see him again. In my eight years at Old Farm he came once on the fly and we went shooting down the tar road to a tavern in Collinsville. Looking for atmosphere downstate, he said, for a picture on Illinois gang wars. Coming back, I was prepared to jump from his high-powered Hertz as he passed my lane, so great was his hurry. He never returned.

At Christmas I get a card addressed in a woman's hand; his secretary, no doubt. A while back the mail brought birthday greetings too, though I wondered why he bothered to remind me I had turned seventy. He'd missed better birthdays.

Christopher was always a little different—another one of your basic facts. Norma married and went east after her schooling in Champaign. Her kid brother looked west, heading out as soon as he finished up at Magellan High. He took a degree in film arts on the Coast and went into Warner's script department. In a year his salary was double mine. Good for him, I thought, and still do, even if he won't come see me.

California was Christopher's oyster and he got a reputation in the film industry overnight. But he didn't marry and didn't marry, which upset his mother. Then, by his own account, he met a girl called Rosamond at a Halloween party in fifty-five and they took up together like thieves. Dorothy was pleased but kept her eye on the main game. "You're twenty-seven and not getting any younger," she wrote. "You haven't got forever to find a wife, you know." Mothers will meddle, especially strong-minded ones.

Rosamond was a plain girl with washed-out blue eyes, pale skin and unremarkable brown hair. They married in June of the next year and Meghan arrived in July. We weren't invited to the wedding. The visit to Magellan when Meghan was four became the only time I saw my daughter-in-law as well as her child. Rosamond, a shy one who tried to be friendly, got her name from the desert hamlet where she was born. We liked her.

They were divorced the next year and in four months Rosamond had remarried and gone with her child and new husband to live in Santa Monica. There was no question of custody. By then Christopher was in San Francisco and involved in "moving Hollywood north," as the catchy line, which once appeared on *Time*'s cover, expressed it. The picture business was in Southern California, everybody knew, but this bunch of renegades, my son included, was bent on hauling it up to San Francisco. *Time* used his name twice and spelled it right in both instances, something important to an old journalist. Except they called him C.C.

The young Turks haven't done badly, by Christopher's account. "We've got four studios there now," he bragged. *Halfway to the Bridge*, made in San Francisco, won Best Picture, though Christopher had to remind me of that. "And you remember they gave Hank an Oscar for his San Francisco picture."

Hank Fonda, yes. From Christopher's talk you might think the stars have no last names. Bob and Paul and Jimmy. That's Redford and Newman, no doubt, and I guess Jimmy goes with Stewart but I became tired of asking. You can be fairly sure it is not Jimmy the Greek, that's all.

So I'm resigned to not seeing my granddaughter again, which hurts more than a little. I wouldn't mind seeing Rosamond either. She was a colorless little thing but sweet when we knew her so briefly, and we felt sorry for her. She hadn't much to offer but Christopher should have paid more attention.

I was halfway to the phone to call Norma and tell her to rush down to see her brother, but Christopher stopped me. "Don't bother," he said. "I haven't got long and she'd get excited and want me to come out. I'll see her next time." Whenever that might be.

"She could be here in ten minutes," I told him, considerably shrinking reality. "She'll be hurt if she doesn't see you."

"Forget it, Pop," he said in his adamant way. "Clyde the Hun might be there and I sure don't want to run into him. How's he doing? Still got his blockhead haircut?" Christopher and Clyde have never been especially close.

I have a feeling that Christopher wasn't anxious for Norma to meet his friend. That's right, C.C. brought a friend along—another of your basic facts. A thin, gangly chap of no more than twenty-five, curly red hair and a love chain round his neck, all loose limbs and double joints.

"This is Ralph, my assistant," Christopher said by way of introduction. I shook a delicate hand, no more strength than a newt's kiss. He had on a smashing shirt patterned in little red roses, pale-blue jeans and sandals. They're big in California, I am sure, but you don't see many of them at the Arms.

Ralph had little to say. He sat and drank a ginger ale from my fridge and laughed at Christopher's barbed remarks. My son has always had a sharp tongue, and sometimes he looked to Ralph for appreciation. Ralph's adoring brown eyes followed his every move, and once, when Christopher was in the bathroom, I asked him what he does as my son's assistant.

"Not much," he answered, picking up a *Geographic*. Hardly a loquacious soul, though his cologne spoke loudly enough, something in the Musky Night genera, guaranteed to open your nasal passages twice as fast as Dristan. Presently he stirred and asked, "What do you do, Pops?"

That is not a name I like, and I thought my lack of occupation was self-evident, but it was no time to complain. "Hmmm," I said with a chuckle, " 'bout the same as you, I guess."

He was reading his magazine again, no hint of a smile.

Before I knew about the limo, whose driver lounged in the sitting room and wowed the ladies with tales of famous people he's driven, I had this idea about where Christopher could stay the night. We have rentals right here at the Arms, very like hotel rooms, where visitors can put up overnight. I mentioned this to Christopher, but of course he was off for supper at Sardi's with his angel.

I trusted he was going to change before supper. He came here wearing fancy Western clothes, a loud blue silk shirt and brown-and-black striped pants such as mean cattle barons wear in the movies. His belt buckle could serve as the plaque on some foreign embassy's door. Youthful threads for a man of forty-seven, I thought. He's handsome, I'd have to say, though the bushy mustache and long hair don't add much.

After we'd talked a while I thought it was as well that they weren't staying. Now I can do what's required as well as the next man. But my heart wouldn't have been in going to the front desk to arrange for a room with a double bed for two men.

Christopher is back on the Coast again now, maybe with lots of money for his picture. I wouldn't know. His visit upset me to the point where I skipped supper and had a tray sent up. Margie brought it and stood around a while in her starched pink uniform, cracking her gum and staring at the milk pitcher and the prints on my walls. Farm scenes and sailboats for the most part, Dorothy's favorites.

"Casing the joint for a midnight heist?" I asked.

She ignored that. "Who was t'two faggots come seeya t'day?"

Some investment people, I told her, and she went away.

Emily came rushing in then to find out who those people were. The driver's stories had circulated through the Arms like hurricane winds, and he spoke the right names—Cary Grant and Gary Cooper and Katharine Hepburn. He said the older man he'd brought here was a famous producer but he left off the name. His idea of circumspection.

Emily was bubbling over when I let her in. "Bennnn!" she cried. "I didn't know you knew famous people."

I told her fast enough who the famous man was and how the visit had gone. "I suppose I should be glad it's over," I said.

"Oh but, Ben, you can't be. He's your son."

"That's true, and I'm not really," I said. "As a matter of fact, I wish C.C. were coming back tomorrow."

22

Lloyd Axelrod, our Greek pirate, retired, has made the paper. Yesterday morning they brought him home in the Eagle Crate and Rufe helped him inside and up to his flat. He's painfully stove up, they say, a sticking-plaster on his head and a bashed knee where he fell. Rumor has him doing a bust-out, though I haven't talked to him. He has trays sent up and lies there and moans, Margie told me. My spy.

Lloyd's trouble is he did it all wrong. Imagine tottering well-dressed in the dark around the train station. They found him bleeding and semiconscious, the victim of muggers. His pockets were emptied even to the little knife to clean his fingernails. So said the *Mail*'s item under Police Reports. I admire their attention to detail.

Now I may not be as bright as your everyday genius but I do know enough to stay off the streets at night. "Marlow is nothing like as savage as New York," Norma told me, "but you stay in after dark anyway." I'm a believer.

Even homey old Magellan began to have street crimes before I was hauled away to the East, and it's a shame. In our young days Dorothy and I loved strolls in the night after the afternoon heat had dissipated. They'd be waiting for us now, I suppose. You feel lucky to have known those gentler times, though remembering them requires you to have attained a certain antiquity.

Lucy keeps an eye out for those about to be unwise, and when somebody must be out after dark she arranges company. In a crowd old codgers feel safe. No doubt it's a false safety, for eighteen of them together couldn't do much with a young tough holding a knife.

"The best help we can get is on mezz," Emily said.

I asked her what that meant.

"The chapel," she said, laughing. "Praying can't hurt."

I've never put much stock in chapels myself. This one is nonsectarian and they have guest preachers sometimes. Since boyhood I have kept the basic belief in God that was instilled in me very early, but most of my faith was vested in Dorothy. I was sure she could hold the world together and save us both in the bargain. Her belief ran as deep as artesian waters, but she was taken away early anyway, and I've been peeved with Him ever since. Local papers up there, please copy.

And so, with trembling faith inside the Arms and muggers without, here we hover like a peep of hens listening for the weasel. Staring eyes, indrawn breath, the air redolent with fear. Fletch would say I am exaggerating, and I am. Nevertheless it is infuriating to remember that as a child you could not stay out after dark, and now to know that, near the end, that rule formulated by the big people of the world applies once again.

&23

Take my word for it, peeve Numero Uno at the Arms is this: the kids don't come see me enough. I've said it myself sometimes, once to Fletch.

"I got a niece in Massachusetts won't ever come see me," he said.

"She that mad at you?" My assigned line, like "Who's there?"

"No. They won't let her out of the nursing home," he cackled, slapping his leg. Your family accounts are mighty short when they read *one niece*. His wife is long dead, I know, and I gather their son was lost in the war. Fletch talked once of a stone tablet near the Kasserine Pass that lists John Pepper amidst a multitude of names of the missing.

In view of his situation it seems small to complain, but I do it anyway. When I was a newcomer Norma dropped in more days than not. Now I don't see her once in a fortnight. Clyde's been in twice, I think it is, that last time screwing the lid down on my oj to the extent that I had to get Rufe to undo it. I could call Norma, or take a hack out and ring her bell. But you try not to bother. She leads her own life, and having Papa underfoot would rate no better than a visit by the narcs. Rodney's expression.

Now, having met the grouching requirements of the aged, I can deal with yesterday, which was Sunday and auspicious for an outing in the country. Norma and Clyde and Rodney came and picked me up for lunch at a restaurant over in Westchester. I paid of course, but expected to.

Norma and I sat in back. "I want you to see the foliage, Papa," she told me. "Clyde, go slow so Papa can see." It is early autumn now and they have nice yellow and red leaves.

Clyde promised he would, and he did, and even smiled, which is not your everyday phenomenon. He takes life very seriously. Only once have I known him to tell a joke, and it wasn't funny. Dorothy laughed, but mothers think they have to play up to the man who marries their daughter so he'll do right by her.

"We get more color here than in Illinois," Norma informed me, "because we have sugar maples. It is the sugar in the leaves that makes them turn."

They looked like plain hard maples to me, but Norma

says no. She has picked up an admirable amount of Eastern nature lore and thinks of Marlow as home. Why not? She's been here long enough. It was the same with me: Magellan became home and Kansas only a dim memory.

At one point Norma squeezed my hand and said, "Oh, Papa, it's wonderful to have you close to us. It's something I missed all these years."

A lump formed in my throat and a thought in my mind. If you feel that way why don't you come see me oftener? Which I did not voice of course, managing some bromide or other.

In Stamford we turned off on a narrow tar track and then another and before us opened a vista as bedazzling as the Land of Oz.

Norma roared with laughter. "It's the Kingdom of Kansas City, Papa! I've been waiting to see your reaction." Forty years and more ago we made occasional motor trips to Kansas City to see relatives and invariably were stupefied by the immense showy houses we found there. It was Dorothy who began referring to the Kingdom, and soon the term came to apply to any house where you can see the owner believes an ounce of pretension is worth a pound of gold.

The Connecticut houses I've seen run to colonials and ranches and capes with, here and there, an authentic salt-box. Norma has pointed them out to me. But this scene confronting us yesterday is like a whole street transported by twister from the Kingdom of Kansas City, huge houses of the sort they show on TV as the digs of Texans with more money than taste. Tara wouldn't rate outhouse status amongst them. In style they look like, well, money.

Rodney joined in our laughter but Clyde looked around with slitted eyes. "Oh, Clyde," Norma said, "we're only joking. Come on and laugh." But he wouldn't; he's from there.

Pretty soon we were across the line in Bedford, a village that goes way back. "Boy, look at these old houses," Rodney said, turning to face me. "Can you imagine living in something like that?"

It seems to me that my grandson has severely restricted tastes in housing, liking neither old nor new. "At least they look comfortable," I answered. The older ones were built when they heated with fireplaces, Norma says. They're nice to look at and well kept. Mixed with the old ones are big gingerbready places from the last century. White pickets are strewn about as if a hotshot salesman from a fence factory had done a job on the locals.

Clyde, without prompting, pulled up to a sign beside a park. I wrote down what it said.

> *Bedford Green. Part of a common*
> *laid out in March 1681 for grazing*
> *cattle, horses and swine.*

"Of course, you can never trust signs, especially in the East," I commented.

"It's the truth, Papa," Norma answered, and I guess she knows.

"Anyway it beats hell out of Eagle Arms for scenery," I said.

"Oh, you'll get used to it, Papa. I like to think sometimes how they care for you, and you in your own apartment."

"Flat," I told her, "and it bores me out of my gourd."

"Dad's going to California tomorrow," Rodney announced without preamble.

"Never mind," said his father, "you talk too much."

We went on down to a restaurant in Dobbs Ferry called Dick's Cabin. A massive fireplace and dark paneling, a dog that came round to say hello. You don't see hospitality like that back home.

Clyde ordered a Martini, extra dry. Norma and I took

white wine and Rodney fussed about beer but accepted ginger ale.

"Where you going to in California?" I asked.

"L.A.," he answered, lighting a cigarette. "Actually, a little place south of there, Newport Beach."

"Dad's gonna stop by and kill this guy while he's there," Rodney offered, with a laugh.

"Rod!" Norma scolded. "That's a terrible thing to say."

"Well, he'd like to anyway."

Clyde sighed like a man beset with carbuncles. "A little office politics," he said.

"We used to have that at the *Times,* reporters wanting all the big assignments. Nobody asked for obits or the weather."

Clyde got the olive down and ordered another, looking grim about the mouth. "A little matter of jurisdiction. We have a sales office in Los Angeles run by a jerk named Joel Novik, a brilliant MBA who hasn't got sense enough to pour piss out of a boot."

"The bright-young-man manifestation," I said. "I've seen it myself."

"This jerk wants to run everything west of the Mississippi, and now he has this guy from the Head Office, me, coming out to do a system right under his nose. Oh, he raised a lot of hell, even went in to bitch to the President. Seems like Hans told him to drop dead." A scuffing in the throat resembling a chuckle.

"Clyde is the best there is with big systems," Norma put in.

"While he's there he's going to throw a bomb through Novik's window," Rodney informed us, giggling.

"That's enough, Rod," said Clyde. "Not that I'm not tempted. Someday I'm going to dump him on his ass, get him fired. I have that much influence, you know."

I was not one to doubt him, no sir. "Sometimes you

have to play rough, I suppose," I said. "I was never in that position myself. All the power at the *Times* belonged to Clint Bradly, and what we wanted was his approval and some hope of more money."

"It's different in big business," he said, and I could see that. "The stakes are high and the knives fly."

I didn't doubt that either. You have to admire a man who plays that kind of game and keeps his head. All I ever wanted was to be a good journalist. The power to fire does not enthuse me.

By the third Martini Clyde had forgotten about Novik and asked what the sign in Bedford had said. Luckily I had it in my pocket or I might have found a bomb under my chair.

I took lasagne, which was delicious with their crusty bread. Norma talked me into a dessert of frothy egg yolks and brandy and sweet wine. I should have settled for tea. The dish was wonderful but rich as sin and played Old Ned with my pipes. I came home and finished off with baking soda in water.

As we drove home it struck me that in Norma's house she must have a box of soda, and that I might go there and spend a little more time with them. But I said nothing, Clyde being powerfully anxious to get me back here. Maybe he was worried about packing his bag, not wanting to omit the grenade.

So that was my outing, a nice affair with my loved ones, even if he had three Martinis and a beer. I should feel happy but don't. What I want is for them to come by today and take me somewhere else. I know—old people can be demanding.

We started early and by noon we were running south out of St. Louis on the new federal highway, bound for inspection by Dorothy's people. The paving was red brick held in place between white strips of concrete. On hillsides the concrete cupped into rain gutters and, going fast, you drove carefully to stay out of them. Hooking a wheel, they could turn you over.

Newly leaved trees lined the fence rows like sentinels and we could see green shoots of corn struggling up out of the brown fields. Roadside poles swarmed with telephone wires.

We were flying, the side curtains off and the wind whipping through. Coasting down hills, the speedometer rolled around to forty-five and, with good runs, I made it up most grades in high.

We'd stayed on the east side, dropping down through Illinois and not crossing the river until the Eads Bridge to miss some of the traffic. I did not like city driving, and I became impatient on the long drag down Broadway. But we inched through and by the time we were even with Lemay the city was behind us. Later there were signs for Jefferson Barracks, the vertical lettering molded into the sides of square concrete posts. You had to be quick of eye to read them on the fly.

Dorothy was excited, giggling spontaneously and urging me to go faster. Her clothes were suitable for a visit to a palace, a royal blue dress, light-blue spring coat and her pillbox held on with pins. It was May and warm but the wind in open cars required a wrap. I had on a tie and a gray suit and a pullover under my jacket. My high-cut patent shoes shone like polished marble.

We were young, in love and having a lark. Of all our trips, none ever matched that one in joy and intensity of feelings. In villages there was farm traffic, for Saturday is market day in the country, and wagons slowed me sometimes on the highway but mostly we swept along, the gas lever right at the bottom.

By three we had reached the twin towns of Festus and Crystal City, passed the glassworks and later turned off the bricks onto a road of river gravel which soon petered out and left us struggling along a dirt track. It was dusty and bumpy and every hill took low gear. Our high-speed run was over. Soon we were dropping into creek bottoms and creeping through water up to the running boards until we could find the track mounting the bank again. Twice I got out to open wire cattle gaps, which did little for my spiffy shoes. They slurped at every step.

The parallel raw brown wheel tracks slanted up across a hill pasture of spring-green grass and Dorothy sprang out to open a gate. "It's Daddy's, our Big Wooden Gate!" she shouted. "Oh, Ben, we're almost home!" Gates and pastures and gullies acquire proper nouns on a farm. At the top I drove through a wood lot of oaks and we came out on a field where ankle-high corn nodded in the wind and the sunlight. She pointed across the valley. "That's it!" she said breathlessly, bouncing with excitement like Dorothy going home to Kansas.

I saw a brick house of two stories, built foursquare with a porch across the front, quite a nice place, with catalpas on the side and a towering oak in the corner of the yard. A rusting barn stood some distance behind the house.

Lizzie groaned up the Simpsons' lane, which, close to the house, was nicely graveled, and we parked at the gate of woven wire and gas pipe. The spring latch went clang-clang and made me feel at home. We had its mate in Kansas. Dorothy took my arm and we marched along the walk, a giggle spilling from her throat. The door with its big glass opened and out came her mother and father; terror seized me. Decorum disappeared as Dorothy went flying up the steps to hug and kiss and wipe tears from her eyes. She was very glad to be home.

The Simpsons were warmly welcoming and my fears passed. He was tall with brown wavy hair, and it was easy to see where Dorothy got her looks: her mother was dusky-skinned too, with heavy black hair and gypsy eyes. I suspected Mexican blood but as yet had never asked Dorothy what gave her such an exotic cast. The world was reticent then, and I more than most.

"Jaime? Where's Jaime?" Dorothy asked.

"Afraid to come out," Mrs. Simpson said, laughing.

Eventually Jaime did appear, a boy of four or so clad in overalls. He slipped out of the door and trotted barefoot up to Dorothy. More hugging and kissing, and he turned his face away when she introduced us. "This is Jaime," she said, "and he's shy with strangers."

"Our surprise package," said Mrs. Simpson.

In good time Jaime felt well enough acquainted to take me to see his car, a set of upright cart wheels and a box where he sat to steer on imaginary journeys. A stick had become his gas lever, a flat rock his brake pedal.

Every meal at the Simpsons' was like threshing dinner, Dorothy's mother covering the table with dishes to welcome the guest of the house. My mother would have done the same; country people like to see visitors stuffed until their eyes bulge. I had not tasted smokehouse ham since Kansas, and early dock and polk greens were served with drippings and vinegar.

That first night I milked the Jersey to surprise Mr. Simpson and talked knowingly, I hoped, about the Anguses that made his living.

"Don't see many college boys milking cows," he observed dryly.

"I grew up on a farm, Mr. Simpson." He seemed pleased.

On Sunday I intended to be up with the roosters to prove myself a man of the soil but it was after eight when I was awakened by the voices of Mrs. Simpson and Dorothy as they talked of farm things in the kitchen below. Ever so faintly in the background I could hear their radio playing music. They had an early model with A, B and C batteries and kept the earphone in a washtub to amplify the sound.

I crept down the stairs, hoping to appear suddenly, like a ghost materialized, but nobody was fooled and I got teased roundly for being a sleepyhead. In this setting Dorothy had become as talkative as Connie Livingston with a gin-and-It in her hand.

Dorothy's father came in from feeding while I was bent over a bowl of shredded wheat at the kitchen table. He wore gum boots smelling of manure and carried a pail of milk. Breakfast for him had come two hours ago but he sat with me to drink sweet white coffee and complain of the scours amongst his calves. Later, he said, we'd go to the hill pasture and count the cattle.

"Have to do it every Sunday," he explained, "to see how many has got out and whether Willie has turned his cows in again. Likes to use my bull on the sly." He displayed an earthy humor on the rare occasions when he wanted and later, when we were viewing the loose-boweled calves in his paddock, he told me they were "shittin theirselves into perdition."

The women left us to our man-talk and went off to make the beds. Now was the time. Drawing a deep breath, I announced: "Dorothy and I want to get married, Mr. Simpson."

"So I heard. Told Dorothy she oughtn't rush into nothing. She says you got a good job there in Illinois." He put a "noise" in it, always did.

"I'm a reporter," I said with pride.

"Oh?" he said in his flat voice, and that ended the discussion. Not another word about marriage was spoken.

We left on Monday after noon dinner, Mr. Simpson coming in from the fields to eat with us. I knew we'd be in the dark getting back but Dorothy was reluctant to leave. When we did get off she was seized by despair—at leaving, I hoped, and not because I'd been rejected. I had no time to ask, being engaged in negotiating the creeks and hillsides, and in forebodings about Lizzie's weak yellow beams that later would have to light our way to Magellan.

We were bumping through a village called Barnhart when Dorothy pointed to a roadside park with a flagpole and a wooden-wheeled cannon from the war. "Let's stop here a minute, Ben," she said, "stop and talk." Parks, even small ones, did not go flying past as they do now, particularly if you were in a T Model, and I turned in on a gravel apron.

"Nice visit we had," I said. "I liked your parents. You tired?" An uttered hope flung out to ward off rejection.

"Worried," she said, her eyes brimming. "Oh, Ben, how could I have done this to you?"

So they had found against me. I, whose natural reaction would have been hurt and a feeling of defeat, became furious instead. "So who cares what they think," I told her. "I'm not marrying them, I'm marrying you. If you still want me."

"It's not that," she said miserably. "I misled you, Ben, and now it's caught up with me. Jaime isn't really Mama's child. He's mine."

Ghostly black smudges swept through my mind; my mouth tasted of buzzard's feet, but I set my jaw and said, "So what? If he's yours then he needs a father, and I'm your man. A boy in the neighborhood, was it?"

"No. I've been married before. Oh, I've deceived you so, Ben." She was crying into her fingers by then.

I put my arm around her. "You divorced now?"

She nodded.

"Then it doesn't matter. That's all yesterday, and I want you as you are right now."

Her sobs slowly died away. "He was a traveling salesman," she said, "you know, what they call a drummer. I was working in St. Louis then and he came to town to sell this line of fly sprayers to hardware stores. Took orders, you know. He said his name was Jaime Stillman, and he talked so smooth and nice. And he had so much money, Ben, more than I'd ever seen. I guess he just swept me off my feet."

She married him in a week and in four months he was gone, driving away one morning never to return. That kind of tale was prevalent in the days when police stopped at state lines and there was no agency to track down errant husbands. A salesman might stay a few weeks in a town, marry a local girl to keep his bed warm and leave her behind when he moved on, knowing there was no one to come after him.

"Did you even get a letter?" I asked.

"Not a word. He just left me flat and that was it."

"And you still named the baby after him?"

"Well, it was his child too, and I thought he would be back. But he didn't and he didn't, and then I didn't want him to. Mama took the baby and said it was hers. After all that, do you still want me, Ben? I'm secondhand merchandise, you know."

"Oh, Dorothy, look, of course I want you. With your Spanish blood and my coloring we can produce some great-looking brothers and sisters for Jaime." In those days marriage still meant children.

"Ben, you're wonderful!" she exclaimed, hugging and kissing, tears streaming down her cheeks. "But wherever did you get that about Spanish blood? Me squaw, not Spanish. Gramma went and got herself captured by one big Cherokee out in Oklahoma."

"I've heard about those kidnappings," I said. The

days when Plains Indians preyed on settlers was barely forty years gone by. "So how do you feel about Indians now?"

Dorothy laughed. "Indians? Indians is me, paleface. You want to lose your hair? I'm from a scalping tribe, you know. It was no kidnapping, Ben. What Grandpa captured was Gramma's heart. She fell in love with him and they went to live in Oklahoma Territory, happy as clams." So Dorothy's mother was half Cherokee, Dorothy a quarter. But she looked more.

"You have anything against Indians?" she asked.

"No. In fact I'm in love with one."

"All right then, let's go up to Maxville and get ourselves a cabin. I saw some there when we came past."

"But you don't have to . . ." I began, suddenly frightened. I had never been with a woman, and Dorothy knew everything.

How it must have cost her to say what she did, a person even shyer than I, and with a stricter sense of what's right and what's not.

"I want to, Ben," she answered. "I want you to know everything possible about me, and then you can decide. If you still want me after that I'll never deceive you again."

So far as I know, she never did.

That was the twenty-third of May. We were married June sixth.

☙25

You keep trying to do something of value, to force mankind to acknowledge your existence on this young planet even though you dwell beyond the Gray Veil.

Some little time ago my talents were spurned by that

celebrated publisher George Harmon. But he knows naught of journalism, or precious little else, so I decided to try the professional market. I have the time to invest in the project—it's all spare, so to speak. So I collected solicitations from magazines directed at me and my peers, of which there are enough to come up to your kazoo. It appears that God puts you on the geezer list the instant you pass sixty-five. I chose a publication called *Golden Ages*, a term I detest, which means, I see now, that I should have known better.

My query said I'm a retired journalist and I want to do an article for you, a piece called "Rack of Ages." All about the second-oldest scam known to man, newer only than pimping. Torturing the Kids, it's called. Poor Cain was the first victim, his parents no sooner reaching a ripe age than they were on him.

"Your father and I don't ask much," said Eve in a whine, "but this place you put us in is a hog wallow compared to the Garden."

We with the washboard faces do feel twinges of guilt, but not often. The temptation is overwhelming, the rewards sweet indeed. All that attention—if you can just manage to get them to worry themselves silly about you.

DAUGHTER: How are you, Mother dear?

MOTHER (thin, weak voice): Oh, as well as can be expected after that stroke last night.

DAUGHTER (horrified): Stroke! Oh, my lord, what did the doctor say?

MOTHER: Doctor? Doctors don't help anybody, honey; they just take your money. Besides, those awful pains went away about three. Could have been gas, I guess.

That was the gist of my query, cruelty as practiced by geriatric parents on their children.

An answer came back today, one turned out by a printing press even to the editor's signature, and it starts with a joke. A rejection slip that calls you Contributor is the kind of humor known only to the IRS and *Golden Ages*.

Dear Contributor:

Thank you for your recent query. The material you kindly offer is not in keeping with our present editorial needs, so we must say, "No, thank you." I must inform you that all our material is prepared by professionals.

I note that you are not enrolled in our Golden Assurance Society, which offers such wonderful benefits to retirees. I'll see that a packet of information is sent to you immediately.

Sometimes you learn a lot in a hurry. Such as that forty-three years as a journalist does not make me a "professional," an idea that caused wisps of smoke to appear at my ears, and that these *Golden Ages* people have a scam of their own going on the old folks.

I found a copy of the magazine in our library, and it turns out to be worse than I expected. There is a scattering of articles on such exciting topics as crossing the street alone, selecting comfortable shoes, having your eyes checked annually. I figure if you haven't learned those things in six or seven decades you're not likely to get smart off *Golden Ages*.

All the rest of the editorial matter concerns itself with old codgers playing golf, sunning in Mexico, riding asses in Arizona and the like. Reading the captions, you discover everybody pictured is on a Golden Ages Tour. Later we see a man seated at fireside reading a book ordered from the Golden Ages Book Club, and a woman unwrapping a package from the Golden Ages Mail Pharmacy with a pyramid peering over her shoulder.

Golden Ages, I came to realize, is no magazine at all. Instead it is a sales catalogue for this Golden Ages outfit of greed and rapacity. Their only goal is to get your money—for travel, books, drugs, life "assurance," shoes, most anything you want that would turn a profit for them. Soon, they tell us, we will be able to invest—presumably our life savings—in their Golden Coast condominiums in Florida. The pinnacle, if that is the word, of their offerings is saccharine landscapes described as having "bright colors for easy viewing." In other words, Coke-bottle glasses need not deter you from sending in your money.

So ends my flirtation with fame as a *Golden Ages* author and my idea of a piece by somebody who has been to the country of the aged and writes of his experiences. *Golden Ages* no doubt prefers authors under thirty so their viewpoint is not tainted by personal knowledge.

You don't find the kind of information I'm talking about anywhere. Libraries have no books for the old by the old. You find out how to be eighty by going cold turkey past seventy-nine. There's a reason, I suppose. When you're through with the aging experience you're in no condition to write your memoirs.

26

In the autumn of the year when war came, not one in fifty knew of Pearl Harbor, or Hawaii either. Globes hanging in schoolroom corners showed a few spots in a blotter of blue marked "Hawaiian I.," but the world has many spots and there was little reason to ponder these.

I knew of Pearl Harbor, for the *Times* carried wire dispatches from our Pacific fleet headquarters, and the Japs were threatening. Besides, I had a son out there. We did. Jaime, who became my son by court process, had left us the year before for a hitch in the Naval Air Corps. Only seventeen when he finished high school in forty, he was a restless child who wanted to be out and doing.

There was money for college, carefully saved, but Jaime was born with traveling shoes and by July he was in San Diego wearing what he called a "monkey suit." We saw him once in September when the train brought him back on leave, his hair all scalped off, his hat squared, his blue uniform fitted neatly to his body. He weighed a hundred and thirty and stood five ten. We were very proud.

Jaime had been accepted for training as a waist gunner on a plane called a "PBY" and in a week and a half he was gone again, never to return.

Even yet, when I think of my three children, it is Jaime who seems special in my mind, the one I spoiled most. Christopher was crafty and plotting, Norma sensible and straightforward. Jaime, like neither of his half-siblings, was imbued with an ineffable fey quality, a pixie spirit as ungraspable as a reflection in a dew pond.

Blessed with the most brilliant mind in the family, Jaime bothered only enough to get by in school. But he had more friends than Christopher and Norma together. He cultivated his peers, sometimes manipulated them as well, though no one thought the less of him for it. Smiles, always smiles, his mouth going forty to the dozen. Sometimes I fancy I see in Rodney a bit of Uncle Jaime.

Dorothy and I said, "Where does he get all that?" when we saw him holding center stage, and he seemed to have been born with wanderlust. There was an answer of course, but the name of Jaime Stillman was not mentioned in our house. I've wondered whether that was right, but it is done now and I was as eager as Dorothy to erase a bad memory.

By the summer of forty-one Jaime was on Ford Island

at Pearl, as he called it. Ford swarmed with "ships" like his, which was the PBY5A amphibious type. He made belittling remarks about the plainer PBY5, which was only a seaplane, while his could come down on land or water. They seldom made sea landings though, and once when they did the hull popped thirty-some rivets. After the war had been going a while people called his kind of plane the Flying Coffin, but by then it was too late to matter to us.

Jaime sent a picture, and there were wings on his uniform. By his letters, the port gun bucked and smoked in his hands; he shot down a drone and laced a sleeve with bullet holes.

We'd had our midday meal on that Sunday and I sat reading the comics in the *Post-Dispatch*. I wore my brown cardigan and Dorothy, with the Country Section, sat in the wing chair in a lavender pullover and the plaid skirt she called her "Rug." The weather was almost tropically mild for December and before noon I had worked in the garden in my shirt sleeves. We had not yet taken our heavy coats out of the cedar closet, and now the radio told us the Japs had attacked Pearl Harbor. On momentous occasions you remember the tiny details of life.

"Oh my God, Jaime could be dead now!" Dorothy screamed.

Later the radio sought to reassure us, minimizing destruction and loss of life. But Dorothy was right: Jaime was dead.

Not until two weeks later did we know. No answer came to our airmail letter or our cable, and there was no way to call a man in service even if long distance had been reliable.

One evening after the sun had set and winter darkness was coming on fast I heard Dorothy's voice at the door and she came through into the kitchen with a yellow envelope in her hand. Two red spots had been stamped on the flap. Inside was a telegram from the War Department, brief but devastating. The aftereffects, as from a crippling accident, never went away.

Two years later the captain of Jaime's plane, on leave in Seattle, sent us a letter. Our son, he said, had been climbing the access ladder into his blister when a strafing plane hit him in the back. He died a hero in the service of his country, said the captain, and added praise for Jaime's bravery. It mattered little. We had lost a son.

◆27

Pulse normal, hemorrhoids somnolent, blood pressure slightly elevated.

This morning I went to Norma's rich doctor and got two hundred dollars' worth of his opinion. He may not have been rich before but he is now. I didn't bother asking for the blood-pressure numbers, being too concerned at the time about my posterior. I bent over for his examination and before I knew his intentions he'd slipped on a glove and, humming to himself, gave my hemorrhoids the poking of their lives. An outraged groan escaped my mouth. Oooaaauugh!

"Sorry, Mr. Carpenter, but it's required."

Not by my medical rules. "Christ, Doc, do you have to use your thumb?"

He'd finished by then and I caught a fleeting smile on his lips, if not a smirk. "Very good, Mr. Carpenter."

"After that, it's a wonder they're not sticking out like purple balloons."

"What'd he say?" Norma asked when we were in the car again.

"About five dollars' worth but he charged two hundred. Don't you know a doctor who drives a Volkswagen and is not into serious torture?"

Norma looked blank and then did her little-girl laugh. "Oh, that, Papa, your piles. What about them?"

"He said he always enjoys playing with them."

"Oh, Papa, you're impossible! Aren't you going to tell me?"

"It's a secret between me and Snodgrass."

"Dr. Greenglas, Papa." Her laugh was rife with insincerity. Norma was piqued because her little boy wouldn't tell his secret.

We went shopping at Bloomingdale's in Stamford and ate lunch there. Norma bought two sheets, king size, and on the moving stair she leaned over and whispered, "They have nice rest rooms in case you have to go before we eat."

"Don't have to," I said. "When you weren't looking I peed in some lady's handbag."

"You're being naughty today," she said, shushing me. "Sure you don't want to?"

Lordy lordy, I was eight again and being shepherded by my mommie. Why do our kids treat us like nincompoops whose mittens need pinning and whose weewee levels require periodic checking? In truth I felt like going right then but the idea of having your daughter schedule your pissoir stops is odious to me. One glass of wine later, plus some slurps of water and a cup of tea, and Mother Nature was sending me alarming signals.

So after lunch I hobbled after Norma into the parking lot, my radiator sloshing, a prayer on my lips that I would not be led by any still waters or, God be praised, especially any gushing fountains.

"What'd you say, Papa?" She was opening the door for me.

"Said I noticed you didn't weewee after we ate. Sure you don't want to?"

She giggled like a little girl reincarnate and patted my shoulder. "I take after my father, thank you; big bladders run in my family."

"Yeah, we Carpenters hardly ever pee."

I thought I was going to, in my pants. Norma obviously inherited from her mother, because the Carpenter bladder present was about to breach the levee. I wondered what she'd say if I left a puddle on her maroon seat.

"So you're all right, Papa?"

"Sure, fine."

How was I to know her wicked intentions? Our route avoided dangerous waters but led straight to an immense discount grocery. Now they have public toilets in filling stations, in department stores, even in courthouses, but who ever heard of one in a grocery?

"I don't get over here often," Norma announced, "and when I do I like to pick up some basics. Wonderful bargains here. We'll just nip in and nip out."

More like rolling in, an ocean wave swamping a beach. The place was awash, so to speak, with housewives swooping down on bargains, the aisles rocketing with maniacal drivers trying out for Daytona. I tell you, I was scared stiff watching cart jockeys bounce off shelves and crash their buggies together without a word of apology. In some aisle or other I knew we'd find bodies with dusty Bascart tracks up their backs.

I steered in Norma's wake, keeping to the side and watching them go by, these nicely attired ladies with white-knuckle grips on the handles, their eyes riveted on some distant can of vegetables, their teeth set so hard their jaw muscles looked like Mr. America's biceps.

They don't care who you are; take your time getting out of their way and you may wind up stuffed headfirst into their baskets amongst the slabs of meat and bags of potatoes.

Norma's bargains looked like doctor bills to me. She

paid more for a Family Pak of beef than I used to spend in a week with a family of five, and there was a plastic laundry bag stuffed with thirty green peppers she couldn't resist.

"What in hell you going to do with all those peppers?" I asked. "Take in Mexican boarders maybe?"

"They're such a bargain, Papa. You can't beat the price."

Probably not, but those three are going to have the pall of a tree snake by next week. Then into the basket fell a block of whiting with the feel of a concrete slab.

"Funny how, in the East, they sell petrified fish right in the stores," I said, but she wasn't listening. The Bottled Juices had her attention. Disaster very nearly struck as I cowed behind her cart, wondering when the waters would break and create the first tidal wave in the short ugly history of this madhouse.

I had a flash image, like the shadow of a passing hawk, and then the crash came. An overflowing gondola slammed my cart against the shelves and jerked the handle from my hands. Luckily my grip was light or I might have wound up on a shelf next to Complete Pasta Selection. A blubbery face looked at me momentarily over a beefy pink plastic shoulder. "Watch what you're doing, Pops," a shrill nasal voice shouted.

"Why, you coming back?" I called, but she was long gone.

"Now, Papa, don't get into a fracas with the ladies," Norma cautioned, finding humor in the incident.

"Fracas, my foot, Norma; these crazies are trying to kill me."

Later I glimpsed an old number dressed in black, a cane dangling from her handle, her eyes glazed in bewilderment, as if she'd come this far but now, out of breath, she could not go on. I thought of offering a kind word but there was no time.

"Come on, Papa," Norma commanded. "I don't want this to take all day."

Our load approaching the gunwales, I said, "Honey, I think you've already got enough for a regiment."

"Just a little while longer. I need some bathroom rolls."

A cruel thing to mention to a man drowning internally. In the check-out line she left to dash for eggs. Alone, surrounded by frenzied women, I felt old and dwindled, a man condensed by time from a quart to one of those metric bottles that looks the same but gives you six drinks less. Spanish words, snarled in shouts in the line ahead, and waving hands full of food stamps got my mind off myself momentarily.

"Some excitement for a change, huh?" said a voice at my ear. Norma had returned unnoticed, a box of three dozen eggs in her hands.

"Do they kill many here in a week?"

She laughed, suffused with happiness over conquered bargains. "It's good for you, Papa, to get out in the real world sometimes."

"You think having your life threatened puts pink in your cheeks, huh, Norma?"

On the way home she brought up my will. "Have you had it changed yet, Papa? Clyde thinks it's really important."

"I'll bet he does," I said, smiling brightly to confuse her. "I haven't done anything yet, no, but I'm thinking maybe to simplify it I'll just leave everything to Meghan."

"*Meghan?*" A look of horror at the mention of the niece she's never seen.

My laughter, which did unutterable things to my suffering bladder, told her I was joking, but she seemed none too sure of the message. I have no desire to treat my daughter with anything but kindness but a little meddling goes a long way with me, even if she is a loved one.

Soon Rodney came in for his cuffs, a poor student because he won't apply himself, a boy who won't do a thing she tells him. My condition by that time dictated simple answers. "Ummm." "Ummm?" "Ummm!"

I was sitting later on my love seat, my radiator drained and my shoes off, when my door thudded as if hit by a low-flying woodpecker and in came Fletch. He shuffled across the carpet, his bow tie centered exactly, his black gabardine suit neat enough for instant burial. He took in my stockinged feet.

"Big time, huh, Ben? I heard you went off with your daughter."

"A very dangerous afternoon, Fletch. It's my advice that if you value your life you stay out of supermarkets."

"Welllll," he said, drawing it out, "seems like the whooooole worrrrrld out there has filled up with weirdos since we came in here."

~28

Mrs. Collins is dying.

She is my next-door neighbor but one, her door around the corner past Mrs. Longo's. I hardly know the lady; once I tipped my hat to her in the hall but didn't know who she was until I heard her door click behind me. Three months ago, on the elevator, we said hello, and I haven't seen her since.

Emily went to see Mrs. Collins once, after she quit going down for meals, a little wisp of a woman with gold-rim glasses, gray hair and a cane, her talk, Emily says, as sparse as her looks. But she's rich. So far as anyone knows, Mrs. Collins never had a visitor. Ellie Longo, one evening when we came up together in the elevator, said as we passed Mrs. Collins's door, "Poor woman, nobody ever comes to see her, no visitors at all."

That is the ultimate put-down here: she never has visitors. Some of our old crocks keep close track, as if guarding a daughter's virginity. Of course by their rules you'd have to go around accompanied by a football team before they could be sure you "have visitors."

I've been thinking it was some strange unreasoned fear that drove Mrs. Collins to cover, which was not kind of me, or the truth. She has cancer, the female kind.

Fear made Mrs. Collins strange though, fear of losing her valuables and finding herself without money before the clock runs down for her. We all know that fear, of being on the far slope and your money gone. You may wish, like old Frank Simmons, that the mortal coil would be kind and let you go before then. The nightmare of the aged is to have more life than money.

Emily's visit was a favor to Mr. Harmon, whom she unaccountably admires. She thinks he's handsome and I don't tell her different, though she's aware he is not my dish of tea. What he wanted to know was how sick Mrs. Collins was. She had barred her door to him and hung up when he called.

Mr. Harmon is being gored fore and aft by this one. Mrs. Collins is a Lifetime Resident, having bought in for twenty thousand when the Arms was brand new. Now the price is thirty. Lifetimes are assured a home until the end, though they still pay monthlies just like us renters. What they receive extra is end care. If you get down at the last and have to go out to a nursing home or the hospital, Eagle Arms pays all. It's in their contract.

So if Mrs. Collins went out it would cost the Owners some money. On the other hand, it's bad business to have people die here—the Death House syndrome. An ambulance is not a welcome sight out front; a hearse might stop

Mr. Harmon's ticker permanently. So he's caught between fire and brimstone. What makes the Owners happy, I suppose, is a Lifetime who takes a hack to the hospital after breakfast and dies before they can put on a lunch charge.

Mrs. Collins was cordial enough to Emily after she got the four locks on her door undone. Inside, Emily saw locks added to bathroom, linen closet and walk-in. A flat of locks.

Emily was there only a few minutes, finding her hostess worn and tired. "It's down here, you know," said Mrs. Collins. "I've always had it hard like that, cramps and pains, and now this."

She knew what Mr. Harmon was after, had it fixed in her mind. Since Lifetimes had gone to thirty thousand he wants the extra ten, she is sure. Nothing Emily said could dissuade her.

"I'm so afraid I won't have enough to last," she said. Her furnishings, by Emily's account, suggest otherwise, her flat being beautifully done and filled with expensive-looking antiques. And Emily found out about the locks. They protect her jewelry and stock certificates. Mrs. Collins said her valuables were her last defense against starvation, a dramatic declaration but not unusual amongst people our age. The idea of the three locks inside is on the barmy side but clever too. Behind one lock are her assets, giving a burglar only one chance in three of getting it right the first time.

Mr. Harmon's questions were dutifully posed. Did Mrs. Collins want to be taken to the hospital? Or to see a doctor?"

"No," the lady said. "I'm dying and I know it. This is my home, and here I'll stay to the end. And, if you would, my dear, remind that Harmon of my written instructions."

The instructions, it developed, forbid Eagle Arms to contact any of her relatives while she is alive, she apparently abhorring deathbed scenes, especially with kin who never bothered to visit her when she was well.

He went back on her of course.

I was awakened this morning before six by voices outside my door. I seldom hear conversations from outside, and voices never linger as these did. First there was a man and a woman in conversation, joined at length by a second man.

I put on my robe and listened at the door, feeling vaguely threatened.

"Then there's the old farm in Wisconsin," a male voice said.

"In Wisconsin?" asked the woman.

"Grandma Jefferson's place, you know; Aunt Edna still owns it."

"I forgot about that," the second man said, "Francie and me did. She remembered that GM stock though. Loren left the old lady well off."

"And all that jewelry," said the woman, "more than I ever saw. Rings and brooches and things." The hot breath of greed was as palpable as a ten-ton rock.

I undid my chain and opened the door a crack. The woman, her back to me, started in fright. She was enormous, her rain-barrel body hung with butchered beef quarters for arms.

"Good morning," one of the men said. "I hope we haven't disturbed you."

The hall was aswarm with people, I saw when I stuck my head out. There must have been a dozen men and women, and three children, on this side of the corner alone. They were strung along the wall like waiting vultures.

"So it's Mrs. Collins, is it?" I said.

"It's so tragic," whimpered the fat woman, wiping away tears with a huge hand.

"We're her relatives, Aunt Edna's family," the man said.

"I'm her second cousin Lucille," said the woman, her voice cracking and her body shaking with sobs.

I'd discerned no crying when they were discussing the land and the jewelry and the stocks.

I closed the door, took an early shower and went round the other way to breakfast. They're still out there and from what I overheard they've tried the locks already and found the right one, all of them assembled to divvy up her possessions as soon as she's gone.

Not one of them appeared when she was well.

May you go quickly, Mrs. Collins.

≈29

You'd think I kidnapped some child. Norma was on the phone bright and early to screech like an owl: "You lure him over there just so you can spoil him, Papa. He ought to have been home studying yesterday, but was he? Nooo, he was goofing off with his grandpa. This has to stop, now!"

"Norma, sweetie, calm yourself. If Rodney wants to visit his grandfather there's nothing wrong with that. Lord knows you don't show your face often." Like two cats.

"I'm busy all the time, Papa, and Rodney has too much schoolwork to fool around down there. He's barely passing, you know."

"But he *is* passing, Norma, told me so himself, and that's enough. What's with you, child?"

In the end she made me agree, next time Rodney appears, to tell him to shove off and go study. Regardless of day or time, I judge. On her end, she agreed not to strangle him with her bare hands. "I'm going to speak to him again though, you can be sure," she said. His hair may be singed by her speakings.

"Remember that Rodney is pretty well formed," I

told her, "a young man going on seventeen. You have to begin treating him like an adult, not some toddler who still wets his pants."

That did not go over well and she hung up soon enough.

All this because he came to see me again a couple of days ago and took the Connbus home. Few events are as joyous to old fogies as visits by grandkids, and the boy had quite a lot to say. Which I did not tell Norma, even when she asked. Grandpa smershed the answer, a trick of the elderly wherein we pretend to sudden senility.

I could tell from the start that things were not right.

"What, no girl this time?" I asked him at the door.

"I want to talk to you alone, Grandpa."

Hoo boy, me having a heart-to-heart with a teen-ager. What do I know about teen life these days? Besides, I've served my time as father of adolescents, and two hitches surely are not required in one lifetime. "Sounds dramatic," I told him. "Come on in and have a pop and we'll talk."

I got us cream sodas and Rodney sighed like a man on death row. "What's your big problem now?" I asked.

"I got a plan I want to talk to you about, Grandpa. School is drivin me nuts, that's what. Ain't doin so good neither."

"Especially in grammar," I said with a laugh. "They let you use words like ain't these days?"

"It's just what we say; don't mean nuthin."

"Sounds to me like you're bored," I told him.

He ran the cold pop bottle across his forehead dramatically. "Yeah, probably it, just bored. I know the stuff but a lot of times I give wrong answers anyway."

"How can you do that if you know your lessons?"

"Easy, Grandpa. Just act stupid and say the wrong thing."

It must be some kind of disease they have here in the East, I thought, perhaps known locally as the wackos. "I can figure out *how* one does it, Rodney. What I want to know is *why?*"

"Why? So's I don't show up the other kids."

"So you give wrong answers?" I shook my head in disbelief.

"Look, Grandpa, I only want to get out of Marlow High, that's all. Have a few friends and get the hell out. They didn't like me when I made better grades than they did."

"Look, Rodney, every teen-ager goes through the outcast thing. They get pimples, think they're ugly, have no friends, they say. It's just not true. I've seen you get on wonderfully well with others."

"Grownups, Grandpa, but not kids my own age."

I'd heard about that from Dorothy, another only child who said she did fine with adults but it took years to come to terms with her peers. Maybe looks are not all of Rodney's inheritance from Grandma.

"About all I can tell you," I said, feeling helpless, "is that trying hard is best, whatever you're doing."

Rodney shook his head. "It's not like that now. Kids are kinky today and you have to do things just right."

"You ever talk to your parents about this?"

"Mom and Dad? No, never. I tried once with Mom but she told me I was being silly. You're the first person I ever really told, Grandpa."

A dubious honor for me. "What about your father, Rodney?"

"He don't notice nuthin, Grandpa. I could sprout another head and he'd never know."

"You said you had a plan when you came in. Let's hear it."

He smiled brightly, and I felt better. Listening to your grandson's woes is no upper, as they say, when you can't do a thing to help.

"It's about Old Farm, Grandpa. You still own it, don't you?"

"What's left of it, yes. The house is sort of toasted inside."

"I've been thinkin, Grandpa, what I need is a goal. I think I could get through school some way if I had something to look forward to afterwards."

"I'm getting a little confused between school and Old Farm, Rodney."

"Look, try this one on: school will be out about the same time your year is up here. I've been thinkin you and me could go out to Old Farm and run it again. Wouldn't you like that?"

Whoooeee, now there's one for you, a child and an old man making a living on Old Farm's scant forty acres. Nobody could do that these days, not even with a mule thrown in, though I did not say so. Why confuse my grandson with the sorry state of our economy?

"I'm not sure it's habitable," I said, "not after that last bonfire I had."

Rodney laughed. "That's the point, Grandpa. We could fix it up just the way we want it. I'm a good carpenter, you know, and you could tell me what to do now that you can't do it yourself anymore."

What, me too feeble to lift a hammer? "I want you to know, young sprout, that I'm something of a carpenter too. Why, I once added a whole room to the old home place, the one Christopher was born in."

More laughter. Evidently I was playing into his hands and didn't know it. "That's wonderful, Grandpa. So we could work together on the house. You know I've always loved that place, a real farm with a barn and everything. That's what I want to be, a farmer, and we can grow our own cereal grains and have cows for meat and some swine in a pen. We could make our own cottonseed cakes and dig our own tubers, all kinds of things. Me and you, Grandpa, partners!"

I laughed, but not enough to hurt his feelings, and I

didn't tell him that it is steers you eat, or that Old Farm is more suited to the support of crows than people. "Where'd you get all these ideas?" I asked.

"In the library. I've been readin about agriculture and country life."

Sounds to me as if he's got his hands on some Agriculture Department bulletins from half a century back. "I thought you'd maybe want to be a businessman someday, like your Dad. Or do something with your French.

"Yeah, but I took all the courses they have, Grandpa, and I sure don't want to go into business. Yuk."

I thought I might as well go on with the official Kemp party line and see what happened. "Businessmen make good money, Rodney. Look at your father." I discovered it not to be a wise thing to say.

"You look at him, Grandpa. I might throw up if I did. You know what Dad did? He sold out to the establishment, that's what, way back there. I'll never do what Dad did."

How do you handle a grandson carrying on like that? Gingerly. "A lot of people are attracted to farming, son, but it's mainly because they've never farmed. I was raised on a farm and I know about the flaws, the principal one being agonizing, backbreaking labor. Nobody with all his marbles chooses to work himself to death."

"But I *like* hard work, Grandpa."

Because he's never done any. "We can talk about it some more later on, Rodney. Right now you'd best get a decent education, and give them the right answer when you know it."

I was beginning to tire of the discussion. Puberty and its problems are not engrossing for a septuagenarian, even when it's your grandson.

Rodney slowed not one whit. "Do you know any books about farming I could read, Grandpa?"

"Well, Thomas Jefferson was a farmer in Virginia and

his stuff isn't bad. Why don't you start with the Declaration of Independence?"

"Oh, Grandpa!" Exasperated. "Jefferson was no farmer, and he sold out too. Look at the size of his house on a nickel."

"All right, I'll give you a serious answer. Probably our best-known writer-farmer lately was Louis Bromfield. He had a spread in Ohio and did some nice books, like one called *The Rains Came*."

Rodney wrote it down carefully and left to catch his bus. I went along as far as the front desk.

"One other thing, Grandpa," he said brightly. "We can put up a wind-charger and generate our own electricity."

Lucy gave him a sweet smile and told him good-bye. "Sounds like you and your grandson are mad at the power company," she said, laughing, when he had gone.

"No no. It's farming we're into. We're going to be Carpenter & Grandson, Purveyors of Fine Cottonseed Cakes, Swine and Tubers, whatever they are."

⚡30

Love and sex and those good things amongst the young nowadays are not unlike roman candles in their fiery beginning and fading embers. He's living with her this week, with somebody else next week. In my time our affairs sparked and smoldered more like punk sticks and, now that I'm this age, romance goes even slower.

Emily and I are involved in a romantic relationship. We get together once or twice a week and feel comfortable with each other, though more like close friends than lovers. We feel none of the wretched yearning that makes young love such agonizing pleasure, and at our age stabs of pain come not to the heart but to the bursitic shoulder. No one at the Arms seems the wiser, which is uncanny in a place where you can't change your mind without note being taken.

A dark secret from Emily's past, furtively hidden away by her, has come my way and I am exercising all the courtesy and tact I can to help her bruised spirit. Life would have been simpler had she kept it to herself but one of the encumbrances of friendship requires you to listen and offer sympathy. Our previous lives, to me, count for naught, and all we have lies between today and the grave. But Emily wanted to tell.

An old letter did it. We sat on the edge of her bed last evening, having accomplished what to me has remained remarkable ever since a certain night spent in a tourist cabin with pretty young Dorothy Simpson, when my eye fell on a stack of papers at the corner of her writing desk. Emily noticed and her fine white hand shot out and turned the top piece onto its face.

"Maybe you shouldn't see that," she said. "It got left out by accident."

"An old love letter, eh? Or maybe a new one?" A feeling of unease flickered through me at that thought; there are some core reactions you never lose.

"Nothing of the sort, Ben. You are the only man I keep company with. Here, look if you like."

She held the envelope before me. By squinting I could make out the top line, "Mrs. James A. Walrod, Incompetent." The address looked to be one of those B towns—Bridgeport or Baltimore or Buffalo.

"Your husband's mother?" I asked. "She's still alive, is she?"

"No, Ben. I'm Mrs. James A. Walrod."

I scarcely knew how to respond. "But you're not . . ." I could not get the word out.

"Incompetent? No, I'm not, nor stark raving mad either. But that's not what the records down in Maryland say. That's where Jim and I lived, you know."

"Yes. He was a chicken farmer, you said. But you don't have to explain this to me. Your past is your past and mine is mine."

"Oh, but I want to tell you, Ben; I *have* to tell somebody. I've had it all bottled up so long. Will you listen?"

We dressed and went to sit on her sofa with cups of tea—only one, so the caffeine would not keep us awake later—and she told me her story of tender love and terrible greed. I'll put on my reporter's cap and type it out.

Emily Cynthia Goodson, daughter of a Chicago accountant, was a graceful, pliant girl, beautiful too, from the relics still observable. Her mother yearned for gentility but hardly achieved it in Chicago. Her hopes fell to her daughter, who was sent east to school, first at Poughkeepsie and then Charlottesville.

At the university Emily studied hard and by nineteen had finished two years toward being an English teacher and carried a B-plus average. In the spring of the second year she met someone even brighter, and it was the end of classes for her. This was Jim Walrod, an ag student who at twenty-five was taking a Ph.D. in animal husbandry. Presumably his studies had given him familiarity with many animals, but only one mattered to him, the chicken.

They married a week after he got his degree and set about fashioning reality out of his dream. A small bank loan and a modest advance from his father, a Montana rancher, secured sixty-eight acres for them on the Eastern

Shore and gave Jim a start in the egg business. Egg factories are everywhere today but at that time the concept was nothing short of revolutionary. Success came quickly as Jim exerted copious amounts of brilliance and energy; soon he added a scheme for selling chickens on the foot, and then they were hauled to market in ice. Frank Perdue was still lisping through first grade when Jim Walrod made the Eastern Shore famous for fresh poultry.

Money flowed in and Jim added land and more land, eventually owning something over two thousand acres. Their place, at the lower end of the Shore, was flat except for a ridge running from north to south through the middle. Jim named it Walrod's Mountain.

Emily knew nothing of the country but quickly grew to love the life of a chicken farmer's wife, and especially the farmer himself. He was a man of singular passions.

"I was like a little girl with her first doll," Mrs. Walrod remembers now, blushing becomingly, "a doll with passionate desires. It was wonderful."

Obsessions can be attractive. Besides chickens and his wife, Jim had entrancing interests in oysters, roses and wasps. For the wasps, he built trap-nests, using precise metric drills imported from Europe, and the homestead at length was adorned by nearly a thousand roses. His passion for oysters was more singular still.

"It sounds simply gluttonous," Mrs. Walrod says, "but I came to enjoy our oyster binges as much as my husband did." In autumn Jim waited until the water cooled to firm up an oyster's flesh and then he and his young wife set off on a sampling trip, first to Crisfield, then north to Saint Michaels and Grasonville. When the right oyster was found they put a whole barrel in the car and went home.

"With the barrel on the back porch, where it was cold, we ate oysters three or four times a day," says Mrs. Walrod. "We had stews and fritters and roasts but mainly we took them from the shell with a squeeze of lemon." So went their oyster madness.

Children were late coming and when the first arrived it was a terrible birthing and there could be no more. The child was a daughter and they called her Cindy. The parents were happy indeed, finding Cindy beautiful and perfect. All idylls, it should be written, have short lives. In the summer of forty-one Cindy wandered into a laying house, came too close to a feed conveyor and was killed when her clothing became entangled. In a way, she was a victim of her father's visionary brilliance, which had produced automated feeders long before their time.

The dream thus ended, and a nightmare began for the Walrods. They had been ebullient people who believed they could weather anything, not reckoning on the wrecking force of a child's death. For months they suffered a dark night of the soul, going nowhere, seeing no one.

The lights came on again for Jim when his sister's son, a boy named Norman Campbell, just out of Yale and a boyhood in Montana, came to the Eastern Shore and bought land nearby. (I should imagine he settled there with the expectation of becoming rich like his Uncle Jim, though I forgot to ask Emily. After decades of asking why? why? why? I forgot to ask why. Old fire horses may never forget; old reporters do.)

Norman, it developed, was nothing like as bright as his uncle, had studied fine arts instead of agriculture and knew only sketchily about how eggs come to be. None of this was a major problem: Uncle Jim, just then desperately in need of family, was delighted to supply advice, money, even his own hired hands. A year after Cindy's death Jim told his wife he had got over the tragedy.

"I told him a lie then," Mrs. Walrod recalls, "the only one of our married life. I told him I was as good as new too." The truth was considerably different, and she now had Norman to contend with as he lured her husband's attention away from herself.

In the middle of the war Jim went off to serve in the Army, rising to captain and then major. In the Solomons and later in the Philippines he kept a few hens and became a micro-legend by supplying fresh eggs to GIs far from home. Jim came back after two and a half years, gray at the temples, his face newly lined. Life resumed as before, Emily and Jim renewing their oyster binges, and there were new nests for wasps. Emily learned to cope with Norman Campbell's intruding presence, though she never developed a liking for him.

The fifties came and went, and then the sixties expired. One day in the early seventies as Jim strolled back from a look atop Walrod's Mountain he fell on the rutted lane beside a barley field. Norman found him face down, victim of a heart attack.

Life went into reruns for the inconsolable widow. She saw no one except Norman, who had married and by that time was the father of two. He brought groceries and did such other shopping as she required.

"I was terrified," says Mrs. Walrod. "I knew the widow's lot and was certain I'd die of hunger. Even in the daytime I kept the shades drawn for fear someone might want to kill me. I wrote no letters, and never answered the phone, and I opened the door only when I was sure it was my husband's nephew." She seems even now not to acknowledge him as her relative as well.

Norman was ever solicitous and often urged drives upon her. She refused, explaining, "I have to have time to pull myself together." Lonely, beset by imagined horrors, she licked her wounds—and licked and licked. Emily Walrod was fifty-nine at the time.

One morning Norman appeared with another man, a stranger who wanted to rent a field. She sent him packing, suspecting his motives were otherwise. More followed, always escorted by Norman. They wished to buy land, eggs, chickens, even the empty oyster barrels by the brood house. Emily distrusted them all.

Over many weeks Norman wore down his aunt's resistance and she got into his station wagon to be taken for a ride. She cried at seeing the outside world again, and the drive stretched on and on, leading finally to a tunnel. Emily knew they were entering Baltimore and demanded to be taken home. Norman drove on, giving no answer at all.

As if in a trance, Emily found herself led into a neat brick building with a plaque identifying it as the Riverview Nursing Home, and they were expecting her. Papers already on hand identified her as Mrs. James A. Walrod, Incompetent.

Emily has yet to learn the chain of events that took her to Riverview, for an incompetent has no rights, can make no legal demands. She was a victim of course of Norman Campbell, and the men who came to her house with him were not interested in buying anything, Papers at Riverview, she says, made reference to two court proceedings about which she knew nothing, and they named him conservator of her estate and guardian of her person.

Riverview is no ordinary nursing home. It specializes in unbalanced women from wealthy families who are willing to buy an alternative to a state institution.

"I raised all kinds of hell," says Mrs. Walrod, "but it only made them more sure I was crazy. I took a handful of pills to kill myself and woke up with a headache. Nothing worked."

After two years Norman, perhaps suffering unaccustomed twinges of conscience, offered her a deal. He now lived in her house and enjoyed the fruits of her husband's labors. His proposition was two hundred thousand in cash to last her out if she agreed to leave the state and live elsewhere. In fact, he had the elsewhere picked out—his former college town.

Though once worth millions, Emily had no alternative. After two months in a hospital in New Haven, where

Norman had studied fine arts, she was released and came to Eagle Arms.

As I said, a story of tender love and terrible greed.

31

You see, and hear, and take part in some strange and remarkable happenings on the far side of the hill. It is because, in these years of our lives, with million-dollar stock-market kills and seeing our copy chopped up by the City Desk far behind, we have time to pay attention to what we never noticed before.

On a warm day last week thirty of us, chaperoned by Rufe and Nursey, were taken by bus to New York and given a Circle Line cruise. As many sights were discovered aboard as ashore. Our crowd, with Andy Kelly and myself the only men, charged for the rail immediately to lock up the best viewing points. Regular tourists and a few children scattered before us. The elderly demanding the best, you know.

The boat had not got halfway down the island before clouds appeared, a breeze sprang up and the boat began to roll. To my left I saw one of our ladies heaving over the rail, joined instantly by nearly all in our party, creating our own barf-in.

"Tell them to take us back!" shouted one lady.

"Rufe, go tell the Captain!" commanded a second.

He and Nursey got us inside and gave us sips of water

in paper cups to settle our innards. Rufe procured a sweet pop for me to sip.

Not until Eagle Arms—the very place we'd paid money and misery to escape—came into view did we feel safe again. Maybe what they say is true: being old in itself means you've got some screws loose.

Mr. Harmon was at the center of our latest Happening, and I saw again why the ladies call him Harmon the Jarman, give *heil* salutes behind his back and sometimes place two fingers under their noses for a mustache.

It was Mrs. Abernathy, squinting upward through her horn-rims, who discovered a leak in our sitting room and alerted Lucy and Mr. Harmon. He appeared in a natty suntan epauletted shirt and black tie, his Storm Trooper habit, and took charge. A crowd ringed the scene of action and marveled at the yellow hard hat on our Executive Director's head. It seemed to be a promotional gimmick by the phone company, a blue bell appearing on its front. Or maybe he swiped it when its owner was up a pole. Soon Rufe appeared, his massive arms cradling a giant stepladder as if it were made of soda straws.

"Go up and have a look, Rufe," Mr. Harmon commanded.

"Better hope it's not from the sanitary side," said a squeaky voice. Ah yes, Fletch, the frustrated plumber.

"What?" Mr. Harmon said gruffly, and might have asked a question but caught himself in time. Did God seek advice while sticking the world together?

A quivering hand swept out and caught a drop. Fletch sniffed his fingers. Lucy, her mind contemplating the drainings from upstairs, curled her lip away from her teeth. "Smells sweet enough," said Fletch. "You're lucky, Mr. Harmon. Except I think what you need is a plumber."

Ignoring the advice, Mr. Harmon turned to Rufe. "We'll have to make an inspection hole, Rufe."

"We call plomer, Mist Horrmonn?"

"Don't need a plumber, but you might get that friend of yours from Martin Manor to help you. Owes you some work, doesn't he?"

"Hinojosa? He know lessn me 'bout pip."

Martin Manor is two high rises at the foot of the hill, and Hinojosa their super. He and Rufe trade work. They're strange about names around here. Rufe, being black, has no last name; Hinojosa, as a Puerto Rican, has no front name.

Soon Rufe was perched on one ladder and clinging to the second was Hinojosa, about third grader in size, clad in a near-defunct suit jacket and black felt hat with the brim turned up all around. Chomp chomp chomp. Chomp chomp chomp. Their wrecking bars dotted the carpeting with ceiling tiles and released cascades of water.

Rufe, ceasing his blows, asked Hinojosa, "Wotchoo do dere den?"

"Make beeg hole, man."

"Den wot?"

"You de boss."

"Boss don know wot."

Hinojosa was right; the hole was beeg, and soon beeger.

Fletch sidled up to Mr. Harmon. "Frankly, I think you're working at the wrong place," he said. "The water's coming from above. Go up to about five and feel the gallery walls for dampness."

Mr. Harmon dismissed him quickly enough. "I've consulted on some really big projects, Doctor."

The script was right out of the Three Stooges. Finding water flowing down the outside of a large copper pipe on one, Mr. Harmon and his gang, taking their audience along with them, tore a hole in the wall on mezz and then one on two. They finally found the leak on four, my floor, but thankfully around the corner from me. Mrs. Forrest's front wall soon appeared to have been attacked by terrorists with bombs.

Fletch said the trouble was in a three-inch journal, whatever that is, and yard-long wrenches were sticking out of the wall, Rufe tugging on one, Hinojosa the other. Next I observed, as coached witnesses tell juries, water shooting out like Old Faithful. Everything had to be shut off and, three hours later, with no flushes and no drinking water, two plumbers appeared, to make the fix. Next week drywallers are supposed to arrive.

At supper Fletch shook his head sadly. "I could have saved him a lot of trouble. Wonder why he won't listen?"

"Maybe 'cause you're eighty-seven years old."

"Eighty-six, Ben. Don't make it worse than it is."

Then there was the afternoon when my grandson came sweeping in here all of three minutes after Marlow High let out, and he was furious. "That book by Bromfield," he said accusingly, "I got it out of the library and it's not on farming at all. It's about India, for cripe sakes, and this Ranchipur, crap like that."

Having a grandson close is better than not, and I feel pride when Residents mention his visits, but this one may yet drive me out of my gourd. "Sit down and cool off, my boy," I said, chuckling. "You want a bottle of pop?"

"Beer, please, and I'm mad at you, Grandpa. You tricked me." He looked like a pit bull with his foot stepped on. "Why'd you do that, Grandpa?"

He settled for root beer and I tiptoed on his eggshells. "Just because you're old doesn't mean you never play tricks," I said. "I thought you'd be amused when you found out."

"Well, I wasn't, and just because I'm young doesn't mean I don't have problems."

"I know, Rodney. Same thing when you're my age."

Mollified, he pulled a huge sheet out of his valise.

"Mmmm, what have we here?" I asked.

He waved a hand expansively. "All my plans for Old House."

I put on my specs and examined his sketches seriously, and seriously wondered what the hell I was going to do next. I can't tell him his idea is loony, can't crush his dream. The accuracy of his memory was revealed on his sheet. The bedrooms were there, the kitchen with its fireplace and my big table of weathered wood. At the back corner my eye spotted an error. "What's that?" I asked. "Old House doesn't stick out like that."

"The new bathroom, Grandpa. See the stool and the square tub?" They were there, all right, except the room had grown like Topsy.

"But you've put your tub out in the yard, son."

"That's our addition, Grandpa. For the tub, see, a big one like the Romans had. You know about additions so it will be your very own project."

Rodney had given me my own work to do, instead of watching others, and you can't beat that kind of treatment when you're my age. "A nice set of plans," I said, pulling off my glasses.

"We'll have a real gueam bath, Grandpa."

"Gueam, huh? Is that like hunky-dory?"

"I guess. We'll go out and start soon as school is out, okay?"

"Have to wait and see what shape I'm in, whether I'm still around." A standard dodge for old gaffers.

"Mom said you're in wonderful shape for your age."

"That's like saying, 'He's a great fiddler for a man with one arm.' "

Rodney laughed, in good spirits, and folded his paper. "What about a book on farming, Grandpa? Will you give me a straight answer now?"

I thought a while and then told him: "My first idea wasn't really so bad, even though I did mean it as a joke."

"That Indian book?" Disbelieving.

"But it truly is about farming, Rodney, even if in India, and more than that, it's about people. You can't separate land from people."

"Honest?" A skeptical little rat. "But it's so old. Aren't there any new books about life in the country?"

"Not that I know of. Authors these days can't get beyond spies and sex and mystery thrillers."

"All right, I'll try to read it then."

He came in mad, went away pleased, his head filled with plans. Meanwhile, Grandpa finds himself in hot water. What am I going to do next?

～32

Lordy lordy, Alice, the world is getting curiouser and curiouser. My son-in-law, on the sly, has been taking lout lessons from Mr. Harmon. I've long suspected he could be a dolt if the notion took him. The other day he was took.

I suppose it has to do with his job. A cloud of black dots hovers around his head these days—ghosts of things that went wrong in California, if you ask me. He has said not one word about the Coast though, and I sure haven't asked.

Pumpkin time, an annual rite like picking persimmons in Kansas, has come to Connecticut. On a certain Sunday the natives, like wildebeest in migration, take to the motor to seek out pumpkins, munch lunch and breathe the country air. Their problem is the same as the wildebeest's: everybody does it at the same time.

Last Sunday traffic on the back roads looked like St.

Louis on Saturday night when there were no signals. The three Kemps came by for me and Rodney, learner's permit in his pocket, did the driving. I had no hint of the lad's having made his chauffeur's bones when Norma called, but I'd have gone anyway. We Residents would jump at the chance to see a man bathe a Dalmatian with a garden hose if it were in the outside world. Al Capone's giving a party? Sounds great. An invitation from Rudolph the Red-Nosed Reindeer? Righto.

They came for me at midmorning in the Olds. *"He's* going to drive?" I gasped when my grandson helped me in nicely, thank you, and settled himself behind the wheel.

"Oh, sure, Papa," Norma said, climbing in back with me. "Rod can probably drive better than they do at Indy."

"That's what scares me," I said, fumbling for my seat belt.

Norma and Rodney laughed and Clyde came in for a grunt or two. Huh huh.

Rodney was polite on the road, which is more than I used to be. We went along Route 7 and turned off on some lanes where the tree limbs form canopies over the roadway. The last of the leaves are still on and the scenery was pretty in the frosted sunlight. Somewhere up about Danbury Norma told Rodney to pull in at a roadside stand. Clyde, who had not uttered a word, went along with us to where rows of pumpkins were strewn on the ground like fat twists of orange taffy.

"What do you think, Papa?" Norma wanted to know.

I pointed with my stick. "That one is the best of the lot," I said, "but they'd all be culls at Old Farm."

"You're right, Grandpa," said my grandson, the agriculturalist, "they're runty."

Clyde grunted.

Norma took a gallon of cider and we went for lunch to a place they knew, a gray clapboard restaurant with a French name and big prices. Our waiter came on with an accent and Rodney exchanged some words with him in French.

"You speak that very well," I said, pleased with my grandson.

"He's from Canada, Grandpa, and they got a patois up there, so I couldn't understand too much." My grandson, the linguist. In French.

I was searching the menu for a chicken dish while we waited for our drinks. Chicken is cheap and safer than things like Hungarian stuffed cabbage and three-alarm tacos, which assault aged pipes like boiling acid. I asked for white wine and Clyde ordered a Martini, extra dry. Norma took a whiskey sour and Rodney swiped some sips.

"Coq au vin," I said. "I've had that and it's good."

"Rooster in wine," Rodney translated.

"Oh, Rod, you and your French," Norma teased.

Rodney smiled sheepishly. "Guess I show off sometimes."

"Sure do," said Clyde in his first words since the trip began. "I don't know what in hell you're gonna do with that French. It's not like business or engineering. They got jobs for those people."

That was the way it went, Clyde grumping and having another Martini, the rest of us making weak humor. One sourpuss can put the kibosh on any outing. Clyde didn't offer at check time, but I had expected to pay. I didn't know he had though. Four lunches for forty-seven dollars. They don't half mind charging around here.

Norma and I were trailing Rodney and his father out to the car when Clyde said over his shoulder, "Let's not drag this out, Norma. Have to get back and get my numbers together for that job in Lyons."

"Can't you rest for just one day?" Norma asked, both vexed and concerned.

Clyde, dropping back to my side, said, "New system in Lyons. That's a little place in south central France."

"Oh?" I replied, not bothering to add that I know

where Lyons is. You let yourself be told a lot when you're old. They think everything has to be explained to you.

At a garden center it was the same, flocks of pumpkins hardly as large as my head. Truck gardeners in these parts have not yet learned of fertilizer.

"Maybe we ought to try Illinois," Norma said, laughing.

Stewing again, Clyde followed her off to a half-barrel of gourds. I heard him muttering like a bull with a stomach ache, and then came some words that were distinct enough. "I don't have *time*, Norma, to spend the whole damned day riding around until that old fart finds a pumpkin that pleases him."

I pretended I hadn't heard, nor Norma when she told him I was having a good time. I had been too, until then.

You can be sure Carpenter & Grandson quickly discovered a specimen exactly to their specifications.

Toward the end of this torturous day of pleasure driving Rodney stopped for gas and we had another scene. The attendant, as they will, told our driver, "That's fourteen and a quarter."

Rodney turned to his father, but Father was busy staring out his window. "He wants your card, Dad."

"You're driving," Clyde said in a near scoff, "so you pay."

"I don't even have three dollars, Dad."

"For Christ's sake, Clyde, *give him your card!*" Her voice could have shattered a Pepsi bottle.

"Here, I'll pay," I said, passing a twenty up to Rodney. I've never had a gas card myself.

A sea of silence roared around us as the car pulled away. Presently Rodney, uncomfortable, piped up, "Grandpa, what kind of pumpkin is that we got?"

"Looks like what they call a Small Sugar," I answered.

"I thought you'd know," he said, delighted. "Did you grow them at Old Farm?"

"Mostly Large Common Field out there," I answered,

and was relieved when he did not bring up his plans for our return to Old Farm. I could imagine the reaction.

I suppose Clyde simply had an off day. I've always got along with my son-in-law, and actually I'm fond of him even though he sure is a hard cuss to love.

We got back at four and I promptly went into the sitting room and made a fool of myself. Five Residents were having a nice gam when I took over and talked a blue streak about my nice outing in the country. They must have wondered why this man who usually says little had suddenly turned into a garrulous old bore, but not one of them let on. By the time you've reached our age you've learned how to listen, even to babbling nitwits.

That Lloyd Axelrod busted out again last night, this time watched over by a lucky star that kept the muggers at bay. He didn't get away of course; they never do.

We're living here at the Arms under a duress we blame on our children even while knowing better, for it is the passing of years that holds us prisoner, not our kids. Most of the time we conveniently forget to see it that way, and in our barnacled brains getting away becomes a starkly simple proposition: by fleeing the Arms we also escape the demeaning process of aging.

I too would be gone, and some time back made a declaration on walking out with my daughter's approval. Words come easy, but thus far I have not managed to broach the subject to Norma, having yet an aversion to the smell of sulphur and singed hair, especially my own.

Lloyd turned his bust-out into a trick worthy of Edward G. and Bogie. He packed no rod and no beautiful woman awaited him, but scram he did. We got the word after breakfast when Rufe, checking the silver fingers set on our doors by the night guard at two in the morning, discovered that Lloyd's had not been tripped. When he didn't answer his phone Mr. Harmon went in with his passkey expecting, I imagine, to find a stilled body. What he saw was an unslept-in bed.

Where was Lloyd Axelrod? Had anyone seen him go out last night? Had he been to supper? Did he act strange? Scotland Yard at work right here in Marlow.

At nine Rufe went to unlock the back door and found a paper bag over the TV monitor. The night watchman's log revealed an entry noting the "failure" of the camera. Failure nothing, it was Lloyd Axelrod who blinded the beast and left his pocket knife protruding from the box that sets off an alarm if the door is opened. Oh, he was foxy, all right, finally putting his engineering experience to some use again.

French leave is wondrously appealing in a place where daily life is quiet, drab and repetitive. Outside doings, whatever they are, take on an allure we never knew before. Arriving at a hotel desk to register is heady stuff to a man who ordinarily goes nowhere and does nothing. The crumbling old Marlow Hotel has attained near spa status, and I've known Residents who checked in, got discovered by one phone call from here and were left to overnight it. Rufe and the Eagle Crate go down in the morning to haul them back at a dollar and a half a head. Plus something for him, he keeps hoping.

Lloyd Axelrod's goal was farther afield—HoJo's down in Stamford. A phone call got him too. Eight of us were in the sitting room thrilling over details of the escape when Rufe brought him in this morning. You could have mistaken him for a prisoner being returned to Stateville.

Lloyd's face showed a mixture of triumph and sheep-ishness, as if he was unable to make up his mind whether he was a bad boy being brought home or a hero returning after knocking six home runs. There was an old Gladstone in his hand; I don't suppose heroes carry them much any-more.

"What'd you do with the leg chains?" Fletch called to him.

"Filed em off," he said, guffawing.

We had a sort of reunion and told him we are glad he's back. In Lloyd's mind, I think, the attention made his abortive bust-out worthwhile. To tell the truth, I felt sorry for him. You're on the desperate side if you have to run away from home to get yourself noticed.

34

I was reading yesterday in the *Geographic* about Kalimantan, which used to be Borneo, and feeling full of good spirits, having at lunch got myself seated with two Baptist ladies so I could hog the wine, when the phone rang.

"Ben? This is Fletch," the voice said. "Can you come right up? Got something I have to tell you."

Uh oh. You have to be leery of ancients who are afflicted with urges to unburden themselves, those who want, after all this time, to confess some infidelity five decades back or a theft at the dime store at age six. I went of course. Confessions, as men of the cloth know, can be interesting.

Fletch put his hand on the back of a chair and waved

me to it, the dentist receiving his patient. "You'll take an ale, won't you?"

"After three glasses of red I shouldn't. But I will, yes."

"What I thought." He cackled into his icebox amongst his ice cubes and oj and half a dozen Ballantine's, and got one out for himself too. We sat across his marble coffee table, circa ought-two.

"Cheers," I said, "and what do you want to tell me?"

"What? Oh, that." Momentary forgetfulness.

"Said you wanted to tell me something."

"Well, Ben, it's funny but you know as I get older 'n' older I think more and more about the war. For years it was hardly in my memory at all." A'tall, that is.

"It's never far from mine, Fletch. Losing a son is as bad a thing as can happen."

"Oh, that one. Yes, it was tragic too, but the World War is the one I been thinking about, back before I rightly learnt what tragic was."

So, the first war. He hasn't bothered to change his terminology simply because of the second one twenty years later.

"I was only about thirteen then," I told him. "All I remember is cartoons of Kaiser Bill and pictures of the parades when the boys came home. I suppose you, being older, can recall a lot more."

"Used to could, yeah, when I wasn't trying. But now when I try there's a lot missing. Sometimes I can get their last name but not their first. Like Bauman from St. Louis, your part of the country. His first name is just gone, Ben."

By that time he had me going too. I thought it was the ale on top of the wine. "How's that, Fletch?"

"This Bauman, he hung on most an hour with both legs gone and one hand, but I can't get his first name."

"You in it, Fletch? You a veteran?" Why hadn't he mentioned it? I still don't know the answer.

"Oh, sure, I was over there. Now Bauman, you can

remember that, can't you? Bauman from St. Louis? Then there was the big Pole from Chicago. After they went out at Saint-Mihiel and got pushed back he crawled in with eleven machine-gun bullets in his belly. We got him to the communications trench before he died, and I wrote a letter to his mother. Now he's got no name at all."

His tales of gore unsettled me. I've seen blood in accidents and shootings but Fletch's recital seemed pointless. "War stories, is that what you want to tell me?" I said. "You all right today, Fletch?" He had me worried.

"Fine, sure, except my memory seems to slip away a little each day. Ben, I need your help."

"In what way?"

"Well, in the war, you know, we got an awful lot killed. Like in the Argonne, twenty-some days and so many dead you couldn't begin to count em. The Heinies were good shots, but our boys were better. Good boys, they were, and so many dead."

"You always lose your best men in war, Fletch."

He took a sip of ale and sat back in his chair. I was relieved, having feared he might have an attack, perhaps had already had one.

"It was such a con game, that's what gets me. We were told again and again how we were fighting for democracy, to make the world safe. Dying on the battlefield was a glorious sacrifice, they said, like hardly dying at all because we'd live on forever in the memories of our countrymen. Now I see the flaw, Ben."

"Death is not glorious, that's for sure," I said. "Being shot up on a battlefield hardly helps the victim."

"It's the memories, Ben. They lied when they sent them over to France. You see, the memories of those men can live only as long as the ones who knew them. There aren't many of us left anymore, Ben, and then who will remember? You can't remember a man you never knew."

"I hadn't thought of that."

"Most people haven't. Now let me tell you what I want. You got a much younger mind than I have, Ben. If I told you about some of these men I knew that died over there, suppose you could remember them after I'm gone?"

I had a feeling that I might have fallen down a rabbit hole. "Their names? You mean I should be able to recite their names? That kind of thing can be written down, Fletch."

"That's not it, no. I want you to remember the boys and the way they were, that's all. Suppose you could?"

Hoo boy. "Sure," I told him, "I'll do my best."

So Fletch went into his list. Bauman from St. Louis. The Pole from Chicago (what a way to be remembered, but it was the best Fletch could do). Captain O'Hara, Medal of Honor, who used a German machine gun on the Heinies themselves.

Czescik from a Wisconsin farm. The Draftee from Wichita, who rose above his lowly status for not having enlisted by bayonetting eleven of the enemy before they got him. Blond Jones from Little Rock. Fat-Ass Bruno, who volunteered so he could escape Gary's mills.

Spurgeon, whose credentials I've already forgotten; a fine friend I am: he carried the memory around sixty years and I lose it in one day. Old Charlie, who'd been with Teddy at San Juan and twenty years later carried a wounded comrade to the lip of the trench before both were vaporized by a direct hit.

That is the list, nine men, I think. Nine whose memory, after Fletch goes, will live on for a while in my mind and thus will not have died in vain. Or so he believes. I did not mention the flaw in his scheme: what if I die first?

"What part did you play in all this?" I asked finally. "Was this before you went to dental college?"

"No no. I started practice in Lynn before the war. Then one day I went down and enlisted to get away from Mother." A rueful laugh. "Thought I was going to fill teeth for the rest of the war but first thing I knew they sent me to England. Then it was France, and when the Great Medical Shortage came along they shipped everybody that knew anything about medicine up into the trenches, even vets. Hell, Ben, I was a captain and they had me carrying litters. Can you believe that?"

I assured him I could.

"And the Great Medical Shortage, you know about that?"

Of course, everybody knows about that, I told him.

In truth, I never heard of it, but he was quieting down, having unburdened himself, and I thought it prudent to skip all questions.

~35

Excuse me, Remington, while I drink this glass of fizz. Let us both hope Alka-Seltzer delivers on its promises. My head feels in need of a transplant and all because I went to a party last evening and they used real booze. At breakfast the dining room was filled with moans like a battlefield of wounded.

In my palmier days I was fond of saying I'd never seen a party I didn't loathe. Usually I had in mind Clint Bradly's Christmas soirees in the City Room, given in lieu of bonuses. They were bad during Prohibition, when he served grape juice and pop, got worse when the real goods came back. Nehi spiked with white lightning was preferable.

Now I've been to two parties in a week, the first one delightful, the last a killer. A few days ago nine of us got together in the card room to help Emily, who looks fifty or less, celebrate her sixty-third birthday. We had champagne, purchased with collected money, and the kitchen sent up a one-candle cake. Somebody switched on the FM and we had a go at dancing. Fletch did a nice two-step with the birthday girl and only staggered once. Afterwards she and I went to her flat for our own observance, but it was not my evening and I felt bad.

"Don't worry about it, Ben," she said. "At our age it doesn't always happen. The touching and cuddling are enough."

Having no alternative, I took her word for it.

This bash last night should have been killed before it grew. We of the crock brigade, more used to red or white, should have known better than to tackle the hard stuff. Of course it wasn't meant for us, or the party either. We crashed it, you might say, right here in Eagle Arms.

In Magellan they'd be laughing about this one for months; in Marlow nobody seems to notice such insane foolishness as Mr. Harmon giving himself a party to get himself past his fiftieth birthday. Letting the Arms pick up the tab of course. For days rumors had filtered in from outside about big doings coming up, but no one here seemed to know anything for sure.

Day before yesterday Margie dropped a whisper at supper: "It's f'doctors."

"What?"

"Shhh, you'll see. I ain't sposed t'know."

Eventually, we discovered she was right, and that it was by Harmon for Harmon. The guest list was limited to local doctors, two dentists, a few lawyers and some bigwigs from Rotary, wherein Mr. Harmon has Aspirations. All this we found out while being told last evening's supper would be in boxes passed out in the sun room. The dining room would be closed for the party.

Even a spurned woman hath no fury equal to a Resident kept from a party in her own Residence. Amongst the men only Fletch seemed to care: he favored throwing the passel of them out so they'd go to a hotel for their doings and leave us alone. The ladies were something else, gathering around the front desk like a flock of enraged hens and glaring at Lucy. I felt sorry for her, being left to face their ire while Mr. Harmon hid under his desk, his ear cocked for the sounds of mutiny from outside.

You could wonder why esteemed doctors would want to hang around with the likes of George Harmon. Don't bother—the reason is starkly simple, the same one that caused Agnew to leave town and every year swells Stateville's head count with politicians. Money.

We Residents, rife with infirmities and hypochondria, are a nest of golden eggs for physicians. But there's a catch: in order to visit a Resident a doctor must obtain Mr. Harmon's approval. The reasoning is not as lunatic as might first appear: we can't have Doc Brinkley grafting goat glands in the card room or loonies peddling potions door to door. The result gives Mr. Harmon a strange power over the medical profession hereabouts, so invitations to his wacko party did not go unanswered.

By noon everybody knew the maddening truth and the dining room seethed like a brawl aborning. Sometime in the afternoon Mr. Harmon, realizing that his fiftieth birthday might be his last if our ladies caught him, sent word out through Lucy that there had been an oversight, he was sorry, and all Residents were invited. The ladies were elated. A party!

Except Mr. Harmon forgot to pull the booze and his new arrangements smelled of asininity. From five to five-thirty the party would be private, for Mr. Harmon and his "close friends." Then everyone was invited in and, as planned, box lunches would be passed out in the sun room. They must have enough left to feed half the town. I myself felt lucky making it to four, let alone trying for twelve.

While Mr. Harmon and his close friends were getting together, our Residents milled around in front of the gates and contemplated the fun coming up. A case of extreme anticipation. By five, the lobby was filled with a mob not unlike those at the Tower when beheadings were announced, the ladies in their finest, the men neatly suited and wondering what a real drink would taste like. The dignity and decorum of the aged flew the coop last night, scared silly by the idea of a childish fling with no cleaning-up later. Nobody gave two hoots about Mr. Harmon's birthday, but a party—halleluiah and thank the Lord.

At precisely five-thirty Margie opened the gates and ran for her life. Mr. Harmon and his doctors watched, aghast, as Residents swarmed in like a cloud of moths and went to work on the canapés and the booze. The room echoed with giggles, peals of laughter and shrieks, one of them from Mr. Harmon when he spotted some ladies zeroing in on this monster cake that stood as high as my head, draped at the top with a wisp of diaphanous silk.

"Not yet! Not yet!" he shouted. "We'll unveil it later!"

The food, brought in by caterers, was delicious—little biscuits with caviar, herring, deviled eggs, ham, cubes of cheese—and the drinks even better. I put down two Scotches and was tapering off on sherry when I found Emily with her fingers clenching a bottle of Spanish brandy and helped her do it just honors.

"Haven't seen anything like this since our house parties at school," Emily said, giggling like a coed. By then I could see two of everybody, and Emily's eyes, all four of them, showed a wild gleam. We were smashed.

The white-jacketed bartender gave up early and leaned against the wall to watch the melee. In half an hour the food had been snaffled up and the bar was going dry fast. Mrs. Moore held a bottle to the light and, finding it empty, tossed it over her shoulder. It smashed tinklingly against the wall but nobody noticed. A lady from eight clung to the liquor table and guffawed loudly enough to be heard in Dallas: "Just like blind pig days!" She drank straight from a bottle of Gordon's, coughed and giggled and sputtered, the most fun she'd had in years.

Mr. Harmon and close friends huddled in a corner, painful smiles pasted on their faces. Eventually, he came out, waved his arms and attempted to shush the crowd. Snickering and giggling proceeded much as before and we did a chorus of "Happy Birthday" that ended with "Dear Georrrrrrrrgie." Naughty naughty.

A table was helping keep me upright and the chairs were splotted with pastel party dresses, their occupants trying to focus on our honoree. He came on with a slurred tongue, for he had been making good use of his time too, and spoke words as moving as a parking sign. All about starting his second fifty ("Diaper that kid!" called his audience) and how honored he was ("More booze!"). Captivated by his own words, he tipped up on the balls of his feet and I expected him to slide a Napoleonic hand under his jacket. He flattered the ladies and announced with a wink that he has attained the prime of his life, a regular rooster strutting around before us. I think he imagines himself very macho, a sort of cultured brute.

The unveiling occasioned shrieks and whoops, for on top of the cake stood a foot-high sugar nude, flesh-colored and complete with a smudge of black for pubic hair. That George Harmon has taste.

"Cut the cake!" shouted the audience.

"I will, I will, but where do I start?" Then, pointing to one of the doctors: "Charlie, you're a gynecologist, where do I cut first?"

The doctor shrugged, embarrassed, while the audience whooped. Perfect humor for a bunch of drunks.

Seizing a two-foot knife, Mr. Harmon moved in for the kill. "All right, a piece for everyone!" he shouted, winking grotesquely. "And you just know what part I'm going to eat first!" Plunging the knife into the cake like a matador, he swept the candy lady off with his left hand and, good as his word, chomped down on her erogenous zone.

The last I saw Birthday Boy one of his green-tinted lenses was flipped up and his toup had twisted so his hair pointed rakishly toward one ear. At the time he was still trying to clear the dining room of wobbly packages of silk and satin that giggled and asked for more drinks.

36

It is the holidays concomitant with tribal rites, I see, that are difficult. This Thanksgiving business yesterday, with me in the bosom of my loved ones, made me yearn for Old Farm, where I could invite a friend or two in for a meal and some meaningless talk. At clan gatherings words come to weigh three pounds apiece.

Norma was nice about it. Knowing of our friendship, she wanted me to invite Emily, which I did.

"I wouldn't feel right about it," Emily said. "I'd be horning in on your family, so I'll stay here."

Nothing could change her mind, so she and eighteen or twenty others got their Thanksgiving dinners out of boxes, the kitchen being closed. It sounded dismal to me but she was happy enough.

Rodney and Clyde picked me up at a quarter past ten. The day was fine, chilly and bright, the air fresh as dawn on the prairies. Traffic was light and Rodney drove easily along the state highway that meanders into their hills. The trees, bare now for the winter, spread their towering racks of limbs handsomely against the high autumn sky in the pretty sunshine. Marlow's beginnings go way back, and timber has had a long while to recover from ancient loggings.

Amidst sugar maples, Rodney turned off on their road, a narrow macadam track that wanders crookedly as it ascends a high ridge. Coming out on top, the road straightens and their house, red clapboard and old, sits on the left.

When we first went inside out of the chill air our cheeks were pink, and the aroma from the kitchen was lovely indeed. Norma inherits from her mother in cooking matters.

The four of us sat in the living room and my daughter and I fell to talking about the days when Dorothy was alive and roasting her Thanksgiving turkeys with their herbed oyster stuffing. Clyde was treating himself to a period of silence, his mind doubtlessly ranging through the office and setting things to rights.

After they married and moved east Norma and Clyde never returned for a holiday that I could recall. I asked if that were true.

"We were there once on the Fourth," she answered. "It was right after we came to Marlow. Don't you remember? Tim Morton, down on the corner, fired off a rocket in his room and set their house afire."

"Oh, yes, the firemen came and flooded Sid's house and drank all his beer."

"And Mr. Morton said, 'First my house, then my beer.' "

I chuckled and remembered the incident as clearly as yesterday; when the beer-drinking firemen had gone I took over a case of Falstaff. One detail was missing though: I have no recollection whatever of Norma's and Clyde's presence. The memory is a strange instrument, with many barren patches amongst the mooring posts.

"You know," I said, "when you moved away your

mother and I thought you'd be back on visits all the time."

"We wanted to, but there was no time."

"We even thought you'd come back to live someday."

"I know; you've said that before, Papa. But it was a fantasy you and Mama created, don't you see? Kids go away now. We even thought once of getting Clyde transferred to UBM Australia." She laughed in reflection. "At least we didn't go that far."

"Could have been a great opportunity," said Clyde, roused from hibernation.

"But it was really better this way," Norma said. "Clyde could hardly have done better than he has here."

"Well, that's true," Clyde said, a flicker of smile revealing his pleasure at having his success mentioned.

Toward noon Clyde got us drinks and Norma returned to the kitchen. Rodney watched Macy's parade on TV and Clyde, sipping earnestly, threw desultory glances toward the screen. A second Martini produced definite signs of animation, even jollity.

"I remember this one Thanksgiving"—huh huh, dry chuckles—"at Great Lakes, and there was a farm family up by Kenosha that had three of us boots up for the day. Real good time." He smiled to himself and lapsed into reverie, a rare occurrence for him. Oh, he has more silences than Cal Coolidge, but you find out later that it was the office that his mind contemplated, not pleasant images from yesteryear such as most people like to call up.

There are pronouncements about Clyde to be made, but you always do your best by the man who marries your daughter. I was not enchanted by her choice, wouldn't have been, said Dorothy, if it was Tyrone Power she was marrying. Well, said I, it is not Tyrone Power, for sure; more in Trigger's category. Dorothy was not amused, and always found forgiveness for Clyde's shortcomings so long as he provided well for her daughter.

Clyde hails from Kansas City and grits his teeth when Norma and I joke about the Western World's Capital of Pretension. In the same way I tend to be defensive about Magellan, I suppose, but I am quick to admit it has boils and scabs. Clyde went to college a couple of years and then did a Navy hitch to get more money. He came back to finish up—and met my daughter.

A mastery of office politics has got Clyde where he is, but his conduct of in-law politics has been something else. Right off, he gave Dorothy a big photograph of himself in uniform, and you could see his Midwestern German background in it. There stood this rotund sailor in horn-rims, his ears giving the appearance of a convertible parked with the doors open, his hair cut like a skinned rabbit, his perfectly round white cap set squarely on his head like a lifesaver on a torpedo. He told us he had been an RT, which means Radar Technician, a rating which, I learned, was a source of humor to other sailors. RTs were the squares of the service, and in the picture Clyde looked it, his chubby hands and forearms folded complacently in front of his short-sleeved whites.

"Handsome in his uniform, isn't he?" Dorothy commented, holding the picture up.

Good God, I thought, but dare not say. "Who is it?" I asked, glancing up from my paper as if I had no idea what she was getting on about.

"Norma's husband-to-be," she answered, and went to hang the picture on our bedroom wall. I could hear the quick taps of her tack hammer and knew the Pope's feelings when he heard of Martin Luther's work.

Inside a week the picture mysteriously crashed to the floor, its glass shattered. "I'll take it downtown and get it fixed," I said, ever so solicitous. Dorothy was not fooled but kept her peace, even when I put the picture in my desk at the *Times* and left it there for years.

Norma married him anyway.

"They took us hunting in the pastures after we ate."

"What?" Ten minutes must have passed, and I'd got caught up in watching this giant Bullwinkle float along the avenue.

"They gave us dinner and then we went out and I killed three rabbits with three shots. One of those little four-tens, that's what the farmer lent me. Said I was the best rabbit shot he'd ever seen."

"That's some shooting, Clyde, especially with a four-ten. Did you hunt a lot as a boy?"

He laughed—happily, I'd say. "Me? No no, not me. I was a city boy, you know, and it was only the second time I'd fired a gun."

"What's a four-ten?" Rodney asked.

"Little bitty shotgun," his father said. "The shells are about the size of your finger."

Rodney's finger; Clyde's are in the twelve-gauge range. His blimp has been inflating inexorably since the day he got Norma to tend his range. A man's waistline is his own business, I am aware, but I've always been slow to cotton to a man who lets his hands get pushed out by his own blubber.

Inevitably, the talk got around to the office. Clyde impressed on me the price of twenty million he had quoted for the job in France, and once more located it for me: "It's in Lyons, a small place south of Paris."

The wine had loosened my tongue too. "Yes," I said, "I know where Lyons is. You know where Nice is? I have a friend in Nice."

"In Nice?" he looked startled, as if I'd claimed kinship to Hermann Goering.

"Sure. Maurice Delacroix. He came over in the early part of the war and worked with me at the *Times*, a refugee. We still write once in a great while."

"Oh yeah, I've heard about him from Norma. Came to your house sometimes when she was a girl."

Rodney heard and dashed over to lean on my chair back. "You got a friend in France?" he asked, hardly believing. "Why didn't you tell me, Grandpa?"

"It just never came up, son, and I don't think about him often anymore. It's been a long time."

"How'd you talk to him? You don't know French."

"Oh, he knows English only too well. He wrote for our paper, a reporter like me. Actually, he did teach me some French, but not the kind of things you say in company."

Rodney laughed and went off to the bathroom, which was what I had in mind, the wine having percolated rapidly. Presently he came out and I dashed in to find a strange smoky odor hanging in the air. I could guess what it was. Well, I thought, they say all the kids do it now. Except I never considered my grandson merely another kid. Put down another fielding error for Grandpa.

Norma's table was beautiful, spread with crystal and her bone china, the bird glowing gold on a silver platter to Clyde's left. The second Martini had made him jolly; the third had helped nothing. His tongue worked none too well and the deck he walked on heaved beneath his feet. Norma showed symptoms of a private stock in the kitchen.

She gave the blessing and Clyde began the host's rite by knocking his filled wine glass flat. That cleaned up, he set upon the poor turkey like a fireman hacking through a roof.

Oh, well, I thought, we're all family here.

A strange gleam had appeared in Rodney's eyes, the shine of some religious zealot and, looking at me, he went into a series of giggles.

"Rod's so happy to have his grandpa for Thanksgiving," Norma said lovingly.

"Well, it's nice," I began but could not go on, being seized myself by giggles at the thought of what was really fueling Rodney's laugh box.

"Grandpa has a friend in France," Rodney announced.

"I know, dear, Mr. Delacroix. I remember him."

Rodney chattered like an excited squirrel about how wonderful it would be if Monsieur Delacroix came to visit, finally lapsed into French and began stuffing food into his mouth as if he hadn't eaten since July. Norma and Clyde seemed unaware of their child's wildly spinning wheels.

"Hear you and the kid are goin out and live at Old Farm come spring," Clyde said with a snort, reaching into his supply of weighted words. Norma's laugh was high on the mockery scale.

"We've talked about it, haven't we, Rodney?"

"Uh-huh." His mouth was full.

"You can't be *serious*," Norma said. "I just got you out of that place, and Rod's only a boy."

"Can you imagine that?" Clyde said. "Them two livin by themselves on that old farm? Ha ha ha ha."

"We'll have to see," I said, pride offended. "I'm not fond of Eagle Arms, you know."

"Why, that's a dandy place, just dandy," said Clyde, muttering and scowling.

"You must give yourself time to get used to it, Papa," said Norma. "Why you've already made friends and I know you're having fun but you just won't admit it, will you?" A tentative laugh.

"Too stubborn, ha ha ha ha."

"Rodney," I said, "would you mind closing your eyes? It can be harmful for a boy to see his father stabbed with a turkey fork."

Peals of laughter, except from me, and Rodney heard nothing funny until his parents began ripping the air apart. Then he joined in with sounds that suggested a howler monkey drunk on fermented coconuts. His mouth unfortunately was full and the little devil choked. We had great snortings and gaggings and back-pounding by Norma. "Hold your arms up!" she commanded.

Eventually, he got his breath and she told him to take a sip of water. Rodney reeled in her wine glass and quaffed half of it, neither parent seeming to notice.

"A barrel of laughs," I said.

"Papa!" Norma scolded. "It's not funny when somebody chokes."

"I was talking about Eagle Arms, sweetie. A barrel of laughs."

"Oh." She finds it necessary to nourish this fantasy of wonderfully happy Papa sitting around Eagle Arms with his buddies, telling raunchy jokes, swilling beer, playing poker, his days filled with amusements.

"Wonder what they do on Thanksgiving in Lyons," Clyde mused.

"Better, I should think," I said.

🐟37

The morning mail brought a letter postmarked St. Louis and forwarded at Magellan, from a Mrs. C. L. Eckstein, or "Dottie," as she signs herself in quote marks. Her mother is dead, she says, Mrs. Arthur Fischer, who once was Constance Livingston, and I am filled with sadness. The lively ones, it seems, go first. Dullards hang on forever.

When you are my age your mailbox exerts a magnetic attraction to messages of death. Sometimes the survivor doesn't feel up to writing and encloses a newspaper clipping instead, or the envelope is addressed in spidery ink and you know the other one is getting on toward the end too.

The nomadism that overtakes the old means we seldom die where we lived. Connie was different, from St. Louis originally, returned there from Magellan when she married and now has died there, presumably in her fine house in Huntleigh Village. Her sojourn at the *Times* was courtesy of her uncle in Granite City, a crony of Clint Bradly's father; one of those deals. Husband-hunting was on Connie's itinerary but her window of admissions, as they say, was as narrow as a castle firing slit, featuring money at its center. When young Dr. Fischer, fresh out of a residency in dermatology, came in pursuit she disappeared from our midst almost overnight.

For thirty years, well into middle age, Dorothy and Connie wrote sweet, loving letters and met in the week before Christmas to have lunch and shop at Famous-Barr and Stix and Scruggs. Dorothy would come home on the trolley, her arms laden with presents, and stagger into the City Room. We'd divide the load and go out to our stop on the bus.

Connie's wryly humorous letters amused me, but the Fischers and the Carpenters remained distant. He became rich and successful as a curer of acne and skin rashes; I plodded on at the *Times*. Only our family emissaries met, as those of the Montagues and Capulets might have. Dorothy invited them once but they refused; Connie said it was because he was a Jew and limited their social friends to his own kind. Which, as Dorothy pointed out, hardly made sense. He'd married a Livingston, hadn't he? And it was Christmas shopping his wife was doing, wasn't it?

We heard about but never saw their estate in the woods, and I was not to meet Dr. Fischer. Dorothy was dead and I'd moved to Old Farm before I saw Connie again. She drove in one summer day in her motor, an impressive Cadillac, as if she'd done it fifty times before. I'd been hoeing peppers across the way and came in at noon, sweaty and dirt-smeared, to fry up a hamburger. The skillet was crackling when I heard tires on the gravel and Smutty erupted in fierce yips.

"Shush," I told him, "it might be somebody rich come to give us something." When you live alone conversations with your dog come natural.

It was somebody rich, all right, but at first I didn't know who. Smutty and I went out the screen door and saw this shining monster with fins like a jet.

"Hello there!" called a voice, and a hand waved from the window. "This where the famous journalist lives?" I think she would have said more but was overcome by rolling peals of laughter. Smutty sniffed at a front tire and peed on it.

I put my hand on the sill and looked in. A warm soft hand descended on mine. "Hello," I said uncertainly.

"Oh, Ben, don't you know me?" A huffing at the mouth and more laughter.

Then I saw it in her face, the even teeth, the wonderful complexion, the pale-green eyes. All the original parts were there, along with some major additions, big jowls and cascading chins and meaty ear lobes. I'd never seen a person get fat in the lobes before. It was as if she'd dropped by a station with Free Air and sucked on the hose a while, her lovely baby face inflating to a hundred and fifty pounds.

"Of course," I said, "and it's wonderful to see you so pretty still, as lovely as ever." They don't notice how nervous you are if you flatter them enough.

Smutty growled when the door opened, evidently casting his vote otherwise.

"Oh, you old flatterer you," she said amidst fresh brays of laughter. Connie found more amusement in the world than anyone I ever knew, and I admire her for it. "It's nice to hear you say it though, and lovely to see you again."

"A nice surprise, Connie, and what brings you here?"

"You of course, silly; I came to see you."

She stood then, a figure dressed in some immense silky thing that hung from her shoulders like an expired parachute. It was pretty material, little flowers on a blush of pink, but the yardage was enough to keep ten Chinese busy for a month.

Indeed it was pleasant to see her, fat or not, which I told her, leaving the fat part out. But I could not resist adding, "See you've been eating well, Connie."

"Oh, Ben, I'm so embarrassed to have you see me this way," she fretted, though I saw no hints of embarrassment.

"We all have our vices, Connie."

"I didn't use to—oh, I had vices enough"—booming laughter—"but not eating. I was slender as a reed until my husband died, and then I just let myself go."

"Sorry to hear about your husband. When did he die?"

"Arthur? In March it was. What's that—four months ago?" It appeared to me she'd been pigging out a mite longer, like ten years longer. You don't turn into a dirigible in any four months.

"Dorothy's dead too," I told her. "In February."

"You sent me a letter, Ben. Don't you remember?"

"No, but it doesn't matter. What matters is that they're both gone."

"I was devastated when I heard about Dorothy, but I couldn't answer. Arthur was so sick, cancer of the prostate."

"I know about cancer. Dorothy had it too. Come on in and let's stop the sad talk."

"Yes, Ben, let's. I'm sorry the subject came up. I wanted so much to please you." An early warning, you might say, one I did not heed. Smutty and I followed her along the brick walk, watching her waddle on legs like beer kegs. Her pocketbook was white and the size of my pillow, filled perhaps with sandwiches and chocolate bars for between restaurant stops.

"My, Ben! What's that I smell?" Shades of Norma.

I did my sixty-five-style sprint inside and got to my

burger before the house went up. My dinner looked like some reject from the crematorium.

"I think you've overcooked it," Connie said amidst loud laughter. "Why don't you let me do it for you? I'm a good cook, you know."

"I thought you probably hired a cook."

"Oh, I've always had a cook, sure, but she's getting too old to do much anymore. What did this used to be?"

"A hamburger, if you can believe it. That's what I usually fix at noon when I've been gardening. I put on lots of onion and pickle slices and mustard, and have some beans with right sharp pepper sauce." My piping was in better shape in those days.

"Sounds delicious, Ben, a real he-man's lunch. I'd love one myself if you have enough. Got any gin?"

"I never heard of doing them with gin," I said seriously. I was no Escoffier, and maybe he did use gin for all I knew.

Connie nearly collapsed, splot, on my kitchen floor before she could stop laughing. "Still have that wonderful sense of humor, I see," she cried, wiping her eyes with the back of a hand.

"There's a bottle of Gordon's here somewhere," I said.

"Goodie! We can have a drink like old times and then I'll fix lunch. Remember how we used to drink all those gin-and-Its?"

Indeed I did, most of them put down by her. We had the same this time, though now called Martinis, and she was as good as her promise on the burgers. They were done to a turn, and the cook took only one. I think she held back to impress me with her canary appetite. Ordinarily, I suspected, Connie could quaff up a hamburger as if it were finger food.

"Sooo good, Ben," she said, "and such a he-man's lunch. You always were so virile."

I failed to discern that signal as well, too innocent for

my own good. "Me virile? At sixteen maybe, but it's been downhill ever since."

"Oh no, Ben, that evening when you wrecked your motor and I took you home I could hardly keep my hands off you. You were so handsome and sexy-looking."

The news is very slow arriving, I thought, and considerably doctored as well. I was unable to forget my status as a small fish brought home to her shy roommate. "You're bananas," I said, laughing. We were finishing our beers at the kitchen table, and the penny had fallen.

She put her hand on mine. "I'm serious, Ben. I came over to see you because I've always thought you were so wonderful, and I care so about you. Can't you see it? Don't you feel the same way about me, Ben? We're both so alone in the world."

Connie had it all worked out in her mind, and I do not want to be disrespectful of the memory of a girl just dead. She was a good woman, and beautiful before fat took her. To her, I came to realize, it was such a simple and sensible idea for me to leave my shack and move in with her in her huge manse, a Caddie in the garage, and a Jaguar too that had been left behind by her husband who, it appeared to me, had been the virile one. We could marry later, she said, but only if we wanted. Connie was always a free thinker.

A vicious time warp assaulted me. Here was a woman, one of the great beauties of her day, for whom I, to put words on it, once had the extreme hots, and now, in a new guise, she was making passionate, outrageously flattering pleas for my affection, a princess come, decades late and swollen a hundredweight, to claim her wizened prince. Like entreaties of love from Sophia Loren, but fifty years down the line.

I told Connie gently of my admiration for her. "But we're such opposites," I said. "We weren't right for each other way back then, nor are we now. Besides, I am not going to marry again, or take up with any woman after Dorothy. But I'll always think fondly of you." And I have.

All right, she said, as simple as that, and went to the bathroom. When she came out she kissed me on the ear.

I couldn't disappoint her in all ways. Connie was only the second woman I ever went to bed with, an almost nonexistent score, and suddenly I appreciated all those years of knowing Dorothy's slender body. Now my box spring groaned as if assaulted by walruses, and the mattress remained cupped in the middle to the day Norma and I dragged it out to our throw-away pile.

Connie left about eight and, exhausted, I fell asleep before nine, my conscience clear but my mind befogged by the way fate had arranged my life.

38

When you hang out with that Fletcher Pepper you can't tell what may happen next. Yesterday, in late afternoon, he called me. "Ben, can you come right up?"

"What now, another list to memorize?"

"What? A list?" He's forgotten, and just as well, since I'm now down to Bauman from St. Louis and the Pole from Chicago.

I found him sitting on the floor of his hallway amidst a tide of souvenirs that, smelling of mothballs, flowed from his linen closet.

"Thought you might like to see these things from the World War," he said brightly. "Thinking of throwing em all down the incinerator."

I lowered myself by degrees and he showed me a French 75 casing of brass and a clip of rifle cartridges, which made me wonder about his incinerator idea. But I said nothing; he's the expert on all instruments of war. Bits of canvas fell away when he picked up his gas-mask bag.

"Rotten as hell," he said, "but I suppose I won't be needing it real soon. Now here's this stuff"—displaying a stick that looked like aged lard—"that we rubbed on our eyepieces so they didn't fog up." We went on pawing through the pile. His putees, neatly rolled but swiss-cheesed with moth holes, his brimmed helmet, a chunk of stainless steel for a shaving mirror.

"You've got me beat," I told him. "I'm a pack rat myself, and my daughter too, but we couldn't hold a candle to you."

He cackled and shook his head. "You never can tell when you might run into a cloud of phosgene, Ben. But out she goes. When you gonna toss your stuff?"

"I got rid of most of it when I came here, with my daughter's help, and I guess she'll get what's left."

"What'll she do with it?"

"Likely she'll put it out at roadside on trash day."

"Might be the best, Ben."

"My son-in-law has a name for what we're doing, Fletch. He calls it an audit. 'Norma, let's go audit the refrigerator,' I heard him say once, and thought he had snacks in mind. What he was really talking about, it turned out, was totting up their fortune in chilled goodies."

"Quite an eater, is he?"

"Sometimes, I suppose, but actually more of an adder-upper. Clyde loves to figure how much he's worth."

"Look at this," Fletch said. "Ever see a Heinie grenade? We called em potato mashers."

That's what it looked like, a potato masher, except iron and ugly. "Is this thing loaded?" I asked. "You know, can it go off?"

"Well, whatever was in it is still there, yes."

"Fletch," I said, exasperated, I'm afraid, "you better give em time to evacuate the Arms before you toss this stuff down the incinerator."

He threw back his head and cackled. "Never thought of that, Ben. They're all so old and everything, but you're probably right. They might make for a hot time down around the furnace room."

"At least my stuff is not dangerous, Fletch. Living with you is like having a retired terrorist in the house with all his keepsakes."

He wanted to know about my collection of memorabilia. Half a lifetime ago I wondered how I could live with fewer possessions than I had, was sure I could not. I shouldn't have worried; as the years go by the sloughing-off comes in good time. The way you feel about something at forty is not the way you'll feel at seventy.

I remember Dorothy, at Old Farm, coming across a framed photograph. "It's such a nice old picture of Gramma," she said, the picture being of Dorothy's mother, "we can't throw this away."

"Well, chick," I said, "she'll never look that good again." The old lady had been dead thirty years. We kept the picture.

I have a snapshot too of a smiling Dorothy in sailor blouse, a babe on her lap. Jaime. She sits on their porch swing, happiness on her face and no hint of hurt. I hadn't met her yet then, didn't know she existed. The picture could be from last week except beyond the fence in the background there stands a 1911 Simplex long ago reduced to flecks of rust.

I described for Fletch the nickel clippers on the shelf of my walk-in which Dorothy used to cut our hair when we couldn't afford the barber. And my mother's buttonhook, Dorothy's nail buffer.

"Norma wound up with the copper kettle that

Gramma made soap in," I said. "Otherwise I'd be taking swan dives into it on the way to the bathroom at night."

My most prized possession sits on its own shelf in the living room, a milk pitcher probably worth five bucks on the antiques market. Dorothy bought it before anything else, a brown pitcher mottled with cream spots, a squat thing with laurel leaves and circles and a girl's face in bas relief. She said it took the place of the bottle gourd of her people and would hold the milk of all the babies we would have. I knew nothing of the legends of the Plains Indians but the pitcher was pretty. It cost seventy-nine cents, I remember.

Fletch liked my pitcher story and demanded my promise to show it to him next time he's down. There it sits in plain view, but he's never noticed.

"Lot of people here would rather have some of those milk pitchers like yours instead of what they put on the table now," Fletch observed.

"You drink the wine," I said; "I've seen you. What's all this about milk?"

"Oh, wine's fine with me, but there's some that sure complain."

"Fletch, you can't name a dish around here but somebody objects. Sometimes I think we're living in some commune of food freaks."

"Isn't that the truth though."

And it is. I've never heard the kind of talk I pick up here, a bunch of people evincing a lifelong fascination with their own bowels. Mable Moore complains that lettuce sticks to her entrails and causes what she calls "irregular movements." Anything in fish revolts Inez Bowman, who evidently put her two hundred pounds together on good red meat.

A few Residents are big on sending back. The dish is underdone, they say, or too salty or spicy. I suspect it gives them a feeling of power and grandeur. Not many of us had servants to order about before we came into the Arms.

Fletch and I were having a regular gossip session, not unlike those we talked about, and had got around to those interminable discussions on milk of magnesia and Ex-Lax and Pheenamint, when the phone rang.

"Must be an undertaker wanting to make an appointment," Fletch said, struggling to his feet. I could hear him answer, then he hemmed and said "well" about forty times, and finally, "Oh, all right, send them up."

He came back a changed man, shaken, nervous, looking his age.

"What's wrong, Fletch?"

"My daughter and her husband, they're here."

"You have a daughter?" I exclaimed, delighted. "That's wonderful, Fletch. I never heard you mention any daughter."

He walked around in little circles and cleared his throat, looking terrified. "They're coming here," he said again.

"Don't be nervous," I said. "Your place looks fine, or it will when we get this stuff put back."

"You don't understand, Ben," he said while I tossed his relics into the closet. He seemed incapable of dealing with them, or anything else. "When I came to Eagle Arms I was running away from those two, Ben. I lived with em, see, as long as I could, and then I had to take off." By then he was whimpering like a child, which shocked me because he's normally a stout-hearted little guy.

I put an arm around his shoulders in big-brother fashion. "Don't be afraid," I said. "I'll stay here with you." It's strange, the roles you get asked to play.

"Will you, Ben? It'll make me feel a lot better." He pulled himself together then and wiped his eyes. "They used to steal from me in Framingham, and beat the pee out of me too. Dennison is big and strong, you know, my son-in-law."

"Stop fretting, Fletch. It'll be all right."

I sounded surer than I was. What could we two old crocks do with a healthy, strong man? I thought of pulling a Help switch to summon Rufe; he could take care of six Dennisons. And of calling the police, though Mr. Harmon might not be pleased. In the end I did nothing. His doorbell went blonk-blim and Fletch got up to answer it. I sat in the alcove, where his bed is, out of sight.

"Dad, we found you," said a woman's voice.

"Hi, Pop." A man's voice, gruff. I heard no warmth in their voices.

"Hello, Helen, Dennison. Come on in. How are you?" He had regained his chairside manner.

"Boy, rich-lookin building you got here," said Dennison. "And call me Dan, Pop. They all do now." C.C. Carpenter made over. The man chuckled hollowly.

"Why'd you go off and leave us, Dad?" asked Helen. As straight to the point as her father.

"Like you was runnin away," said Dan.

"Why I had to, or you'd have killed me," Fletch said.

I arose and stepped into the living room. The three were still in the hall. The man wore an aged felt hat, which he had not bothered to remove, and there was an overcoat over his arm. His threadbare gray suit, with old-fashioned wide lapels, was stretched to bursting.

"Hey, who's that?" he asked. "You got a roommate, Pop?"

Fletch steered them toward me. "This is my friend Ben," he said, pointing. "Ben, my daughter Helen and my son-in-law Dennison, er, Dan."

Dan and I shook hands, and Helen came up to offer hers. She was heavy, with a hard face and dirty gray hair, red veins in her nose. Her coat was coarse and cheap-looking.

They were a rough pair, all right, as unlike Fletch as scarecrows. I wondered whether they intended harm but after we had sat down and exchanged a few words I was sure they did not. I have no doubt that when Fletch lived with them they were given to mistreating him, and one cannot forgive them that, but what I saw, instead of cruelty, were the marks of an overwhelming poverty. It was evident that they'd had little for a very long time.

"You scared us that day when you drove off and didn't come back," Helen said reproachfully.

"You call the cops?" Fletch asked.

"No no," said Dan. I suppose they had a pretty good idea what had happened, and there are people who have an aversion to ringing up the police, no matter what.

They stayed half an hour altogether and did not ask for money. When they left it appeared that they were pleased to have found Fletch.

"My daughter has a drinking problem from way back," he explained when they were gone. "I tried to help but she wouldn't let me, and he's as bad as her. Helen's had man problems too, married three times I know of, and every one of em worthless."

"Well they think enough of you to locate you and come see you."

"I don't trust em far, either one, I tell you. They probably did it to see whether I'm off my rocker enough so they could get charge of me, me and what's left. You think I acted sane enough, Ben?"

"Perfectly sane," I assured him.

❧39

Imagine that—I'm still alive.

I went to bed early last evening with a fever of a hundred and one, a sore throat and chills. In these years you figure each time you come down it may be the big one.

Day before yesterday a light rain caught me while I was walking and turned to sleet before I could get back. They have strange weather in Connecticut; it changes so quickly, and they like to talk about nor'easters as if they'd just come ashore from the *Pequod*. Sleet in late November is not uncommon in Illinois, but you get some warning. I was chilled through when I got home and took two cold pills, but they didn't help.

Nursey came back about eleven last night and wanted to know how I felt. Awful, I said, so she gave me some pills and went away, leaving me feeling the end was nigh. She makes night calls cheerfully enough, but only when it's serious. So if you catch her leaning over you after the sun has gone down you right away conjure up some verses from the Good Book to recite as you pass into the next world. It never hurts to be prepared. Fletch and I, in the sitting room one night about ten, saw Nursey go through to the elevators. "Ben, who you reckon she's givin final rites to this time?" he said.

I went back to sleep despite forebodings, figuring I might as well be rested when I go off for my big interview in the sky. It could be a long journey for all I know.

When your step becomes none too firm and you find that walking with a stick is better than without, you keep expecting the old guy with the scythe to drop in at any time. After giving up on plane crashes and racing wrecks, as unlikely endings for me, I got to thinking that I might check out while hoeing lettuce at Old Farm, or maybe after lifting a sundowner to my lips. The latter seemed better. Knowing how quickly Dorothy's time had come, I was sure the knock on my door was only a tick away. I waited and waited and finally, in the spring of the year after she died, I woke up one morning at Old Farm to bird song and lilac blooms outside my kitchen window and I said to myself, "Ben, you old fool, you're going to live after all." I've been at it ever since.

This morning I looked at myself in the mirror and said, "So, still hanging around, huh?" and put on my pants and went down to breakfast. Flirting with eternity makes you powerful hungry.

40

Christmas is coming on and I'm back after a few days in Marlow Hospital—nothing serious, fever and some weakness. In the Army they'd say I'd been on R & R, but in my case I'm not sure from what. Maybe from living, since it's my sole job just now.

I told them at the hospital that it was this damned Eastern weather that is getting me down. We've had days and days of deep cold and what they call snow showers. "Why doesn't God dump a couple of feet on us and be done with it?" I said one day to two nurses changing my bed. "That's what He does out in His own country, in Illinois."

They chuckled mildly but seemed to find little humor in what I said. I found even less in the hospital. You hang around that place long enough and if what you've got doesn't get you the food will. The meals are put up in New York and hauled out in hot-trucks. New Yorkers must cheer when they leave town. They have two dishes: hot and ice cream. Gravy is sloshed over everything hot, and it all tastes the same, pork, beef, mashed potatoes, broccoli. The ice cream is flavored with cardboard but is cooling to the palate.

Emily came to see me twice, leaving me unhappy last time, and Norma came once with Rodney. I could tell I hadn't reached the end of the line when he presented me with his detailed sketches for the refurbishment of Old House. His drawings show everything down to white porcelain knobs on his kitchen cabinets. I always made do with brass pulls myself.

It would be nice if we could do it. Would have been. One of these days I'll find the gumption to tell him his dream is doomed. You hate to disappoint a young lad, particularly when his fantasies include a role for yourself.

Emily took me by surprise. "My lease is coming up for renewal pretty soon, Ben," she said, "and when it does I want to get out of Eagle Arms."

I lay in a state of shock for a moment. "It's coming up?" I asked. "With your birthday and all I thought you'd already renewed." When you're desperate you grab any straw that floats through your mind.

But straws are forever straws, and save nobody. Her contract, she said, has a couple of extra months tacked on for reasons obscure to me.

"You've always said you liked it there," I went on. "If that's true, why leave?"

"Don't fret, Ben," she said, taking my hand. "It's not the end of the world. Eagle Arms was just wonderful after New Haven, and after Baltimore and my husband's nephew. Even a chain gang would have been inviting after that." She laughed a little to cheer me up. "But now I feel different."

"You don't like it anymore?" Ben Carpenter finding it difficult to accept someone's dislike of the Arms—who'd have thought? "You and Mr. Harmon have a tiff maybe?"

She smiled her quiet smile. "I know how you feel about him, Ben, but he had nothing to do with it. I've just decided I came in too young. Especially since I was in perfect health. Quite simply, Ben, I made a mistake."

"You know best, Emily," I said, already resigned, I suppose, to the inevitable. "I had no chance to make a mistake myself. My daughter made it for me. Besides, I'm quite a lot older."

"Poor old Ben," she teased, "you're not that much older any more. I'm catching up to you. And it wasn't age anyway. Careless with fire, that's what you said once."

"Did I say that?"

"And getting lonely at Old Farm."

"I said that too, huh?"

"Look at it from my point of view, Ben. I can still take care of myself, cook my own meals, tidy up my own apartment. If one can, one should. Don't you agree?"

"I suppose, but just where is this new place of yours going to be?"

"Why somewhere here in Marlow of course. I like this town, and you're here. I wouldn't leave you, Ben."

So that was it. She won't be far away—but farther than a few floors up.

In Magellan I knew of cases where the girl was moving away with her parents, or her beau was. So the kids rushed around and got hitched before they could be separated. There were instances too where her parents merely went through the motions to speed the boy's decision. Our shop foreman went so far as to resign, then came back a week after the wedding to reclaim his job.

When you are seventy-three and the object of your affections is moving out, your options are severely limited. Fletch was right—another marriage at my age would be cuckoo. So the best I can do is enjoy her presence while I can. She still has something like six weeks to go on her contract.

41

I'm getting out! I'm getting out! Yep, come June I'm going to leave the Arms. So there's something left in this old life yet.

I can imagine what Norma will say when she hears. Likely raise hell, she will. I told Emily that.

"It's not her life, Ben; it's yours. Yours and mine."

So it is. We worked it out yesterday. The afternoon was bright with sunshine but blustery and cold, a damp wind blowing in off the Sound. We were down at the shore to look at a place for Emily. It's mid-January and she's wild to get out, except she has not been able to find a decent flat.

I went with her to a big new complex that they're still building. It sits beside the Rippowam River, a smallish and foul-looking stream that meanders in from Stamford on its way to the Sound. The place is called Rippowam City, and they have studio flats at decent rents, or so they advertised. We found out why people have nicknamed it Ripoff City, and it doesn't have to do with the rents.

Renting Office, said a sign over a door that was down half a flight. "We'd like to look at one of your studios," I told a man of about thirty, neatly dressed in a blue suit.

His smile was welcoming. "Something for one of your children?"

"Our children?" Emily said. "Oh no, we're only friends. It's for me."

The smile disappeared. "Where do you reside now?"

"Eagle Arms, but my lease is about to expire."

It was the wrong answer; I knew as soon as she'd said it. But he'd have found out anyway.

"I'm sorry, but we don't have anything in that size available at this moment," the rental agent said as smooth as molasses. "But if you like you can leave your name and a number where you can be reached if anything comes up."

The devil got hold of my tongue: "How about something larger? Say one or two bedrooms."

She would have protested, for her desire was for something tiny to make for easy care, but she had no time.

"I'm sorry, but all we have available is some very large units. One of the penthouses, for instance."

"Don't bother with the telephone number," I said to Emily. "They'll never have anything for you at Ripoff City."

They have laws about discrimination. You have to treat blacks right. And Jews and the Irish, even poor people, and women the same as men. But no law seems to apply when your only problem is having lived too long.

"Did you see his face when you mentioned Eagle Arms?" I asked Emily as we walked along toward a pay phone at a gas station to call a hack. The one we'd asked to wait hadn't.

"It wasn't a very friendly look," she said.

"You see, he knows what kind of place Eagle Arms is. If you live there you have to have some money, yes, but it also means you're an old bird. Too old for regular rentals."

"At sixty-three?"

"Sixty-three nothing. The minute you said Eagle Arms you became an old lady to him. Everybody at Eagle Arms, they think, has got to be pushing eighty. Why, if Rodney said he was from the Arms they'd think he's really eighty but his false face fits nicely."

We got out at the foot of the hill and walked up for exercise, and to give Emily time to compose herself. She'd cried in the hack and was shivering from disappointment and terror. It's frightening toward the end when you can't bring something off that would have been a snap twenty years back.

"Have you run into that kind of thing before?" I asked as we turned up our collars and huddled in our coats against the cold.

"Nothing so blatant, no. There were two places up on the hill by the hospital that would have taken me but their rents were so exorbitant. So many have gone condominium, and I don't want a condo."

"Maybe we can make it work out," I said, patting her back. "I'll help, if you want. You've never asked, you know."

"I didn't want to bother you, but I'm asking now, Ben. Please help me find an apartment."

I led her into the library on mezz. There was something I wanted to check out. Rufe had a nice blaze going in the fireplace and I was happy we'd come. No one else was about; it was as if the scene had been arranged just for us.

We took off our coats and sat on the sofa. A cup of tea or a glass of sherry would have been nice but the Arms has no such service. I fetched the evening copy of the *Marlow Mail* and looked in Real Estate. Soon I found what I sought. The ad was big, the aerial view lovely. "For People Who Love the Seaside but Thought They Couldn't Afford It," the copy said. "Try Rippowam City on Marlow's Own Renowned Seacoast." I read it out to Emily.

"I never heard Marlow has a renowned seacoast," Emily said.

"Neither did I but we're both in a foreign land here. Look what it says here now. 'Life style and luxury of New York at a fraction of the cost, and right at the seaside.' Then they list what they call comfortable studios and bigger places. Says so right here."

"Then he was lying to me."

"Of course."

"Why? Why would he do that?"

"That's a rental agent for you, always afraid people might expire before their leases do. It terrifies them."

Emily was furious. "I think I'll call that man up and give him a piece of my mind. What a creep!"

"Don't waste your breath, my dear. Look, do you know where your contract is?"

She did, and we went to six to look at it. I scanned the lines and found it to be identical to my own.

"It says here that you can cancel out at any time with the payment of two months' rent," I told her. "That's what mine says too. How would you like to waste two months' rent?"

"What do you mean?"

"Well, my contract is up in June and I want to get out as much as you do. If you're willing, why don't you sign up again and then, when mine is up in June, we'll both get the hell out of here and find a flat of our own, the two of us."

I doubt the idea had ever occurred to her, and I know it hadn't to me until that second. "Oh, Ben," she said, "you're so nice to offer, but I couldn't put you to all that trouble. I'll find something."

"You're taking the wrong meaning, Emily. It's not a favor I'm offering. I *want* to go someplace and live with you. Don't you know that?"

She was convinced finally, and agreed, and that's how I'm getting out. We are. Even together we probably couldn't get ourselves into the newer and fancier buildings, rental agents all being the same. But we might swing a flat in a converted house, like the one Dorothy and Connie had back in Magellan.

In celebration of our pact, we made love, and it worked. We missed dinner though. When the phone rang Emily told Lucy we were going out to dinner. They do keep close track of you.

I imagine now everybody at the Arms knows all, and has guessed a lot more, but I couldn't care less. What I dread is the storm that is sure to break when Norma hears, and I wonder what Rodney will say about Grandpa taking a flat with Mrs. Walrod rather than going back to Old Farm.

I was late to breakfast this morning and after I sat down at a vacant table I noticed Emily eating with Lloyd Axelrod and Mrs. Abernathy and a lady from ten. A fine-looking woman, I thought to myself, and a new romance for Ben Carpenter. But romances are different on this side of the Gray Veil. Neither of us has said a word about love, or marriage either.

42

Those Eagle Arms renegades, Fletch and Ben, pulled off something this morning that simply isn't done around here. It was his idea but I went along naïvely enough, and the experience was not cheering. Maybe on a few things Mr. Harmon is right.

They took Mabel Moore off to the hospital yesterday after a stroke in the early hours. Her Help switch got the night guard and eventually Nursey, who took a look and called an ambulance. I only heard about this part, but I saw what happened next.

Twirling its red and blue lights, the ambulance parked out front at breakfasttime, when the Residents were hovering over their scrambled eggs and prune juice. But not for long. The dining room emptied like a school-room with a fire drill going. Having an ambulance in front is exciting stuff; a beep on its siren might have produced wet pants all over. Morbid curiosity is rampant at the Arms. A sudden illness or an accident sets tongues going ninety a minute. When there's actually something to see, our gang gets as thrilled as the Romans waiting for the lions to be turned in.

Three attendants, two men and a woman, young and in white, wheeled a stretcher through the front doors and here came Mr. Harmon skipping out of his office to intercept them. "You'll have to go around behind," he told them, "to our service entrance."

I heard shocked intakes of breath and small cries of surprise from the gathered audience.

The man leading the team, chubby, with a black mustache, hardly missed a stride as he came up to our majordomo, who blocked the way like a bull moose protecting his harem. "We take the shortest way," the attendant said. "This is an emergency—all our calls are—so get out of our path and stop interfering. Where's the elevator?"

"Ahead and to the right." A crackly voice, Fletch's.

Despite what you read you don't often see a person pale before your eyes. Well, Mr. Harmon definitely did pale and, retreating to his office, his expression went from fierce to strange. "Looked like he'd been beaned with Irish confetti," said Fletch. It's what they call bricks in Boston, he told me.

"Poor man," said Emily. "Now he's humiliated."

I thought he had it coming but let it go with a shake of my head and a few tongue-cluckings. There was much excited tittering around us. Scenes of humiliation rank right up there with accidents.

Soon an elevator door opened and they brought Mrs. Moore toward the front. She was covered with a sheet and strapped down tightly. The men wheeled the stretcher along and the girl held an IV bottle connected to Mrs. Moore's arm. There was a craning of necks and shouts of

"Good luck, Mabel." And comments: "You see her eyes, all funny?" "Her mouth was drooping on the left side, or was it the right?"

I stood by the front desk and kept quiet, though I stared as much as anyone else.

Mr. Harmon wasn't through yet. The mustachioed attendant stepped on the treadle but the door stayed shut. "Open the door, please," he called.

Lucy leaned out. "I'm sorry," she said, "but our Executive Director says you must use the service entrance."

So here was one of our own being carried out and, hiding in his office, Mr. Harmon was barring the door. Lucy, I could see, was near tears. I was furious. Leaning inward, I spied, beneath the phone console, the small lever that controls the two sets of sliding doors. A nudge with my stick and it flipped over. There was a hiss as the doors opened. Lucy gave me what seemed to be a smile of gratitude. "Tell him I did it," I whispered.

They bore Mrs. Moore away across the hill to St. Elizabeth's, the Catholic hospital.

I thought I might catch hell from Mr. Harmon but since that incident I haven't even seen him. He must be slinking around behind the wall coverings. Emily found a kind word for him of course. "He was only trying to protect us," she said. "It's demoralizing to see one of our own people taken away like that."

Maybe, but more likely he was protecting the Owners and their Investment. No doubt he heard some stiff words from them when Mrs. Collins died here and, next day, the *Mail* listed the Arms as the place of her death. Bad publicity.

All that was yesterday. I've been putting off the events of this day. At breakfast Fletch said, "Let's go over and visit Mabel Moore."

"Me?" I answered. "She and I haven't been particularly close."

"I know, Ben, but she's all right, gossipy or not, and she and I were two of the originals in this place. We go way back."

"Whyn't you go alone then?"

"Couldn't do that; sure way of startin talk around here."

Mrs. Moore is half-dead in the hospital and Fletch has one foot in the grave, yet he's worried about talk. So I went.

We walked over the hilltop and got right in at eleven. She's in a semiprivate with a loony for a roommate, a dark little woman with stringy gray hair who was sitting up in bed as pert as you please.

"We're going into the city tonight," she announced.

"Imagine so," Fletch said out of the corner of his mouth.

"The theater, *My Fair Lady*. My son got the tickets. He lives in a penthouse overlooking Central Park."

"Good for him," Fletch said as we scampered beyond the privacy curtain. I'm no expert on Broadway but even I know *My Fair Lady* has been closed a while.

Mrs. Moore stared at us without recognition. There was an IV with two bags, and an oxygen tube came down from the wall and clipped into her nose.

"Feeling a little better?" Fletch asked, stepping close.

"Oh, it's Dr. Pepper," she said indistinctly. The left side of her face was drawn down and her dentures rested in a glass on her table. One hand lay lifeless but the right held a wad of tissues that she used to wipe drool from her mouth.

"Looks like you've got good care, Mabel," Fletch told her.

Some words formed but were difficult to understand. "Ood oo kuk." Maybe "Good of you to come." You couldn't tell.

Her eyes wandered up to the ceiling. I don't believe

she was aware of my presence, nor did she respond when a middle-aged man came in. Her son. We shook hands and he motioned to someone at the door.

In came a boy of twelve or so, her grandson. "Hello, Grandmother," he said, and touched her wrist.

"Grant," she said distinctly, dropping the tissues and finding his hand. Her eyes soon found his face. I've heard about that, the old and dying responding to the young.

Fletch and I left soon and came walking down the slope to the Arms. "Maybe Mr. Harmon is right," I said.

"About what?"

"Oh, the way he and the rest of them don't seem to want us to visit Residents in the hospital. It sure can be depressing."

Fletch did not respond right away but I could tell he was thinking. Finally he had it in his mind and started out, "You know, Ben, you know death is . . . death is . . ." It wouldn't come.

"Damned final," I said.

"No, let me think." His ailment was holding him back, I suppose. "The accouterments—that's it—the accounterments of death are not becoming at all to an old body like that."

"Or to anybody else's," I answered.

"You seen a lot of dead people, Ben?"

"Enough. Not laid out on a battlefield like you, no, but when I was a reporter I saw a lot of young ones dead in their cars and beside their motorcycles. If anything, death looks more horrible on them."

"The Greeks and Romans thought death was ever so becoming to the young, Ben. Plato said there was nothing more beautiful than the death of young men in battle."

"Fletch," I said, "did it ever occur to you that Plato might be full of baloney?"

He cackled loudly and fell into a coughing fit that sounded like he'd inhaled a frog. "I guess we are too," he

193

said finally, "both full of baloney. Death is terrible, that's all."

So far as I know, Mabel Moore is still alive at this minute, but Fletch evidently divined more of her condition than I could. If it's death that has settled in with her, he's sure making a mess of the poor lady before taking her away.

43

Around the Arms they think we're an item now, the subject of as much gossip as Liz Taylor. Oh, we give them reason for their talk, going around together much of late, and we have taken to having supper together, usually with Fletch as a third and whoever Jackie brings over for a fourth.

Fletch knows there is something going on, but doesn't seem to suspect how much. He might disapprove if he knew—or might not. They say old people are terribly set in their ways, and no doubt some are, but most of us are as capable as anyone else of changing our opinions or our feelings. Fletch appears to have softened toward Emily; more specifically, toward the idea of our being, well, involved with each other.

When I first came to the Arms, I realize now, my thoughts of those around me ran to starkness. In my mind I disapproved of Mrs. Bowman's plumpness, of Jackie's sweetness and the gossipy ways of poor Mrs. Moore, who still lies over there in the hospital in bad shape. Now my feelings are tempered. Not that I'm trying for sainthood—it's just that, what the hell, we're all going through this together and we might as well make it as easy as we can for those we're thrown in with for the great descent on the far side of the hill.

I wonder, though, what Fletch would say if he knew about the flat, or the others. We found it last Tuesday, still occupied but coming up late in May. Norma hasn't heard yet either, and when she does I may have to pull a Lloyd Axelrod and flee in my nightshirt to refuge in some embassy by the UN.

For a couple—how strange to use that word—so accustomed to endless empty days with nothing happening, Emily and I find a powerful stimulant in all this excitement. Other Residents are mostly happy about our close friendship, while wondering how far we have gone. Emily has been asked whether I'm fun to be with, and you know what they have in mind. He's very pleasant to go shopping with, she told one yesterday, and he helped me pick out a face powder at the drugstore.

A deposit was required on the flat, and I signed the lease with a happy smile. It was afterward that we found the fly in our ointment. My signature alone is not good enough for them, nor Emily's either. She didn't even get asked. What they want is a co-signer, such as a close relative, one with money. They make no bones about it—I have to line up somebody who will come up with the cash if I croak too soon. The whole world is aflame with fears that some old duffer might die owing them a dollar.

No one vaguely aware of my situation would have difficulty pointing a finger at the logical co-signer, but I'm putting the call off for a while. I can hear it now. "Hello, Norma? Listen, honey, how'd you like to co-sign a lease with your old daddy?"

There is time, it still being February, but I'm having the same feelings as I did when I was afraid to tell Mother about the broken eggs. Only, the parent now is younger than the child.

"You were right about trying the conversions," Emily

said as we walked home after the signing, feeling happy with ourselves.

"Magellan wisdom, you know. They invented the art there."

She laughed and squeezed my arm. "You mean nobody had ever cut a house up into apartments before they did it in Magellan?"

"Must not have; I never heard of it before I got to Magellan."

My idea was to stay away from the high rises that are starting to give Marlow a skyline, and stick with the conversions. We found what we wanted in the third place we looked, up over the hill and down at the foot on Madison Street. That appealed to me, for Magellan's big street, paved with bricks, was Madison, and trolleys ran there. It's still Madison, but the cars are gone, and the bricks too.

Eighty years ago this house was something to behold, and the traces remain, like glimmers of beauty you see in a girl now seventy who once was homecoming queen. It is big, white clapboard and on a spacious lot. That part of town is called Mapleton and in those days, they say, it was a quiet bucolic village with the farms still close by. By now the city has swallowed the village, and Mapleton, if you look it objectively, has become a little seedy. Only a few of the old mansions are left to joust with the high rises, and with the banks and shops, some of which are getting along in years themselves.

The owner and his wife have taken the ground floor as their own, cutting the second floor in half to make two flats. Each has its own outside stair, and I'm reminded of the place Dorothy and Connie once had. We'll have a neat living room with two windows facing the street, and the kitchen, nearly as large, is what they call "eat-in." The grace people used to find in dining rooms is no longer appreciated. There's the bath and bedroom in back, and off to the side a room for boxes and cases.

"I could put a workbench in there and tinker with clocks again," I told Emily. Fixing up aged case-clocks was once my hobby, when I was young and newly married. Emily was tickled at the thought, and talked of getting a machine and stitching up some dresses, as she did in her days as a bride on the Eastern Shore.

It gives me strange feelings, this taking a flat with a new woman and the two of us thinking of things we did when newly wed to others. But life repeats only to a degree: there'll be no wedding this time. We finally got it talked about last night. Emily was the practical one. "Our Social Security would go way down if we married," she said. "We just can't afford to, Ben."

"And living in sin is all right with you?"

She laughed and clapped her hands in front of her nose. "You make it sound so excitingly evil, Ben! I can hardly wait."

So that is how it is going to be. All I have to do is convince Norma to co-sign.

And Rodney. How can I tell him that Grandpa is never going to Old Farm with him?

ꞏ44

I was witness this morning to a sorry scene at St. Elizabeth's.

Mrs. Moore has been in there the thick part of a week now, and Fletch wanted to go visit again. "Might cheer her up," he said. "Must be a strong old girl, holding on this long."

"Tell her hello for me," Emily said. They are friends, you know.

We got there before visiting hours but walked right in anyway. "Look important," Fletch advised. "They won't dare stop us if they think we're somebody."

They didn't either, though that had nothing to do with our look of importance. They very nearly weren't home. We spied a policeman, who was supposed to be at the front door, over in the lounge reading a racing paper. Nobody else was about, and on two we found the nursing station abandoned.

"Looks like they had a fire drill and forgot to come back," Fletch said.

"They forgot the patients too."

We saw them lying in their gowns and johnnie coats, a man reading a magazine, two women watching little television sets suspended on arms. Others stared into the distance, perhaps glimpsing eternity, for Mrs. Moore is on a floor for the elderly. Eventually, a nurse came out of a door down the hall and disappeared around the corner. The scene was eerie, as if we'd dropped into a place of the living dead.

"Florence Nightingale wouldn't think much of this," Fletch said.

"She'd be bored, Fletch. She had this thing about soldiers, you know."

"At least she'd be here."

The loony roommate was still at it, though subdued—literally. Cotton straps at the wrists tied her to the railings. Her face was badly scratched, but her mouth was in good shape.

"We're going to a garden party in East Hampton," she said. "Did they tell you?"

"No, they never tell me anything," Fletch answered. He's quick enough when he's not trying.

"At the Eastmans'," the roommate continued. "All the first families will be there."

You wonder whether it's delusions or scenes from real

life; maybe she did live that way once, this addled old lady. I'll never know but my journalist's blood makes me hanker to find out.

We shut the curtain behind us and beheld the scene, transfixed. Fletch spoke first. "These CVA cases are terrible things," he said, sounding like a medical doctor.

"What's a CVA?" I asked. "And do you really know anything about it?"

"Been around medicine all my life, Ben. CVA is what they call it, cardiovascular accident. By that they mean a stroke."

"I knew she'd had that last week," I said, "but she does look worse, much worse."

Mrs. Moore's condition is stable, they said on the phone, but what a place to stabilize—just above the vegetable level, I'd say, maybe on a par with a jellyfish. She lay inert, her eyes unfocused, her hands also tied to the railings. The worst part was a pinkish-white foam oozing from her mouth.

"We'd better do something, Ben," Fletch said, agitated. "She sure looks bad."

His words frightened me. What I know about medicine wouldn't fill a flea's overnight bag, and I was sure Mrs. Moore was dying at that moment. If only we could stop her. "What'll we do, Fletch? We're not doctors."

He whirled and stalked away at a speed that surprised me. "Get some staff in here," he muttered.

Not being one to face scenes bravely when I don't know what the hell is happening, I trotted along at his heels.

"Lester Lanin is going to play," said the roommate.

At the far end of the hall we saw a man wheeling a patient away on a litter. An old woman in a blue dressing gown sat on a chair against the wall. There was not a nurse in sight, and the hall's strange hush was broken only by faint sounds of TV, no voices at all.

Fletch stalked over to the nursing station and screamed like a madman. "Nurse! Nurse! This instant!" They could have heard him in East Hampton, wherever that is, this famed surgeon demanding action. He got it too.

A door lettered *Dispensary* flew open and out came a nurse, a tray of plastic cups in her hands, and scared shitless, as my grandson would say. Fletch was about to speak when another one came running around from the far hall, black and heavyset and making time. "What is it, sir?" she asked, calm as anything, but winded.

"Get a house doctor up here quick," Fletch told her. "Mrs. Moore in two sixteen is in bad shape. Looks like a hemorrhage in the nasal passages, and she's aspirating her own blood."

After observing what had just happened, I thought the nurse would hop to. She didn't budge. "And you, sir?" she asked him.

"I'm Dr. Fletcher Pepper, retired now, but there's still a doctor in front of my name. Move, *now*."

She did. "Call Dr. Bardwaj," she told the tray nurse, and hurried into Mrs. Moore's room with us following.

"Cocktails on the lawn," said the roommate.

We watched while the nurse removed the oxygen clip from Mrs. Moore's nose, wiped away the foam and felt for her pulse. She knew what she was doing; she saw nothing in me that reminded her of a doctor either. "Perhaps, sir, you could wait outside?"

"Certainly," I answered. "I think I'll go on back, Fletch."

"Visiting hours begin at eleven, sir."

"I'll go too," said Fletch. "Nothing I can do. Thank you for coming so quick, Nurse. I hope I didn't cause a disturbance."

The nurse smiled, looking up from her watch. She'd been counting pulses. "Doctor," she said with a chuckle, "I bet you was one heller when you was still in practice."

We were tapping our way across the hill before Fletch spoke again, a grin on his face. "Had em buffaloed there for a while, didn't I, Ben?"

"You had em hopping like frogs, Fletch. You sure sounded like a man of authority."

"It's only when they don't know, Ben. I didn't notice Harmon doing much hopping in that plumbing mess. I had it once though, back in Lynn. People looked up to me and I was a good dentist to them. Now I'm just another old man." His voice had grown sad.

"That's not like you, Fletch, feeling sorry for yourself."

"Merely a statement of fact, Ben. I don't think she'll last the day."

"What? Oh."

"Strokes are terrible things," he said next, "disabling and altogether wretched. God could have done better."

"Be sure and tell Him that when you see Him."

"The thing about Mabel Moore, she's always been interested in other people. She's nosy, all right, but by God it's better'n sitting around waiting for the shades to fall." His tribute to Mrs. Moore.

The day was fine, one of those February productions with sun and some warmth, a promise of spring in the air. We took our time, determined to enjoy it.

"Lord, deliver me from CVAs," I said. "Cancer might be better if it was quick. My wife died in two weeks, you know."

"In two weeks? You never told me that."

I have, but it didn't matter. "The way I want to go is of a heart attack while chasing a blonde," I said.

He snickered. "That's premature," he said. "I don't want to be taken until I've caught her. That way I wouldn't have to put my socks back on, and my feet are a long ways down these days."

45

When events went badly my father could be heard to mutter, "'i God," no doubt thinking to lessen his blaspheme, for he was a man of piety. Of late I have found his expression useful around here; 'i God but life can turn on you.

"A place of your own?" Her fury gushed from the phone. "Papa, how can you even think of such a stupid thing at your age? And to think of all the trouble I went to to get you into that place. I suppose you think it just happened, like that."

"Norma, honey, they go to a lot of trouble to get people into Stateville too, but that doesn't mean they like it."

"Oh, Papa, I'm so afraid for you, scared you're turning into a crazy old coot, going senile on me."

There was more, and later she apologized for the coot remark. Eventually, she cooled down to something in the slow-cooker range and, still later, said she'd sign. It wouldn't surprise me if she opened a vein to get a suitable writing medium for her signature. I've never known her to be so angry; why, she even threatened to come down here for a face-to-face encounter. A bridge date kept her away and for once I made no suggestion that she might cancel it. I've found it unwise to invite tigers into your home while their tails are still twitching.

I got her to agree that I was to be the one to tell Rodney that Old Farm was out.

Norma's tantrum on the phone was two days ago, and in the morning yesterday word got around that Emily

Walrod, the beauty of the Arms, and that old devil Carpenter are setting up housekeeping together come the last Saturday in May.

Mr. Harmon was first to get the word. From Norma. Why she called him, I don't know, nor did I ask. He is notably displeased and was curt with Emily when they met in the evening. His sticking point no doubt is the usual: money. Having a pretty Resident around is good for business, and now I'm taking her away.

Inez Bowman was jolly and happy in all her avoirdupois and chins and hennaed hair, these days cut into a fright wig. There was talk and titter among the ladies, and Lucy squeezed my hand warmly. Margie bubbled while delivering our lunches, "Hear yez gettin sprung from d'jernt. Ain't love grand? Wisht I had some."

"Don't worry, dear," Emily told her. "With your looks you'll have all the choices you want."

A pleased smile came to Margie's face. "Yeah, but when?" she wanted to know. The girl truly is pretty and if her love life is as drab as she lets on I do not understand it. Surely her accent is not alienating to her own N'yawk kind.

Fletcher Pepper, DDS and scarer of nurses, reversed his field and has decided, now that he knows we're not getting married, to give us his blessing. "Have me over for a drink and I'll fix your teeth free," he said.

This afternoon brought Rodney, his eyes looking as if he'd been tortured with snakes. "Grandpa," he said, "I've been making all these plans about Old Farm and now you go and fink out on me." He was near tears.

So much for Norma's promise to let me be the one who told him. From what Rodney said, it was no big deal to her. She's having a cat fit about Emily and me, but the Old Farm idea held no importance. "Crazy kid stuff dreamed up by my two boys," she told him. I could paddle that girl.

Reality in my flat being on the grim side, I got a beer

and split it with Rodney, which pleased him ever so slightly. But the half-brew didn't make up for his blasted dream, and Grandpa never found it in his heart to explain that sooner or later he'd have had to back out anyway.

Old Farm was dead in his mind before he got here, and I would not say he ranted long before collapsing on the love seat. "What am I going to do now, Grandpa?" he wailed. "I've *got* to get away."

"You sound like me and Eagle Arms," I said. "But away from where? You're not doing time at an institution like I am."

"From school, and away from Mom and Dad too."

"Look, son, you have only one more year and then you'll really be going away, to college. A year's not long."

"A year's forever to me, Grandpa. They mean well but they're driving me crazy. Mom hassles me about school all the time, says I don't work hard enough. I don't even think about college."

"You passing everything, Rodney?"

"Sure, and I did last semester too. It ain't that; Mom wants me on the honor roll, that's what."

"How about your father?"

"He couldn't care less, except he hassles me too when Mom tells him to."

"You could do better in school though, if you wanted to?" I asked.

"Sure, but then I'd get hassled at school."

Until that moment I can't say I had more than a perfunctory appreciation of my grandson's problems. But now I can see the fix he's got himself into—should have been aware of it long ago, I suppose, but the troubles of childhood seem so slight when compared to your own.

"You sound like a man backed into a corner with no way out," I told him.

"Just about." The beer was finished but it hadn't helped the expression on his face.

"Everybody gets that feeling, Rodney, but fortunately things do work out. Once, I was in a place in Magellan where some members of the Shenton Gang from St. Louis were drinking, and the police came for them. They had a regular shoot-out and I thought I was a goner, for sure."

Rodney likes my newspapering stories, and I'd drawn his attention away from his problems. "How did you get out?" he asked.

My grandson now knows the place to hide if you're in a blind pig during a shoot-out is amongst the drainpipes beneath the ice chest, though I'm not sure how much that will help him. He went home on the Connbus with beer on his breath and the rain cloud following closely.

So now my grandson is disappointed. My daughter, who said I sounded dumb when I explained humankind's penchant for pairing off, is furious. And Mr. Harmon thinks I'm some kind of traitor. All this because I want to get away from here and go live with Emily Walrod in our own place. For the life of me I can't understand what's so wrong about that.

'i God.

46

Another week closes at Eagle Arms; like all the others, an idle one, or nearly so. What I wouldn't give to eat a fast breakfast and catch the Connbus down to my desk at the *Marlow Mail*. I'd do obits, I'd do the market page, even the kind of schoolboyish sports they run. I've heard of old rascals who applied for jobs just as if they were regular people. Your answer is likely to be a derisive laugh, as if a drunk had wandered in and asked to run the Wire Desk. They think you're making a joke.

One day Emily and I walked over and looked at what will be our flat. Like Rodney, she did little sketches, and then announced that we'll have to get rid of a sofa and some chairs. Norma will take them, if I know my daughter. Hers are getting threadbare, and I have a feeling about Clyde's reluctance to finance reupholstering.

For days there has been no word from the hills. She's pouting, I gather, and still hasn't signed. It seems that I've committed some mortal sin by wanting out of my life sentence at the Arms.

Just after lunch on Saturday the Kemp youngster dropped in, bringing no glad tidings. I'd managed three glasses of red by getting myself seated again with the Baptist ladies, Fletch having had a tray sent up and Emily being at the dressmaker's, and was contemplating a nap when my visitor was announced. Saturday calls are rare around here, for on that day our kids are out clearing the shelves at supermarkets, raiding hardwares and fiddling with the gutters. Clyde of course stays in his den and writes memos; messages carrying weekend dates make your co-workers nervous.

"Well, what brings you here?" I asked Rodney. He was wearing jeans and an Oral Roberts Swat Team sweatshirt.

"Just thought I'd come see you, Grandpa. Got any beer?"

So that was his game: Grandpa, distributor of beer. "I can't keep giving you beer," I said. "It's illegal, you know, and your mother would have my scalp if she knew."

He laughed and, in a strange loose-jointed movement, flopped on my love seat. "She already wants your scalp, Grandpa. Mom's really pissed."

"Watch your language," I said, splitting a beer; half is only half illegal. "She's mad about the flat and Mrs. Walrod, eh?"

"Not about your girl friend, no. We all liked her at Christmas."

"Even your father?" Tumultuous news.

"Didn't hear him say, but he talked her arm off." And so he had. My son-in-law, charged with three or four White Ladies, as he calls them, ground on endlessly in his serious voice—about how much the food had cost. I'd heard his rants before, but it was new to Emily, hearing that the turkey cost "darn near forty bucks."

"But he couldn't remember the price of cranberries," I'd told her. That had made an impression on me.

"Raging about the flat, is she?" I said to Rodney.

"Yeah, I guess, but you gotta understand her, Grandpa." Elaborate hand gestures. "Mom's an arranger, see, and when she gets things fixed just right she damn well wants em to stay that way. Anybody that moves screws her up."

"That's bright of you, figuring out what makes your mother tick. Boys of sixteen may be getting smarter, I think. Arrangements or not though, I've got to get out of here. You can tell her I said so."

"So do *I*, outa there. I ain't fittin into Mom's arrangements."

"Your mother might have called me at least."

"That's not Mom's way, Grandpa. Gets so mad at Dad sometimes that she don't speak to him for a week."

Ah, yes, the little girl with the temper—inherited from her mother, I used to say, and laugh. Dorothy was of wonderfully even disposition, so the source lay somewhere in my mixture of Irish and English and Scottish and German blood. Thinking of that, my risibles liberated by the wine, I broke into laughter.

"What's so funny, Grandpa?" Rodney asked, falling into a veritable paroxysm of heehaws.

"Oh, just thinking of your mother's temper."

More laughter, much louder now, and some from me. The wine explained my own unlikely conduct, but Rodney had had no wine. I looked closely at him when he had subsided and decided, on viewable evidence, that the little devil was half-swaked. I might have noticed earlier except for my own state. A boy and his grandpa sitting around zonked. Oh my. The behavioral people could make a lot of that, I'll bet.

"How'd you get here?" I asked.

"Connbus."

"I thought maybe you'd driven. Your mother said she lets you take the Pinto sometimes."

"Not this time."

"Why not?"

"Said I'd been drinkin too much."

"Had you?"

"A few."

"Does your mother know about how you drink?"

"Hey, you gonna hassle me now? I get enough of that at home, Grandpa, and you always been my friend, even when I was a little kid."

"I still am your friend, Rodney."

"Then don't hassle me about a few beers."

"It's not really my business, son, but you worry about somebody who's sixteen and acts tight."

"Tight? I ain't tight, Grandpa. Never felt so laid-back as now."

"That's not what I meant. Tight is an old Midwestern word . . ."

"Ah ha!" he fairly shouted. "You mean twisted!"

"I guess." The kids use strange words these days.

"I only had four, I think."

"How do you get beer at your age?"

"Same as you; out of the fridge." He leered at me to see how I'd take his smartiness.

"You know that's not what I meant."

"Oh, all right. What I do is liberate six-packs from the kitchen and put them in that old refrigerator in the basement. Dad thinks it's been unplugged for five years; he just don't know." This time he giggled, mostly to himself.

"Does your mother know?"

"Sure."

"And approves?" I could not imagine Norma ever being that liberal.

"She sort of ignores it, Grandpa. You know, Mom is funny that way. Sometimes she does something real real nice for me and the next minute she wants to beat the shit out of me."

"Rodney, that's not a nice word."

"What I come to see you about is money, Grandpa." A stark declaration if ever there was one. His eyelids drooped slightly.

"What kind of money are you talking about?" I asked.

"Enough to get me to Australia."

"Oh, come on, Rodney, stop horsing around." I was beginning to weary of his antics.

"I'm not kidding. I want to get away from this place and since you finked out on Old Farm I've decided on Australia."

"Emigrate, you mean?" At sixteen kids do get wacky ideas.

"Migrate is what they call it. And check this, Grandpa: they have farms out there with a million acres or more."

"Suppose they won't take you, Rodney. The Australians are fussy about immigrants, and I doubt they're looking for sixteen-year-olds. Not if they're in their right minds, they're not."

He was off and running. "I want to leave this godforsaken country, Grandpa, and never come back. I'm tired of being an American. Democracy sucks. I want to go to a socialist country where they treat you right and you're not always getting shoved around by the big corporations, by Wall Street and General Motors."

There was more, much more, my grandson zipping off

like an elk with a bee under his tail. I'd never heard him rant like that before. Or seen him looped before either. Uh, twisted. When his mouth showed signs of slowing I asked, "Are you sure about Australia? I thought their government was like ours, democratic."

"No no, it's democratic, yes, but it's a social democracy and the big companies don't push you around like here."

He had me there. I pride myself in knowing geography, but I couldn't swear what kind of government they have in Australia. He's not going anyway. Rodney is going to Marlow High School next year if his mother has to take him in handcuffs—supplied by Grandpa.

His knowledge of Australia was impressive. He told me about their gross national product, their per-capita income, their copper and bauxite mines. "And in Darwin they have eighty-ounce beer bottles," he said.

"No wonder you want to go."

I doubt he heard me. Rodney was on a run, as they say in show biz, but all runs eventually wind down, and so did my grandson. I took him to the front desk and put him in a hack and gave the driver eight singles. I heard no outraged protests about the capitalist hacks of this town. Rodney was sad by then, and tired. So was Grandpa. I came up and slept past supper. The telephone woke me.

"So you're not dead yet, huh?" said a voice with a cackle. Fletch.

I was back in bed by ten, and trying for sleep, before I remembered my own father's flirtation with Australia. During the financial panic of nineteen-seven Father and Mother, beset by bad times, got the idea of selling out and moving to Australia. It was a story Father liked to tell, and my question was always the same: why hadn't they? I felt somehow deprived, never having had the chance to ride an ostrich or chase a kangaroo.

"We were mistaken," Father would say. "Times only

seemed so bad because we were living through them. But they always get better, and moving to Australia wouldn't have helped us."

I might have thought of that to tell Rodney, but didn't. Only hours later did my mind offer up that memory. It makes you wonder.

◆ 47

Fletch has a girl friend!

But if you go by the words the little guy speaks, a girl friend is not what he's looking for. She's looking for him though, and hardly the first to do so. A widower with a doctor in front of his name is choice prey beyond the Gray Veil.

Fletch came in and told me his troubles last night. You'd think the Father, Son and Holy Ghost had landed on his doorstep in a rubber dinghy. "Ugh ugh ugh," said he, "have you seen her, Ben?"

"Mrs. Taylor? Sure. Mr. Harmon introduced us. Remember?"

No answer, Fletch being too busy thinking up his next remark: "What a face, what a face! Ben, I tell you, she'd drive a bulldog off a meat wagon." Later he elaborated: "A mud fence for a face, Ben. My God, she looks like Barbra Streisand's ugly sister."

The situation is as perilous as a sailboat in a cyclone, methinks, what with Fletch getting off about her twice in one conversation. I had not known he liked her that much. You have to remember the games of childhood to sort these things out. The girl you liked best was the one you stuck your tongue out at and said what an ugly face, and all those freckles. In Lynn, Massachusetts, the coin of the realm evidently is meat wagons and mud fences.

Since I've known him Fletch has been as gun-shy as a filly under a deer rifle but I have a feeling now that he's acquired a liking for the smell of cordite—or Chanel, of which Mrs. Taylor wears plenty. Now I have observed the lady and found her not wanting. She may be a little touched in the head about retaining her debutantehood— or maybe it's her maidenhood—but you can't fault anyone for wanting to stay young. Nobody ever asked for old age: it's something they give you whether you want it or not. In age, she's up there with the rest of us old coots, but her hair is the color of a crow's pajamas. I'd guess she might admit forty-nine, but no more. Sometimes she wears lipstick on her chin, and green shadows lurk around her eyes. But her features are nice and she's as friendly as a PR agent at his own cocktail party.

I happened to be squinting into my mailbox when she and her children came by on Mr. Harmon's grand tour, the one he gives prospective Residents. "Hi there, Ben," he said with great jollity. His fake voice, obviously.

I waved my Social Security check at them. "Good news, Mr. Harmon. Down in Washington they think I'm still alive." His little entourage laughed dutifully and he joined them with a ho ho ho. I could see he was none too pleased, and leery besides.

"Folks," Mr. Harmon said, "I'd like you to meet our resident comedian. Uh, Mrs. Taylor, this is Ben. Ben, say hello to Mrs. Taylor." His usual.

"Rosalie," she said.

"Carpenter," I said.

"Oh, the Philadelphia Carpenters?"

"No, the Kansas Carpenters."

He forgot her kids entirely. "Mitchell's my name," said this nice-looking man in a business suit. "Her son-in-law."

I was going to ask Mrs. Taylor about a swap of sons-in-law but Mr. Harmon was tolling them onwards. The daughter, unintroduced in any way, was a stunner, a beautiful face, soft wool dress, red, with matching jacket thrown over her shoulders. Mmmm. Her hair was like courthouse ink, and you could see where the old lady got the idea.

Mrs. Taylor's entry into Eagle Arms was typical. Most of us get brought here by our kids for a look-around. "Isn't this nice, Mother?" "So cozy, and you'll have oodles of friends." "I'll be real close any time you need me."

Rodney has an expression for it: buffalo bagels. I asked him where he heard it. On TV, he said. What a place to learn English.

I was shown the same model flat when Norma hauled me down, Clyde being in Minneapolis, or maybe Singapore. It is Mrs. Mead's place up on eight, furnished like Mrs. Astor's summer cottage. I imagine she gets something off for being Mr. Harmon's sample, but later, when he shows you through the echoing empty flat that, like a jail cell, has been chosen for you, it is likely to resemble a broom closet in comparison. It'll look grand when we get furniture in here, the kids tell you. Picked out by them of course.

One can imagine old geeks who have said no, I'll take Sing-Sing instead, but not many. Once you see them looking you can lay money they'll show up soon at the gates. The kids have decided, you see, and the geezer in question discovers that when the voting took place he wasn't given a ballot.

Mrs. Taylor wears expensive clothes and you can smell her before the elevator opens. It's a nice smell, like money. Her husband, it is said, was a breeder of cattle in Nebraska. He must have had a lot of the little critters, to leave her as well fixed as she appears. Fletch could do worse, I thought, and told him so.

"At my age, Ben? What an idiotic idea!" He did not sound overly convincing, I must report. I think she may have his number.

In my dream, before the telephone rang, I walked again on the shady side of Hitt Street, around the corner and to the library. At my side was Kelly Masterson, my already-balding roommate from Texas. The leaves were broad and we wore polo shirts; the snow was above our ankles.

The clock, faint in the gloom, said something after three, and the ringing had been going on for a while. Straight from sleep, your mind has shed the body of age's infirmities and momentarily you are young and nimble again. A too-quick movement of my torso nearly put me on the floor on my head.

A telephone screaming for attention at three in the morning is terrifying. A death in the family? A grievous injury? My mind turning over at very slow idle, I picked up the receiver.

"Papa?" This before I could speak, panic in her voice.

"What is it?"

"Rodney. It's terrible. Rodney's in jail!"

The dichotomy of panic conversations is unfathomable, the mind demanding an obliqueness limiting frontal exposure. "Where?" I asked, as if it mattered.

"Police station."

"How do you know?"

"He called me. Oh, Papa, what can I do?"

"What have they got him for?"

"Drunken driving. I can't believe it. Just a boy."

"He had the car then?"

"I let him, but I never thought this would happen."

"With his learner's permit? I thought they had to have licensed drivers with them." Another subterfuge.

"No no. I mean yes, but he has a regular license now."

"I thought you had to be seventeen."

"No, they only have their learner's permits a couple of months. Papa, tell me what to do. Rodney's in *jail!*"

"What does Clyde say?"

"He's in Pittsburgh. That's what scares me so. I'm here alone."

By then my mind had risen above the forty level in IQ and I mulled over the situation. "They want bail money?" I asked.

"They won't let him out at all, Papa, not tonight."

In Magellan I'd know what to do. A couple of calls and the kid would be sprung. That's how it works in Illinois. In Marlow, Connecticut, I hadn't a clue. "Well, Norma, I'm not familiar with police procedures here but keeping a drunk driver overnight is common practice. They let em sleep it off. Most states take drunken driving pretty seriously these days."

"I know, Connecticut especially. A big fine, and they take your license for thirty days. But it just can't be true, Papa. Rodney would never drink that much and try to drive."

"We'll have to find that out later."

"What can we do?" Her voice was plaintive.

"The best thing, Norma, is to go back to bed and try to sleep some more. You might think about a lawyer too. You and Clyde have one?"

"Yes, but he's real old, and I don't think he handles things like this, only wills and real estate, stuff like that."

"Maybe I can find somebody when it gets light. Emily

215

has a lawyer here, I know, to keep little Norman in line."

"What? Oh, her nephew, yes." Her voice ran down and she whimpered, a sound I haven't heard from her since she was a small girl. "But Rodney, Papa, we can't leave him down there alone."

"He's hardly alone, my child. In fact, I'd say he's the best-protected citizen in Marlow tonight."

"Don't be funny, Papa, please."

"It's the truth. They won't hurt him and he can sleep it off. A night in jail might do our boy some good. I think he's been going a little heavy on the beer lately."

⚓49

The lawyer was about what I expected. "He's a Jew," Emily had said, "very dapper and a very tough guy. But he's my tough guy, and he keeps little Norman scared half to death."

He came out of his office to greet me, a handsome man with dark wavy hair parted in the middle and the complexion of a girl, age about forty. We shook and I silently admired the cut of his blue suit and his rep tie. "Shapiro's my name," he said, "Harlan Shapiro. Come on in, Mr. Carpenter." He led me to a pretty leather chair in front of his desk, real leather.

"It's kind of you to see me," I said. "My daughter's family has this little trouble with the police."

"So Mrs. Walrod tells me. I'm sure we can take care of it. You probably wonder about a Jew with a name like Harlan, don't you?"

"Ummm? I hadn't really thought about it, Mr. Shapiro."

"I mean, you mix a good old Anglo first name with something like Shapiro, and what have you got?"

Holy Moses, I thought, I'm here to get on with the Rodney business and he wants to talk about a funny name for a Jew. They do have the damnedest small talk in the East. Back home we mentioned the weather and how much fly ash. I supposed I had better join in if I wanted to do business with Mr. Harlan Shapiro. "You put Harlan and Shapiro together and you'd probably have a boy," I said, chuckling. "Except nowadays it's harder to tell because you find girls called Mike and Andy and Kevin."

Mr. Shapiro found that acceptable as small talk, and smiled nicely. "My mother was born in Harlan County, Kentucky, Mr. Carpenter, and she named her first-born after the county. Guess you never thought they had Jews out in Kentucky, did you?"

Oh, sure, I wanted to answer, down there they have Jews and infidels and blacks, even a couple of Orientals, but they're just as good as us old Anglos, honest, Mr. Shapiro. In point of fact what I said was my usual, "Mmmm?"

The chitchat having run its prescribed course, we got down to Rodney, who, I told him, was missing school on account of being in jail. "Pretty serious stuff," I said, "a sixteen-year-old picked up for drunken driving."

He pushed his palms together precisely, blew on his fingertips and smiled reassuringly. "Being charged is one thing, Mr. Carpenter, but charges can be reduced, sometimes even dismissed. You needn't worry overly much about your grandson. I'll see that things work out properly. This will require funds though." Already we were getting down to that.

"How much?"

"Five hundred should do it."

My checkbook was out in an instant and I was writing his name on the pay-to line.

"This is not all for me, you understand."

"Oh?"

"First I'll go over and post bail so the child can go to school this afternoon. Let's see, this is Friday, so I should think I can get the case into Police Court on Monday."

"Then he'll miss another day of school," I fretted. "But I guess that's a minor detail in view of the charges."

"No no. The boy will never see the inside of the court. There's a coffee shop across the street, and I'll go there early in the morning. Have a cup of coffee with the police judge, perhaps the arresting officer too. Of your five hundred, Mr. Carpenter, I'll retain perhaps half. Do you understand me?"

I gave him a straight look. "Mr. Shapiro," I said, "I come from Illinois, spent most of my life there."

"You're from *Illinois*?" He laughed gleefully. "Then, Mr. Carpenter, you certainly do understand how such things work." More laughter.

Back home we all knew how things worked, but I hadn't realized outsiders did too. Even here in distant Connecticut they know about Illinois. Fancy that. Mr. Shapiro's reaction was a little too understanding for my liking. You always feel some pride in your state, and I didn't know whether to laugh or be affronted. So I merely smiled thinly.

Emily's Jewish lawyer—I want to get down the right ID for him, since he made such a big deal of his religion—was as good as his word. And my money. Rodney's only offense was making an illegal turn, and twenty bucks took care of the fine.

Illinois could learn something from this town.

~50

After lunch on the day they released Rodney, which was way last week, Norma came on the Connbus to pick up the Pinto and stopped here on the way—nervous, upset, furious, all at once. "Did you even see him this morning?" she asked.

"Rodney? No. Mr. Shapiro said he'd get him out and send him on to school. Said he'd have him call you to tell you he was all right."

"He did call me, Papa. And, you know, he didn't seem upset at all."

"Probably an act, Norma. I imagine he's good and shook." At that time of course, we did not know how his case would turn out. I had faith in Mr. Shapiro, but not that much. Norma no doubt saw her boy moldering in some dungeon until he sprouted a long white beard.

"I could kill that boy, I really could," she seethed. "All this trouble because he wants to act big and drink beer."

I offered her a Bud to calm her nerves. Norma hates beer but she took this one pronto and drank it down furiously, straight from the can. My little girl was that upset.

"I wouldn't be too hard on him," I said. "Rodney's had a rough night, Norma. He must have been scared out of his wits. Did he tell you what happened?"

"A little. He was with this girl Charlene, who is a lot older than Rod."

"Likes them experienced, does he?"

"She's old enough to buy beer, Papa. I think that's why he took her. They sure bought plenty."

It depends on where you are coming from, methinks. Two six-packs wouldn't be much to some people, but for two kids it might be enough to cross their eyes—for me, it sure would. In reality, however, together they drank only one six-pack. The second one is what got them in trouble before they popped a single tab. The store where they went is way down next to the harbor, an area of many one-way streets. There's a place where you can make an illegal left turn and get away easily; otherwise, you have to wind up a hill and back down. Rodney made the left, as dozens of drivers do every day, but a cruiser was watching and bingo, he's in the poky. The girl took a hack home.

Norma eventually got her nerves to stop writhing like snakes, after the second Bud. "I worry so much about Rod," she said. "Someday he's going to kill himself or somebody else if he keeps this up."

"You can't judge the boy by bromides," I told her. "He just may have learned his lesson."

"The thing that makes me so mad is the way he goofs off in school. Now he's drinking beer and getting into trouble. It's all so needless. He could be a normal, good boy, Papa. I don't know what I'm going to do with him."

Hoo boy. I decided to bite the bullet. "The first thing you should do is let up on him, Norma. I don't think you realize what a tough spot Rodney's in."

"Tough spot? Rod's only a child, Papa, and we give him everything you can imagine. We're the ones who had it tough as children, Papa, Clyde and me."

"You're right about his being a child, except you know that children have the worst problems of anybody. Rodney's trying to make good-enough grades to satisfy you, but not so good as to alienate his friends. And he wants friends, needs them. Now you tell me that what he's trying to do is easy."

"You make it sound so complicated."

"Believe me, it is. What Rodney's trying to keep together is a house of soda straws, don't you see?"

"Why can't he just do the best he can, like I did? Like we all used to."

"Times have changed, Norma, and kids are different today. In addition to everything else, you know he feels let down about Old Farm. He had his heart set on going out there with me. He loves Old Farm, you know."

I might have mentioned Old Farm somewhat later, such as twenty years later. I got to hear plenty about leading children astray, but Norma went on down to pick up the Pinto saying she'd think about taking it easier on Rodney. I tried not to think, around four o'clock, of what she might greet him with after his long night and day away.

51

"Well, Benjamin, cat got your tongue?" Emily asked at breakfast, a tinkling laugh betokening inner happiness. Through the windows we could glimpse a nice Sunday morning in April. The weather is chilly by Magellan standards but the sun was bright and the flower beds out front show a pretty border of crocus.

"I'm a little down because of a dream," I answered.

"Oh, one of those," she said simply, patting my hand. "I was afraid you might have had a change of heart."

"Hardly that, Emily," I said, summoning up a smile. "My whole history says I never change on such things."

We decided last evening, sitting on her sofa with teacups and little cakes spread before us, to say we love each other. We hadn't before, largely, I suppose, because love is what you get involved in when you are twenty and filled with hope and the rutting season is upon you. Circumstances at seventy are drastically altered, but we could think of no good excuse not to be in love again. Love amongst the elderly is when you worry as much about her bursitis as your own.

"That's a relief to know," she said. "I know what you mean about dreams. I get them sometimes, bad ones, for no reason at all."

"If I'd been out boozing and chasing women it would be easier to understand why God got His back up."

"If you did that I'd have mine up too, me and God." I did my best to return her warm smile. "My worst dreams are the ones with Jim in them. You'd think I'd be happy to dream about him but I always wake up frightened and depressed."

"I dreamed about Dorothy a lot when she was alive, her and the kids, and sometimes a bad one about Jaime."

"But she's left your dreams now?"

"Pretty much, except this one last night certainly had to do with her."

Dream patterns change. The middle years are gone for me now, and I've never dreamed of myself as the old man I am. The stuff of my dreams is my boyhood on the farm. Mother is there, Father too, the horses and the cultivator with its fenders for spring corn and the hay derrick on its skids. Sometimes I see childhood friends whose very existence I'd forgotten.

Ned appears sometimes, my older brother, and these are always bad. He went hunting when he was sixteen and shot himself in the lungs when he pulled his gun up over a fence of barbed wire. Ned walked back to the house, pale and shaky, pink foam coming from his nose, and said, "Father, I shot myself. Please help me." But there was no help for him.

Some of my nighttime shows are enjoyable and I wake up happy, but most are harmless, pointless and strangely constructed. This one last night though, I hope it does not go into reruns.

I was being drowned in Dorothy's concrete laundry tub in the basement of the old home place, strong hands holding my neck and pushing my face into the soapy water. Once I got my head out and screamed, "Dorothy, stop, you're killing me!"

Resisting with all my strength, I arched my back and stiffened my neck. But I was losing the fight, and knew it. Soon I would be a corpse with its head draped in Dorothy's old tub. Pulling myself together for one last attempt to stay alive, I turned my head to look at my attacker—all the way around, like a meadowlark.

Looking down at me from the other end of this set of huge arms was the face of Clyde Kemp. "You still here, Old Man?" he said angrily.

~52

The news to be recorded here is old now, from a week and a half back. In that interval I have not written a single word, nor do I feel up to it now. But I must.

Wednesday a week began with one of those beautiful and unexpected spring mornings, the kind you get in early April when winter hasn't quite left but the new season is asserting itself anyway. The tulips were all in bloom, the air soft as a child's breath. I call it walking weather. Emily had been going with me of late but said this time she felt poorly so I went alone.

Over west is Victory Gardens Estates, the houses small but neat, the lawns groomed nicely. The name comes from the second war, when the town gave allotments for growing vegetables. The little street leading down into the

Estates is called Halsey. You don't find many places now that retain those names from the war.

I'd been out nearly an hour, looking at the flowers and the greening grass, when I decided to call it a day. Halsey rises gently, so I used my stick to help climb. Halfway up I saw people in front of the building and as I drew closer hands waved at me and there were shouts I could not understand.

Mrs. Bowman and Mrs. Mancuso came around the front bed, still set with yews for winter, crossed over and hurried towards me. Hurrying is a relative term; at our age you have to watch where you put your feet. They came to me all out of breath. "It's your Emily!" Mrs. Bowman gasped, her eyes wide, her hands clutching and unclutching each other.

My heart dropped like a stone and shadows passed in front of my eyes. She'd said "your Emily," and it was the first time I'd heard her name that way, which gave me pleasure even as fright coursed through my veins. "Yes, what about Emily?" I asked.

Mrs. Bowman was unable to continue but Mrs. Mancuso, a thin little woman in a black coat, added, "She got sick and fainted in the hall. They took her to the hospital."

"Which one?"

"Marlow."

The three of us hurried to the driveway. The ambulance had just left and a dozen Residents stood looking down the hill where it had gone, as people will, though the flashing lights were well out of sight. Mrs. Stickney came up and took my hand. "She'll be all right," she said. "I think it was an upset stomach, she vomited so, and then she fainted. She'll be all right."

"You saw it?" I asked, thinking to myself that I might get Rufe and the Eagle Crate to take me in pursuit.

"Well, I live on six too, and I was walking down the hall when she came running out. I guess she got sick inside because she was still throwing up, and then she fell against the wall and fainted. I ran in and pulled her Help switch. I hope that was all right."

"You did exactly right, Mrs. Stickney."

We heard a car approaching then, coming from around back and out through our parking lot. It stopped at the corner, a little black rig I'd never seen. The window slid down and out came Fletch's head.

"I was gonna go look for you," he shouted. "Jump in and I'll run you over there."

So this was his fabled Morris Minor 1000, a pretty little car, spruce and shiny as a black beetle. For months he had talked of taking me for a ride, but fear stopped him; now that ride would be to see Emily, the woman I loved, in the hospital.

The dread that had kept Fletch from behind the wheel was nowhere in evidence as we went down the hill like a Ferrari chased by smokies. "What about Emily?" I shouted, for the engine was roaring like an airplane—and no wonder, at the rate it was turning over.

"Can't tell you much, Ben. Appeared that she was getting up mucous and some food, and her breathing was labored."

"Sick at her stomach, huh?"

"Well, looked more serious than that, but I'm not sure. Now shut up and let me drive. My last drive, Ben." The little guy was working the clutch and the shift and the gas like a race driver, his body jumping all over the place.

"You'll do all right," I said. By the time we got to the first cross street I wasn't so sure. There was a stop sign against us but we roared on across, managing somehow to miss the traffic that was coming from both left and right. At the boulevard beyond, the signal was red but Fletch didn't notice. Fortunately, no vehicles were in the intersection or the drivers might have been scared out of a year's growth. Halfway through Fletch changed his mind and twisted hard left. I heard a screech of tires like pigs on fire and my driver rose in the air over me. We went around on two wheels, something you don't hear about with the new low cars.

"Long time since I did that," Fletch said out of the corner of his mouth.

I was too petrified by then to comment, having visions of this as our last ride in quite a different context. In a minute or so I decided simply to become unfrightened. At my age, and his, you are likely to die of something, I thought, and it would be all right so long as we didn't take anybody with us.

A block later Fletch discovered the horn and we went racing along, dodging around and between cars, one of his hands on the wheel, the other hammering the button. At the corner of the street leading up to the hospital the light was green, though it wouldn't have mattered. We whipped around and went rocketing up the hill past everybody in sight. I had to admire the way Fletch was handling the car.

Up ahead I saw a police cruiser facing us. It had halted for a red light, but Fletch didn't. I watched out the back window for flashing blue lights. If he comes after us, I thought, Fletch will be forced to stop and then the officer can take me on up. I hadn't quite given myself up for dead yet. There were no blue lights; instead, the cruiser pulled slowly away in the opposite direction.

A new thought came to me and I shouted, "My God, don't kill us before I get to see her again!"

"Always been a good driver, Ben," he shouted back.

A sign on the left said *Ambulance Entrance.* More screeching and sliding and Fletch parked us right in front of the ambulance, its lights still going. So was our horn. Fletch couldn't stop pounding. "All right," I told him, "you can quit now. We're here, and you are a very good driver indeed, Fletch."

I asked the girl at Reception about Mrs. Walrod but drew a blank. A youth in a white jacket, of high-school age, hung up a phone and came forward. "That's the patient they just brought into ER," he told the girl.

We could find out no more; no one was sure of anything. Fletch pointed to some chairs and we sat and waited. "These things take a while," he said.

Hours seemed to pass. I stared at the blue vinyl chairs and the other people. There was a hint of low voices but mostly we were a silent gathering waiting with shriveled stomachs for news from inside.

Surely, I thought, surely it can't happen again, not to the second woman I've cared about. And Emily only sixty-three and healthy. It couldn't.

A voice called for Mr. Walrod. Fletch and I went forward to meet a dark little man with a mustache. Dr. Rajai, by the tag on his coat. "Are you Mr. Walrod?" he asked me in the smooth accent of India.

"I'm her fiancé." The word sounded strange to my ear, and apparently to Dr. Rajai's as well, by his expression. I had never before been a proper fiancé, Dorothy and I marrying so quickly as to be scarcely affianced at all.

"I'm sorry to tell you," said Dr. Rajai, "that Mrs. Walrod has expired."

My knees nearly went and I grabbed a chair back to keep from falling. Dots of white floated in front of my eyes and I was unable to speak. Fletch put a hand in the small of my back. "Awful sorry, Ben. Such a wonderful lady. You all right?"

I nodded and managed to say, "Such a terrible shock."

Fletch turned to Dr. Rajai. "What was it, Doctor? The heart?"

Dr. Rajai spoke carefully. "We cannot be sure, sir, but pending an autopsy I should think the cause of death was cardiac arrest, yes."

We went to the car. "Can you drive, Ben?" Fletch

227

asked. "I'm too done in to try." So his last drive became a one-way trip.

I started off all right, except for being rusty on shifting. At Old Farm I'd driven to the last and wasn't completely out of practice, but luck failed me. At the foot of the hospital hill there's a park to the right beside a stream. I was going slowly, trying very hard; by the park I felt the right wheels bump and rise. There were more bumps as the sidewalk passed beneath us. A big sycamore smashed into the light on Fletch's side and crunched up the hood. My chest went into the wheel, and I saw Fletch pulling himself laboriously back into his seat. "You all right?" I asked.

"Oh, sure, too mean to die." He reached over and turned the switch off and we got out, shaky on our feet.

"Sorry I wrecked your car," I told him. "My muscles didn't seem to work. I'll get it fixed for you."

"Oh, pshaw, Ben, stop fussing about Maudie. She's old enough to die anyway."

Some boys ran up and asked if we were hurt.

"We're fine," Fletch told them, holding out some folding money. "Can one of you run and get us a taxi? I got to go home and sit down."

"You go on back, Fletch," I said. "I'll wait until the police get here."

"Fiddlesticks, Ben, we're both going home now. Come on."

"They may get us for leaving the scene, Fletch."

Just then a motorist who had stopped to look at the wreck of our antique car came up to us and offered to drive us to the hospital.

"Just came from there," Fletch said. "But we'd be mighty obliged if you'd give us a lift to Eagle Arms."

"That leaving the scene," he said on the way up, "we'll be all right when they find out who owns the car and come see us. Might be a little touchy at first, but not after they find out I got a doctor in front of my name and I'm eighty-six years old."

"I hope," I said, "but it was me that was driving."

"They won't know that. You got to use things like doctor and your age when you can. Bet I don't even get a ticket."

That's about the way it worked out, except the two officers were friendly and respectful from the start. One asked Fletch if he intended to drive again and, according to Fletch, looked relieved when Fletch said no.

Two days later a man called up and offered five hundred for the wreck.

"Five hundred nothing," Fletch told him (his account), "that car's a classic. Worth every cent of fifteen hundred." He finally took eleven hundred.

Fletch came up with me that evening and had a healthy jolt of brandy, and I cried some. The world had let me down.

"I've been hoping that when I took you for a drive it might make a piece for you to write for your book," Fletch said. "But now, well, it's all so tragic."

"Fletch," I said, "you can count on me. I'll write the very best piece I can anyway."

And I have.

53

April is the cruelest month, they say, and no wonder— it is the only one that begins with a joke.

At the *Times* the back shop used to get off some good ones on Clint Bradly. The news staff didn't like to rile him because we worked within reach of the fire that he breathed, but he was fair game to the printers. Once just after the war they dropped a start-up paper on his desk when he was in the men's room and peered out through the glass in the shop door when he came back and picked it up.

Mr. Bradly, as was his custom, ran his eyes up and down the columns, nodding with satisfaction. Sometimes he hummed as he took in the ads, thinking of the money they were bringing him. He hummed and nodded to the centerfold of Section A, and spread the paper wide to admire Frisco's double-truck ad. Hummm hummm hummm, a *lot* of money. The humming stopped short. Mr. Bradly sat for a minute, stunned, before dashing the paper to the floor and sprinting for the back shop.

"Goddamned idiots, you've got a typo in the Frisco ad!" he screamed, his voice cracking and going off register. "Stop the presses! Stop the presses!"

Stark layouts were big in those days, and the Frisco ad showed nothing but an immensely long flatcar across the bottom of the two pages under huge black letters: SHIP ON THE FRISCO. A situation tailored for the printers on April Fool's Day. The P had turned into a T, and they had Mr. Bradly going off like Vesuvius. He threw the door back so violently the glass cracked.

His screams were met by roars of laughter from the printers and compositors and stereotypers, and a chant, "April Fool! April Fool! April Fool!" that could be heard in St. Louis.

Mr. Bradly came back muttering, "Goddamned idiots," his standard reference to the printers. I don't think he ever forgave them that one, and the crack is there in the glass to this day. They call it Clint's Crack.

The back shop had run off half a dozen copies with the doctored ad before changing stereotype forms. When Mr. Bradly got to thinking of how much the joke had cost him, since stereotype shells were not cheap, he must have felt like gnawing into his desk like a buzz saw.

Such are the thoughts I occupy myself with these days, sitting for hours sometimes to search the past for humorous events I saw or took part in. It is preferable, no doubt, to weeping uncontrollably over there in the red chair, which for a while was nearly all I did.

I was not married to her, nor did we have children together, or even live together, yet this loss seems more difficult than the other. Emily and I got so little of what Dorothy and I had so much of. You expect to find young love, and you do, but love is a scarce commodity for widows and widowers up in years and its loss more tragic.

After Emily's death the Arms witnessed the unprecedented: one evening we held a memorial service for her in the chapel. This in a place where death is a forbidden word. A pastor from down the hill read Scriptures for us and I thought, Oh, God, the youngest and fairest of us all is dead. I doubt a single Resident that evening did not feel the cold hand of the beyond beckoning.

As for me, I'll never be that young again. On my birthday Norma took me to lunch at a Japanese place where they served fried chicken guts and fish that, unnervingly, shudder and moan softly when you poke them with your fork. She gave me a digital watch that would tell me of the tides on Mars if I could manage to get it set. The damned thing is smarter than I am.

Everybody is aging. My grandson has turned seventeen and one day after school he came by with his drawings for Old House. "I know you're not feeling good, account of Mrs. Walrod, but I was thinking maybe now we can really get going again, Grandpa."

The idea had not occurred to me. With Emily gone, he thought, he and I could get back to business. "I have this flat coming up, Rodney," I said. "Your mother signed, you know, and they have my money."

"You don't plan to *live* there, do you, Grandpa? Mom said you and her gotta go down and get rid of it when you're better."

"She did, did she? I'm not sure at all that she's right. I have not made up my mind yet, and you can tell your mother that."

"But this is our perfect opportunity, don't you see? You can go back to Old Farm, just like you've been wanting." His smile was confident, for he thought I couldn't say no, and he had Dorothy's smile, and her complexion and hair. He only missed the eyes.

I had to level with him, was way overdue, in fact. "Listen, Rodney, your Grandpa is not as young as he used to be. My machinery seems to be wearing out and, to tell you the truth, I won't ever be able to go to Old Farm with you. It was a wonderful dream you fashioned for us, son, and I loved it. But I can't, and that's that." I would sooner have shot myself than tell him, but I have no gun and he had to know.

He refused to believe me of course. "Grandpa, you're just feeling low because of Mrs. Walrod. By the time school's out you'll be a new man. We'll brew you some sassafras tea and get your blood going again." All this sprinkled with smiles and hand gestures.

I hadn't realized there was a boy his age who knows about sassafras. "Well," I said.

"Boy, are we gonna have fun out there growing our own produce and milking cows. Maybe we can have some goats too. I read they're good for keeping weeds down."

"And eating the wash off your line," I said, smiling so it felt like my face was cracking in a thousand places. "But don't you see, Rodney? It's a fantasy, and you've got to realize it, a dream that can't come true this year or any other year."

He finally came to believe me, and it was awful. His face showed Dorothy's look when I'd done some damn-fool thing to hurt her and she didn't know why. Tears filled his eyes, and mine too. "You sold out, Grandpa!" he railed. "You're just like everybody else!"

His anger finally worked itself out, leaving a sad and confused boy—and desperate. "Oh, Grandpa, what am I going to *do*?"

"Why, just finish high school like other boys your age," I told him with the assurance, I hoped, of a used-car salesman. "Then you'll go away to college, and you'll really like that. I always did." It was a heinous lie of course. I hated college and couldn't wait to get out, but you always think it's going to be a lark before you go.

"I ain't talkin about way down the line, Grandpa," he said. A year is a mile of time when you're seventeen, I suppose. "I'm talkin 'bout right now, this spring. I think I'm flunkin out of school, and I got hardly any friends there. I'm just gonna forget senior year. To hell with it." He was talking tough but his voice cracked.

"What's happened to you and school, Rodney?" I asked. "Your mother used to write what a good little scholar you were, and now this."

"That was kiddie school, Grandpa. High school is different, pressures, stuff like that."

What he said is true, I have come to realize: pressures are real these days, even for youngsters. It's easy to go wrong with grandkids; they're always babies to you, with no more cares than a sparrow. "Yes, son," I said, "I know about the pressures at school and I don't want to add to them."

"At home too, Grandpa. Mom is so pissed about the Pinto thing she barely speaks to me. You see why I want to get away?"

"Well, she is right, Rodney, in being disappointed when you got arrested. It wasn't very bright of you."

"And Dad, he's plain bananas since then."

"Fussing about the money, is he? I told him not to worry about paying me back."

"Naw, he ain't never made a fuss about not paying

somebody. It's all these things he wants out of me all of a sudden."

"Such as what?" Our conversation was becoming mysterious.

"You know, Grandpa, since I was just a little kid Dad acted like I didn't exist, never played with me, never read me one story. I might as well have been an egg in the icebox. All he did was sit around and write memos."

"He's always worked awfully hard, Rodney," I said, and it is the truth. "He does it all for you and your mother."

"Donkey doo, Grandpa. Dad loves power and telling people where to get off. He'd sell Mom and me both if UBM'd make him vice president."

"Oh, come now, you're being cynical way beyond your years." And brazen too, I thought; donkey doo indeed.

"That ain't the point though, Grandpa. What I'm talking about is now. I got news for you; the old buzzard has finally found out I exist."

"Rodney, you're not saying very nice things about your parents."

He was not slowed one bit. "You know, when he got back from Pittsburgh and heard about me gettin arrested and in jail and all, I thought he'd shit a brick, I really did."

I'd lost the heart to reproach him. "Came down on you hard, did he? I'm not surprised, Rodney. Enough is enough."

"Naw, he ain't said one nasty word. At first I wondered what in hell was going on, thought maybe he'd gone absolutely nuts with all this Rod-this and Rod-that stuff. I couldn't get him off my case, Grandpa. I got myself arrested and he found a son he didn't even know about."

"Better late than never." My bromide factory was going full blast.

"You know what he wants now? He wants me to sit around with him and have these man-to-man talks. Yuk. He tells me all the time that someday I'm gonna be responsible for carrying on the proud Kemp family name. Jeez, it's terrible. I liked it better when he saw me around the house and wondered who that kid was."

I didn't have much to say to that, or time to say it. Rodney put his hands to his face, leaned over his knees and began to cry. "I'm sorry about all this," I said softly. I wanted to go to him and cuddle him and tell him it will work out all right. But you don't do that to a man of seventeen who is crying.

Instead, I fetched a beer, filled a glass and put it by him on the coffee table. "Cry all you want," I said. "I know this is very hard on you, and crying will help work it out."

The tears finally stopped and he wiped his nose on the back of his hand and drank some beer. "I'm sorry," he said.

"Don't be. Never be sorry about crying."

"It's not that so much. I'm sorry to hassle you about Old Farm. It's just that going out there seems such a great way of getting out of Marlow."

"I know," I said.

If God hadn't been out to lunch right then Rodney would have caught the Connbus and that would have been that. But no—He obviously was starting with three Martinis, and Rodney stayed, and Rodney talked, and out came a Rodney I'd never seen before. I'd washed my face and was putting on a tie to go down to the gates when I heard a beer can pop. I came out of the bathroom and there sat Rodney, pretty as you please, sipping from the can.

When push came to shove I decided not to deal with the beer. "I hope we have chicken for supper," I said, a broad hint that he should go.

Then he gave me this straight look across the coffee table and said, "Can you let me have thirty dollars, Grandpa?"

Thirty dollars for my grandson I'd hurt so much was no big deal, so I pulled out my wallet. "Of course. What's it for?"

"I know where I can score some mescaline, Grandpa, a really good buy and good stuff too. The brown powder kind, not those white pills that they may put anything in."

I sat down, the money in my hand. "But, Rodney, that's a drug, isn't it?" I wasn't sure, though I know about reefers and I have seen white bags of heroin in the cage at Magellan Police Headquarters.

"Sure, it's a drug—just like aspirin and whiskey. You can really get off on mescaline though, I mean great."

A new worry; hardly what I needed, or need. "You on drugs, Rodney?"

"Not *on* drugs, no, Grandpa. That's your old-fart thinking. I do em sometimes, that's all. All the kids do. Gets us away from thinking about our rotten moms and dads."

I held onto the money, feeling queasy. "I can't do that, son, can't give my only grandson money to buy drugs. They're killers, you know."

Rodney laughed derisively. "Oh, come on, Grandpa, don't be a wimp on me. We're pals, remember? For thirty bucks I can get a lot of hits."

Rodney did not get the money; Grandpa did not get down to supper. I phoned for a tray, and cried when he had gone.

Margie noticed. "Y'awright, Mr. Carpenter?" she asked solicitously.

"A little stomach upset, that's all."

"I mean y'eyes, Mr. Carpenter. Want me t'call Nursey?"

"I'll be all right. Had a visit from my grandson, that's all."

Yeah, saw im downstairs. Good-looking kid, y'know. Why y'feel bad 'bout him? Y'should be proud. What'd he do?"

"I couldn't tell you that in a million years, Margie."

A bad time at the old Arms.

54

It might be wise of me to stop after those last pages I dropped into my box lid, stop and throw the whole she-bang down the incinerator like Fletch's souvenirs. But I've burned nothing. For two reasons: I am a pack rat, to start, and, like most writers, I sometimes like to reread my stuff, if it isn't too awful. Last Saturday I got out my account of our trip to see Dorothy's parents and found much enjoyment in it. Those were wonderful days.

What I have to put down now is not going to bring joy, ever. My modest hope is to make sense of these alarming events.

They're giving us brunches now on Sundays. You can go from nine right through until two, and have a glass of champagne if you want it. The stuff tastes like the bottom of a Standard Oil tank but I drink it anyway. Two glasses yesterday. Margie noticed and made shaming fingers. Afterwards I felt better than for a while now, and could think of Emily without my eyes tearing up, and when I let myself in I had a nice nap in mind. From the hall I looked through and in the bedroom stood Rodney, a dresser drawer open in front of him.

"Hi, Grandpa, howya doin?" he called breezily, coming to sit on the love seat. The boy showed more brass than a church bell.

I was both furious and sick with worry. "How'd you get in, Rodney?"

"Oh, she didn't say nothin. Told me to come on up."

"I mean the door, how'd you open it?"

"Like you, with a key. Don't you use a key, Grandpa?"

"Rodney," I roared, "don't play smart-ass with me. Where'd you get the key?"

"Why, it's Mom's, Grandpa. I know where she keeps it." He held it up in his fingers.

I went over, my legs shaky, and sat heavily in the red chair. "Rodney, what's come over you? Now I catch you rifling my flat. What's happened to you, boy?"

His bravado deserted him about then. "I'm in a helluva bind, Grandpa," he whimpered, "real trouble, and I need money to get out of it." He slumped where he sat, the stuffing all gone out of him.

"Last time it was for drugs, Rodney. What now?"

"Not exactly drugs, Grandpa. Well, yes and no. You see, I owe some people and they're gettin really nasty about it."

"For drugs?"

"Dope, yeah."

"How much?"

"A hundred and three dollars."

"A hundred and three?" I was incredulous. "How can anybody take that much in drugs?"

"Coke is horribly expensive, Grandpa. It was only a gram."

"Wonder it didn't kill you."

"It kept the two of us wired out a few hours, for sure." He smiled sheepishly. "But now they want their money or they're going to kill me."

What he said shocked me, for none of us ordinary

citizens is used to threats of death, but I retained enough common sense to consider his case objectively. Drug dealers, from what I read, get into wars and kill each other regularly. But they don't kill customers who owe them money if there's a ghost of a chance of collecting. Not if they're smart, they don't, and every last one of them, by managing to conduct that kind of business and stay out of jail, has to be a genius. "They tell you that?" I asked. "Did they actually say they'd kill you?"

"They sure as hell did, these guys down in Stamford, two tough dudes."

"I suppose I'm going to have to get you out of this, Rodney, but you're scaring Grandpa to death. I hate to even think of what you may get yourself into next. But you can take my word for it, those dudes, as you say, aren't about to kill you. Nobody kills his own customers. They're just trying to scare money out of you."

"I wouldn't be too sure, Grandpa. Look at this." He turned around and hoisted up his sweatshirt. A folded white rag was taped amateurishly to his back—but not white anymore. Dried blood made it an awful mess, and there were the yellowish-green stains of his body fluids. "That's what they gave me as a sample," he said.

I was shaken, I tell you, to see what those terrible people had done to my grandson. I went over to have a look. "What'd they use?" I asked. "A knife?"

"Some kind of hook. While I was talking to one the other one walked up and ran his hand down my back, just like that. It hurt like hell, Grandpa, and ripped my shirt all up."

"Could I look?" I asked.

"If you want to."

I pulled the sticking tape off, which wasn't difficult. Rodney had bandaged it himself and you can't do much on your own back. The place had a revolting look, a deep gouge right into the flesh. It began under his left shoulder blade and ran down half a foot. Water and pus oozed out, and the flesh looked septic. "I'd say you have a bad infection coming on," I told him. "We have to get you to a doctor or you're really going to be sick."

"Don't worry, Grandpa, my body is strong."

"You don't know what you're saying, Rodney. You can't see what's going on back here, and I can."

"In the mirror I can."

"Look, it doesn't have to be a doctor. I'll take you down to Nursey."

"That creep? She only knows how to treat old people. Come on, Grandpa, get off my case." His insolence was like a red handkerchief to a bull, perhaps an aging one, but capable of temper nevertheless.

"Sit right down there and shut your trap, young man," I raged. "Enough is enough. There's a lot I want to tell you, beginning with the fact that you're fast on the way to becoming a little creep, and a vast disappointment to your grandfather."

I went on to tell him what a mess he's making of his life, how he's letting his parents down, and trying to kill his grandpa with worry. There was plenty to be said, and I said it all, some of it twice. Until then, I don't believe Rodney had realized what a kettle of fish he's got himself into. To my surprise, he listened intently without a word of back talk. At the end I said, "The games you're playing are for big people. You're not dry behind the ears yet and here you're trying to deal with drug traffickers."

He spoke then for the first time since the beginning of my rant. "Well, I lied to you, Grandpa." He looked meekly down at his hands. "Those two dealers from Stamford do want their money, but it was two kids at school that said they'd kill me, and said this was a sample. I owe em fourteen bucks for hash."

Mescaline, coke, hash—where will it end? "Now kids at school really might do it," I told him. "They're not smart enough to know better. But, my God, how many people do you owe for drugs?"

"Only those two in Stamford and the kids at school, a hundred and seventeen dollars altogether."

I didn't bother to ask whether Norma and Clyde know. Of course they don't; I wouldn't if I hadn't caught him in my bedroom. "Is this just going on and on?" I asked him, disgusted.

"No, it's not, Grandpa, honest. I've learned my lesson now. I can't seem to do drugs and stay out of trouble like some of the kids can. I've got to stop, and I won't lie to you anymore either."

"What about going through my drawers? That's worse than lying."

"I was desperate for money, Grandpa. Still am. I don't want to be killed."

"Rodney, I love you very much. You're my only grandson. But you are breaking my heart. Don't you see?"

"I'm sorry, Grandpa, I didn't mean to hurt you. I just got off on this dope thing but now I'm going to try to pass in school. I'll do my best, I really will. I don't know about next year though. God, I hate Marlow High. That's why Old Farm sounded so good."

"I should have told you sooner, that I'll grant you, Rodney."

"Things didn't get so bad until I found out. I got to get away after school, Grandpa. I've just gotta."

"You can't run away from troubles. They always follow you like bad company."

He looked dejected, like a pullet that falls into a horse trough. I gave him the money, naturally, and only hoped he wasn't going right out and buy more drugs. You never know, not even when he's your grandson. I daubed a lot of Merthiolate on the cut and bandaged it neatly with gauze and tape. I thought later that I might have had Fletch down to take a look. But Rodney had gone by then, and if he could say that about Nursey I could imagine his reaction to a man of eighty-six. I've always thought, for no very good reason, that my grandson was different from most children his age. But I see now that he isn't. Rodney has no more respect for age than the rest of them.

I'm wondering now about how much I should tell his parents. Nothing, I suspect. It's the Eleventh Commandment: Thou shalt not snitch on thy grandson.

55

Norma knows, all right, but not much. She phoned about eight, as I was coming in from breakfast, the smell of bacon still on my fingers. "Papa, Rodney's been in some trouble at school. Did you know that?"

"What?" I was bumfoozled by her rapid chatter.

"I mean, he seems to tell you more than me, even though I'm his mother."

"So you are, Norma, but what kind of trouble is this?" I've always been gun-shy when a grilling seems to be in the works.

"Well, some kids beat him up at school and he has a big cut on his back."

"They did that to him at school? It sounds like a tough place, like old Central High in Magellan."

"Like Central High now maybe, Papa, but when I went there the kids were nice. They've always been at Marlow High too, until now. I mean, they don't beat up their teachers like they do in New York. But this is serious, Papa; what am I going to do? Maybe I should go see the principal. What do you think?"

"I doubt it would do any good, to tell you the truth.

And it might make it worse if they found out. Kids usually settle these things amongst themselves. What does Clyde say?"

"He's been in Chicago for a week now, Papa. Besides, he has this idea that boys will be boys. You know, kids don't have real problems."

"If they're cutting him up at school, he does, for sure."

"Listen, Papa, will you help me? I know you're fond of Rod, and he adores you. So maybe you can think about it and tell me what to do. Will you try?"

"I'll put my mind to it, Norma."

So now, you see, I have an assignment—to come up with the right advice for Norma in the handling of her son. Sometimes I complain about not being needed, but I've never wished for this kind of a job. What do I know about kids in the East?

While I've been typing these lines another thought has come to me. Maybe Norma knows everything but wants to spare me. For my part, I can't fink on my grandson. A ridiculous pass we've come to. Heaven help us all. Especially Rodney.

~56

The world has gone bonkers, and God's hopeful little proposition here in the Milky Way is coming unstuck. My declaration for the day: you heard it here first.

It's Saturday morning at the Arms, and spring-fresh. A shower of warm drops hit me at a quarter past eight while I was out walking—my first stroll in a while, after a period in which I alternated between moping and railing at Whoever is arranging lives. I get the unsettling feeling of being very unpopular with the fates in these fading years. Why, I want to know, am I still hanging around while first one and then the other of the women I loved was taken away? God is going to be lucky, if I ever get up there, not to get a boot in the butt for the mess He's made of this planet.

The sun, I see, is shafting down through the clouds out over the Sound, a pretty scene arranged on high to camouflage the turmoil below. It's an old trick of dictators, putting on a pretty scene, or a particularly gruesome one, to divert attention from the real miseries that are abroad. God knows the ruse of course; only a very inexperienced Almighty wouldn't. After putting down all those comments it might behoove me to write some kind words about some member or other of the Trinity to get credits for myself in the Book of Gold. But frankly, I never heard that God can read, or if so in what language.

You see the mood I'm in. As of now I've been at the Arms near a year, and spent eight years before that at Old Farm, all the time trying, like a good journalist must, to keep up with the world's happenings. At the farm I had TV and a radio, and the *Magellan Times* was brought daily to my box by the postman, for which I paid full rates. Clint Bradly never learned about free. I had a telephone too, though it seldom rang.

I have been thinking all these years that I knew the score. How wrong I was. Now I feel like a man asleep one hundred years, a convict being sprung from Stateville half a life later. The people and the things they do in the outside world are strange indeed, and I'm an alien in my own country. Old Farm was more isolated than I knew.

The world and I started losing contact, I suppose, in my last years at the *Times*. Magellan is a lively little city, not some backwater hamlet, and its citizens enjoy all those benefits of the metropolis—foul air, street crime, dope pushers. But toward the end I didn't see much of that. It was the young reporters who wrote crime and covered the floods. Mr. Bradly, perhaps thinking kindly, or more likely figuring I was over the hill, put me on obits and told me to cover City Council. The Council in forty years had never done anything worth more than a number-three head. The Garden Club tours I wrote about might have required some walking but I covered them on Monday mornings by phone.

Then came Old Farm and I was really out of the action. Oh, I knew about our space travels, and about the riots too, and saw Vietnam end on my television. But those momentous events had as well taken place on Jupiter. The real world was my vegetable garden across the way, my pumpkins and strawberries, and my haunches warmed by good oak splits on my andirons.

Now here I am, a year later, confronted with madness on all sides and wondering where I can shelter to avoid being run over. Rodney's escapade caught me at a bad time, and now there's the problem of the flat down on Madison that awaits me next month. Those are my close-at-hand concerns, but there's more. Maybe life has always been like this in the East, the people forever raging about something.

I've awakened to find everybody out there gone nuts, an old man derailed by zombies on the way to meet his maker.

I see there are protests about nuclear power all over the place, and here in Connecticut they're scared stiff that some nuke might go berserk and do unspeakable things to them. Terror behind the venetian blinds.

In the Middle East they're still arguing and killing each other after a hundred years, and those who try to make peace are reviled. They used to give prizes for that; now it's a kick in the butt.

Marlow beaches are a disgrace, says the *Mail*. Could

be. But, never having seen them, I'll be damned if it worries me.

>*For Sale: Fridge, repainted puce, 20 cu ft, good cond,*
>*Classic '67 Cobra w/blown 289, 400 hp, a steel at*
>*$11,000.*
>*Chev 56 customized, Amphicar fins, street legal*
>*$2600.*
>*Printing done on permises.*
>*Happy birthday Ruby darling much live Mike.*
>*Wanted: Gay roommate, M or F, call Woody.*
>*Wanted: Fleas for training, call Dr Badger,*
>*Bridgeport U.*

It's as if I called earth and got the wrong number.

I suppose my view is colored by my state of mind. B. Carpenter is peeved at one N. Carpenter Kemp, even more at C. Kemp, lout.

Taking my assignment seriously, I gave weighty thought to Rodney's problem for a day, made up my mind and called Norma.

I've had a change of mind, I told her. Staying and facing his problems mayn't be best. I'm thinking now he's right. Send him away for senior year, that's the ticket. So he can start anew with a clean slate far from the fetid halls of Marlow High.

"Oh, Papa," she answered, exasperated, "you're playing right into Rod's hands. That's exactly what he wants to do—run away from everything."

"Because he wants to get away doesn't mean it's wrong, Norma. Use your noodle, girl."

"Well, it's just not right, Papa, and I know Clyde wouldn't agree."

"Why don't you ask him, my child? Get him to think about his son's problem. He going to be home tonight?" With Clyde you never know; he might be in Wichita, maybe in Lyons, a small city south of Paris.

"I'll ask him. You don't need to be snide, Papa."

True, and I apologized.

The next day she rang me up with Clyde's decision: "He doesn't think it's a good idea either, Papa."

"And why not?" I was feeling frustrated, having my best thinking sneered at.

"He thinks Rod should stay here and work his problems out."

"Here we go again, Norma. Isn't there anybody out at that house that can come up with a new idea once in a while? Hell, that's exactly what Cleopatra told Caesar, 'Stay and face your problems, Julie Baby.' Look what happened to him."

"Oh, Papa!"

"Look, I've done the best I can. You asked for advice and I've given it."

"Papa, I know you mean well, but you just side with Rod, and that's that."

Family squabbles on the telephone can give you a pain in the ear. All the entertainment value was taken out of these things when they stopped having party lines. "Look," I said, "why don't you and Clyde and Rodney come down here and we can all talk it over, just like a real family."

She said she might come herself but was sure her husband wouldn't have time. The idea of having Rodney present wasn't even worth discussing, I gathered. My daughter doesn't half mind displaying her talons of steel.

Her visit is supposed to take place this very afternoon, and I have a few things saved up to tell her. Rejecting my advice wasn't enough for her. "I just wish you'd been here when I needed you, Papa," she went on. I'd say it was more of a scold than a lament.

"You've said that," I told her. "What's it supposed to mean this time?"

Her litany faltered not at all, a record pulled inexorably under the needle. "Now that you are here and could be of help, you tell me crazy things, like sending Rod away. That's what they used to do in the Midwest, Papa. If a boy got in trouble they'd send him off to military school, and say it was to make a man of him. We're more civilized than *that* in Connecticut."

"They still do that out home, and there's nothing wrong with it if it solves a child's problem. Military schools get a bad press because there are parents who send their boys away to solve their own problem, which is that they can't be bothered with their kids. But that has nothing to do with Rodney, Norma. Nobody says send him to the Army."

"All I know is you're no more help now than you were when you lived out there."

"You know, Norma, what you really want is for me to play Daddy Warbucks, right?"

"Well, you could be more help, Papa."

"All I'm asking is that you think some more about sending Rodney away to school. Don't lock up your mind and swallow the key this early."

"Clyde doesn't think it's the thing either."

"What'd he say?"

"You really want to know, Papa?"

"That's why I asked."

"I don't think you're going to like this, Papa, but what he said, well, he said, 'That old fool, what does he know? He's out of it.' "

As I say, the world has gone nuts, and I'm going to have plenty to say to Norma, especially about Clyde Henry Kemp.

A momentous meeting, like Dumbarton Oaks with heart. She came about three and stayed until well after the gates opened, leaving behind a flabbergasted father.

The beginning was hardly auspicious, Norma snarling like a dog with a flea in his nose. I came on strong after I'd handed her a grape pop and she went to sit on the fake leather chair. "Look," I said, "Marlow High is getting dangerous for Rodney. We have to send him away." Once, I might have said "*you* have to"; not today, no sir. Ben had on his Godfather suit this time.

"Oh, Papa, let's not start that old argument again. It's impossible. Take my word for it."

"Nothing is impossible if you put your mind to it, child. Don't you remember what your mother taught you?" Dorothy put great stock in anyone's ability to succeed if you care enough and try enough.

"Mama never had any problems like *this*," Norma answered, seemingly incensed. "Only thing she worried about was keeping the house clean and what to cook you for supper. Jaime and Chris and I pretty much took care of ourselves."

"Hah! So much for your memory. Nobody ever could raise three kids without a lot of problems, not even in Eve's day. Course she only had two and one did take care of the other, sort of permanently."

Norma didn't hesitate long enough even to figure out what I'd said. Sometimes, I thought, you cast your best pearls before the swine you love. "Oh, Papa, just stop it. We never got into trouble with the car; we never even heard of drugs. Worst thing we ever did was smoke Jaime's cigars that time."

"Yes, the cigars Jaime stole, you mean. You think that was nothing, three little kids smoking stolen cigars?" They'd been sick as colicky puppies and a chastened Jaime was sent down to the candy store with eight pennies to pay for the cigars and confess his crime. No wonder their faces turned scummy green; twofers could rile a billy goat's innards.

"It was simple as one-two-three," Norma said, snapping her fingers. "Mama spanked us and that was that. Don't you see? Rod's problems won't go away with a spanking, and his grades are real shaky. He's on academic probation, you know."

"He didn't tell me that."

"And he smokes marijuana. Probably does worse too."

Much worse, I thought but didn't say, adhering strictly to the Eleventh Commandment. "I've heard about the pot, yes, but he has not smoked it here. Have you seen him do it?"

"Of course not. I'd skin him alive if I caught him."

"This bickering isn't getting us anywhere, Norma. Why are you so set against sending him away, you and Clyde?"

"There's the expense, for one thing. You seem to think we're made of money, Papa."

"One small family can't spend all Clyde's making. Good heavens, Norma, one year of private school won't cost the earth."

"Eight thousand at least, Clyde says. We might have it, yes, but he wouldn't want to spend it on schooling when we have a free public school. Clyde is saving, you know."

"So I've heard."

"He used to complain about paying for Rod's gym shoes and even his jockstraps. I said it was a good thing public school didn't cost two dollars a week or Rod would have been apprenticed in some factory at ten." She displayed the briefest of smiles, and I accepted her peace offering with a chuckle. "Clyde can be sweet and understanding, Papa, but he does find it necessary to be close with his money."

"Why, for heaven's sake? He have looming debts, does he?" In all these years I've said scarcely a word to them about money, but now I was driven to nosiness by images of Clyde sitting on bags of money with a snarl on his kisser.

"No no, Papa, we're not that poor at managing. There's the house, but it's almost paid off. Clyde gets over forty thousand now with his Christmas bonuses."

"Then what the hell is his problem? Plain cheapness?"

"That's a terrible thing to say, Papa. For your information, he does have money worries."

"Such as what?" I was making up for the years of circumspection—fast.

"Well, he worries about his investments, his stocks and things. Then there's the insurance and he's afraid of getting sick and not being able to keep up. The premiums are enormous, you know."

"No, I know nothing about your affairs, Norma. What kind of insurance is it?"

"What kind? Why, life insurance of course."

"Terrible investment," I said, remembering a series I once did for the market page. "Shares in the Salvation Army would pay better."

"Well, whatever, Papa. He decided to buy a lot a long time ago and now he can't just stop paying in and lose it all."

"How much insurance has he got, for heaven's sake?"

"I'm not too sure, a quarter million, maybe even a half million. He used to come home with new policies all the time. He'd pull them out of his inside pocket to show me, sometimes before he even took his hat off."

"What does he have—some on you, some on Rodney but most of it on himself?"

"None on us, no. It's all on him."

"I'll bet a shrink could have a field day with a man who needs that much insurance on himself. You must be a really nice person, Norma, not to drill him right between the eyes. You'd be the richest Carpenter ever."

She smiled wanly and sighed.

"Look," I said, "I have plenty to last me out, and more, unless I get into some medical disaster. And that doesn't matter anyway where my grandson's health and happiness are concerned. I'll pay for his schooling, glad to."

"*You?*" Genuine surprise. "We couldn't let you do that. He's our son, not yours."

"Fiddlesticks. It's the first time I've had a real opportunity to help one of my grandchildren. I don't suppose I'll ever see Meghan again, so don't deprive an old man of a rare pleasure."

"We just can't, Papa." She went and stood at the window and looked out over the Sound. "It's pretty here, Papa. You have a nice view."

"Yes, it is," I said, "but I've already seen it. If Mount Ranier loomed out there we'd think it was lovely too, but only for the first week. Look, Norma, I don't want to nag, and he *is* your son. But if there's a way I can help, I want to do it. I'd never ask anything in return; you know that."

She turned and came back and went over to my fridge. Stooping, she opened the door and took out a can of Coke. "Don't mind if I have another one, do you, Papa?"

"Of course not; help yourself."

She took a few sips from the can—Norma was never one for straws—and came my way, and I saw tear tracks on her cheeks, and I was alarmed. I had not meant to hurt her. "Norma," I said, "have I said too much? I'm sorry if I have. You know how parents are—always trying to boss things, even when their children are grown. You're always babies to us, you know."

Norma put a hand to her face and sat beside me on the love seat. "No, Papa, it's nothing like that, and I'm the one that should be sorry. Why must everything be so *hard?*" She was crying in great wrenching sobs by then, a driven kind of weeping as if, once the levee had split, everything it was holding must be pushed out.

I patted her back, scarcely knowing what to do. "There there," I said, as if to a child, "it can't be as bad as all that." I had not seen her cry since she was a small child, and not much then. Norma, even as a tot, was too proud to let herself cry; Christopher was the whimperer amongst our children. I have always been a believer, in obedience to my mother's teachings, in the therapeutic benefits of crying. But, faced with my middle-aged daughter who never cries, but was then crying, I was not at all sure Mother was right.

"Papa, Papa," she whimpered, putting her head on my chest, "I know you're doing your best"—more sobs— "and that it hurt you so much when Mrs. Walrod died. I know, I know, and you are sweet and generous and a wonderful father."

I kissed her on the forehead and cuddled her as best I could. She seemed so in need of affection. "It is because you are my wonderful little girl, and I love you," I told her. I'm not much given to saying things like that, but it is true, so why shouldn't I? And why not write it down? Now that I look up and read those words, I'm glad I did.

"Your life here, Papa, it's not really what you want, is it?"

"Nothing wrong with it that couldn't be cured by turning the clock back fifty years, my child. It's true, I'd rather not be here, but I'd most rather not be seventy-four years old. For an old man, I have it better than most. And I know you did your best by me."

Her sobs eventually ran down, and she dried her tears and got herself ready to leave. In some way, she seemed a much softer person as she straightened up her charcoal pants suit, and probably less likely to kick the door down if it failed to open on the first twist.

"You'll think some more about sending him away, will you?" I asked her.

"Yes, Papa, I'll talk to Clyde about it." If I know my son-in-law, I'll owe a year's tuition.

"You know," I added, "since Rodney is so fond of French, we might just go whole hog and send him over to France for his senior year."

She laughed at the idea. "That might be a little far," she said, "and I wouldn't know how to do it anyway."

"Remember Maurice Delacroix, Norma? In Nice? He'd help us, I'll bet."

"You're forgetting, Papa, he's even older than you are. Must be close to eighty now. You're remembering him as he was during the war, but that's a long time ago."

"Old or not, I know he'll help us with advice. Besides, there's his son. I understand he runs the paper now, but I forget his name."

Before she left I had her agreeing to talk to Clyde about France too.

In the morning I am going to write the letter.

~ **58**

It's late now here in the East, as they say on television, and I've had a long, busy day—up at six, breakfast at half after and then a nap. The afternoon called for another snooze, and now the clock is creeping up on eight and I'm thinking of being in bed by nine. A day's length and the stress of its activities depend on who is doing the looking. This one, to me, has been a humdinger. To a lad of twenty-three the day would only now be reaching its most interesting hours. But who's twenty-three anymore?

At lunch Fletch went to eat with Mrs. Taylor and I saw them over there chatting it up. We got lamb and potatoes and green beans, an agreeable meal except Chef Michel cooks the meat until it comes up in color to a chunk of mahogany he keeps in his pocket. All old coots take well-done, he is sure, and we're the biggest bunch of coots he's ever seen. I prefer pink myself, but I wouldn't get it here in a thousand years.

Later I caught Fletch in the sitting room. "Saw you and Mrs. Taylor getting on famously," I said, chuckling.

"Rosalie? She's a nice woman, Ben, and if she wants to be friendly why shouldn't I say hello?"

"A likely story, Fletch, ha ha and ho ho." I couldn't resist, after the way he used to run on about the designs of widder women on us males. He even said it of *her*, but I won't think about that right now. It hurts too much even yet.

"I suppose you and the other young sprouts here think you're watching an old man make a fool of himself, eh?" He was piqued, all right, like any schoolboy being teased about his girl. For myself, I was flattered quite unduly by having myself associated even remotely with the word *young*. I suppose you almost never get too old but what somebody someplace thinks you young. As the years sweep past though, these nice folk become difficult to locate.

"I'm only teasing, Fletch," I told him. "Don't take it so seriously. Personally, I think you and Rosalie make a striking couple."

"Ha!" he snorted. "And what've you got up your sleeve this afternoon?"

"Oh, nothing much," I said, "except I'm going down to that Marlow Travel Service and buy a ticket to France." I tried hard to keep my voice casual. I've never bought a ticket to France, nor anywhere else that people go today. Havana has not been a big destination for years.

"So you're really going to send that boy over there, are you? Thought your daughter wouldn't let him go."

"No no. She came around right away. It was my son-in-law who balked—until he was sure it's not going to cost him anything. Want to go along, Fletch?"

"In this rain?" Another monsoon, this one starting before dawn. "Why not wait a day or so?"

"I just want to get it done, Fletch."

The hack finally came for us; when the weather is heavy they all seem to be elsewhere, as Fletch said. At the travel agency this Irish lady of thirty or so who didn't seem to be doing anything smiled at me, so I said, "Excuse me, miss, I'd like to buy an air ticket to Nice, in France."

She showed us a wonderfully warm smile and her blue eyes sparkled. "And wouldn't we all now? Indeed, a nice ticket to Nice." She had a good laugh at that. "You know, when I got up at half seven this morning it was already at it."

"Yes, a wet day," I said, chuckling with her.

"Now what is it I could do for you boys?" she asked brightly, and I saw that this young lady was very certain that any two old geezers who walked in off the street and demanded a ticket to Nice could not be taken seriously. She was happy to go along with our joke though. People are like that, willing to indulge the elderly in all sorts of outrageous eccentricities. In the high numbers you can be as crotchety as you like, and no one is surprised, or pretend to deafness if there's something you'd as soon not hear. But getting yourself accepted as a regular person—aye, there's the rub, as Mr. Shakespeare might say.

"He wants to buy a ticket to Nice, that's what," Fletch told her with some acerbity. "For his grandson."

"Oh, your grandson it is then," she said to me. "Why didn't you say so already?" A bit of New Yorkese had got mixed someway with her Irish lilt.

The ticket is not quite what I expected in colors, for I had imagined garish shades of red, white and blue. She gave me stapled sheets pale green in color, with the agency's own name at the top. But it's for Air France, for sure—first from what they call "JFK" to DeGaulle, which is in Paris, and then on to Nice. "R. Kemp," it says, and gives Norma's phone number. The little rat is going after all. I made the reservation by phone for the tenth of June, and now I have the ticket to make sure nobody backs out.

What I told Fletch about Clyde's reaction is on the way to being a stretcher. He did not really say yes, or no either. To be exact, my son-in-law wanted to think about it a while, which, with him, might mean a year or two. Norma told me that on the phone, except about the year or two, and I scratched the Eleventh Commandment on the spot. Grandpa finked, that's what, but I saw no other way out, Clyde choosing to hem and haw rather than make a decision. It was a scene badly in need of an ending.

"Rodney," I said, "Rodney, you know, has a problem that is a lot more serious than pot and beer. Have you heard of cocaine, and do you know about mescaline?"

She didn't, but she does now. Oh, Grandpa told all; there's no other way to put it. Norma, horrified, I should think, saw the light right away—and not light powder either. I read that someplace, about what the light at the end of the tunnel is being reflected by.

When he heard about France, Rodney rang up right away, very excited. "Grandpa, you're wonderful!" he exclaimed, and did not add anything about Grandpa being a snitch.

Through the years I have thought often about how I befriended Maurice Delacroix when he came to us during the war, a refugee who couldn't go home while Hitler held his country. There were those in Magellan who were irked at the French over the Vichy business but Maurice had nothing to do with that, and I tried to make him feel welcome.

His answer came by return airmail, and he's not as old as I feared. The letter says he's seventy-six, but now pretty much out of the paper. "I permit Claude to make the decisions now," he writes. "Sometimes I look at the books and make a fuss, for this I must do or he would not remember that I am his father."

Maurice still uses English beautifully. There is much about the warmth of our friendship, though we have not seen each other since the morning in forty-five when he took the trolley out of Magellan on his way back to France. Perhaps it is that we should correspond more frequently than once per annum, he says, now that my precious grandson is to be with him.

Advice was all I asked, advice on a boarding school, but Maurice has much grander ideas. Rodney is to come and stay the summer with him and his wife "to achieve a familiarity with the French language as it is spoken today, which is preposterously unlike the way M. Hugo wrote it. We have become a country of linguistic barbarians, I fear."

In the autumn he and Claude will see that Rodney selects one of three good schools in Nice.

Toward the end he talks of the joy he and his Ulla will find in having a young person around, if only for a while. Ulla is a Dane or Swede who was traveling in Italy when she attracted the eye of the young French journalist who was then a correspondent for his father's paper. They married several years before the war and Maurice's trek to North Africa and the government-in-exile. He came then to America by way of the West Indies, leaving Ulla and Claude and a daughter in Nice, with the idea of joining the U.S. Army, and so to fight Hitler. They turned him down; too old, even then.

So he sought work around St. Louis, a very French

city, he was sure. The closest he got was Magellan, and Maurice was to learn that in St. Louis they speak Missourian, and a little hillbilly. Mr. Bradly was glad to have him, for the draft was depleting our staff, and he stayed three years, convinced to the end that somewhere in St. Louis was an enclave of Frenchmen speaking the native tongue.

Being French, or old, or both, Maurice complains at the way his children treat him. Claude, he says, no longer seeks his advice and his daughter, married to an engineer and living in Zaire, sends a letter only after he writes to remind her that she's not yet an orphan.

Several years ago Maurice went to live in a place called Saint-Paul, which I thought to be a part of Nice. He's enclosed a postcard with an aerial view and Saint-Paul, I understand now, is a separate village on a mountaintop in the foothills of the Alps. They call them *Les Alpes enneigées*, whatever that means. Saint-Paul is a quaint hamlet with red roofs, by the picture, and is enclosed by a wall. Rodney will like it there, and Grandpa will like the idea of his grandson being there.

59

My story is no more than a column-filler. Harry Cassidy, from his position in the slot at the City Desk, used to call out, "Ben, write me a four-line column-filler, will you? The fire story's short." Or five lines, once in a while as few as two, though the compositors could lead out that much when they felt like it. This one is even shorter, though the writing is heavy.

May has come. My flat has gone.

I haven't quite felt myself since that day when Norma and I broke the lease; the cost was dear in dollars, even more in spirit. Those few square feet might have been a haven for Emily and me after our trying journeys alone, but it was not to be. Taking the flat by myself seemed preferable to sticking it out here. In the end Norma won out, Norma and the eroding-away of my self-confidence. I think it is in doing time in a Retirement Residence that you lose faith in yourself. I've been here less than a year and already I have serious doubts that I could get my own meals or clean up after myself. The process works that quickly.

And, by myself, I'd have nobody to bring the trays. Of late I've been skipping supper, and Margie brings them up and gives me worried looks. "I'm only a little upset," I told her last evening. "Don't give it a second thought."

"It ain't like you t'ask f'trays allatime," she said. "You was always so sportin, like y'Old Fart threads last yeah. They was funny." She laughed and patted my hand, a pretty good kid.

For the thousandth time she eyed the milk pitcher. "Y'last chance t'gimme it, Mr. Carpenter." She's heard the legend and wants the pitcher for the day when she becomes a mother.

"What's this last-chance business?" I wanted to know. "You think I'm going to check out tonight?"

"O'course not," she answered, laughing again, "but I just ain't gonna bug you no more is all."

"Promise?"

"Maybe," she said with a giggle, moving then to do her usual survey of the prints and Dorothy's mother-of-pearl hair receiver on the TV. Having a pretty young thing admire your possessions is pleasing, and I'll give her the pitcher tonight. I seem to have no further use for it, and what would Norma do with yet another possession?

Sometimes these days I have pains where they shouldn't be, and I tire so easily. Nursey came and took my blood pressure.

"Rest yourself," she told me.

"You mean I can stay home from work today?" She smiled and pinched my cheek.

Rodney was here Sunday and brought me six cans of cream soda and some ice cream. The pop seems to humor my insides, and I've had two spoonfuls of the ice cream.

"You drive down?" I asked him.

"Mom let me have the Pinto, just like that. I didn't even ask."

"She must trust you again."

"It was the ticket, Grandpa. It makes her feel that I must be grown up if I'm going away." I mailed it out to him in an envelope addressed to Monsieur Rodney Benjamin Kemp, which pleased him mightily. He may be right about the ticket's effect on Norma, but there is more to the equation than that. Even I, who do not see him often, can discern the coming of manhood to my grandson. He is slowly becoming his own person and, if I'd have looked, I suppose I could have seen it as early as last fall when he refused to buckle under to Norma and Clyde in the fuss about the courses he took in school. He took what he wanted, it turned out.

"You get the car quite a bit now, Rodney?" I asked him.

"Sometimes. Why?"

"I thought maybe you'd take me somewhere." My flat is gone, but my Stateville urge isn't.

"Sure, if I can. Where do you want to go, Grandpa?"

"To the bus. They have a depot here somewhere, don't they?"

"Trailways, yeah, down on Jefferson. You taking a trip?"

"I'm thinking seriously about it, yes," and I was. "You

wouldn't have to go with me, Rodney, or anything like that. I feel queasy about starting off alone, that's all. If you get me to the depot I'll be all right after that."

"Where you going, Grandpa?"

"I'll have to see where the bus goes, I suppose."

Rodney thought I was pulling his leg and laughed up a storm.

But I wasn't.

~~~60

We got away just at dark & the plane frightened me at first. Spread out below was a regular Christmas Tree of lights, and I was looking down when the engines went off and we dived, with a cry in my throat that nobody could hear.

"Don't worry Grandpa its only abatement," said Rodney.

Scary as christ on the cross—my brother used to say that before he shot himself in the lung & died. Poor boy, his foam was pink.

"We're gonna have a roman bath." Rodney was excited about going to the farm.

Air France, I said, I didn't know they went to St. Louis

Everywhere, he said. In French but I understood.

The pilot had stripes above his elbows and a plug hat like on the Puerto Rican & I laughed till I saw who it was—Mr Harmon

I turned to tell Rodney but he was gone & Emily spoke to him, too friendly I thought. When I looked back Mr. Harmon was gone and I saw a light blue wall like in my bedroom.

I woke up crying because now even my dreams have turned on me and I do not dream of Kansas nor my parents, only of such hopeless stuff as Air France taking me and Rodney & Emily to Old Farm. I fell on the way to the b'room because my leg is weak that I broke when I was 5 and my left arm wont grip. I got there though & threw up & came and lay down again holding on to furniture & walls.

I write by hand now to rest the remington, a yellow pad & pen. I hold the pad still with the back of my lt hand Phone rang this a.m. but I didnt answer until the door rattled & in came Rufus + Nursey

You all right? Rufe asked. We see telltale up & wonder. Nursey took my fever & said the flu She sent for my doctor to come but I couldnt remember his name. "Norma's, I said. "Your daughter, she asked? I didnt tell her about the foot They always want to know too much.

What are you writing? Nursey asked. Drivel I said & I thought you didnt dream any more when you got old,

"What?" she demanded.

The dreams keep on, I said but the song says you get too old, when is that?

At a hundred and 20 most people do, she said.

Almost there I said

ᘛ61

Special Dispatch—like we put on stories from Alton & Wood River—only this one is from Marlow Hospital where Rufe & Nursey brought me in the Eagle crate. Yesterday I think or the day before—everything is muddled here The Doctor found out about my hand but didn't say boo. I keep

slobbering & can not help it, its so messy & they cant understand good english here. keep asking

Many nurseys but not nice like ours, only scowl & ask
why I want paper Roll a joint I said but she did it anyway
& thinks Im write a letter.

Last night—the worst with my grandson & Norma &
her husband Clyde the usual Im so frstrated I cant write
right—stood like vultures I thought. Norma held my hand
& that nice, Clyde at foot with that hat in hand. Kept
saying lets go honey we're not doing any good here—
without asking me Rodney hugged me & cried, & Grandpa
too, he's going so far away—France. Rodney I said you
know the copy paper in grandpas box—throw it away because the cleaning ladies might be in & see it before I get
back.

He said okay & get well quick dont leave us yet

Shut your face & lets go—Clyde like usual Come on
Norma let the old man get some sleep.

That Idiot thinks Im dying. from the flu of all things
Wish Fletch was here it would cheer me up Or Jaime, a fey
lad his Mother said

BENJAMIN OSRO CARPENTER
April 18, 1905–May 21, 1979